The Road Home

Kat Ryan

The Road Home

Copyright © 2024 Kat Ryan

Published by Red Rims Publishing

ISBN: 979-8-9888609-4-5 (eBook) ISBN: 979-8-9888609-5-2 (Paperback)

Editing by Victory Editing

Cover Design by Elle Maxwell of Elle Maxwell Designs

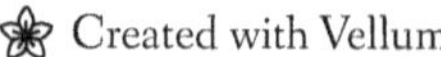 Created with Vellum

In this book, Maeve shows the importance for having a kick-ass group of women around you. I'm blessed with so many. Without naming their actual names, I'll shout them out by group.

Marco Polo/ Mommy Squad
Voxer chats
Quarantine Book Club
The women in my family, my hype squad
My colleagues
And the women in my own 'Highland Falls'

Ladies, thanks for having my back. My heroines wouldn't be able to take on their internal demons or the ones they find in the world without you. Love you always.

Chapter 1

Big Red

Maeve

My girl Taylor belted out lyrics from the speakers as Big Red and I rolled down another long road. Windows in the truck's cab were partially down, my blond hair a mess of tangles blowing in the wind as I sang out in harmony with the song. Only Big Red and I knew if my voice was any good, and as a truck, she certainly didn't care. My spirit needed to sing it out, so I did. I was in my give-no-fucks era. Not sure what album that would align with, but I was certain Taylor would have my back. We girls had to stick together.

My gaze focused down the road where the sky met the barren Central Illinois fields. I wasn't used to the open space of the Midwest, though I was rapidly becoming a fan. My sister often likened me to a fluff of dandelion floating in the wind, and it was true. I hadn't had a "home" since leaving ours at eighteen, though that would have been a generous term for our house growing up. As soon as I could, I'd gotten the hell out of that place and the judgmental attitudes of our parents.

Allyson was the only thing that had kept me from peacing out on my family completely—well, she and our grandmother, whom I called Nan and Allyson called Grandmother.

She'd been Grandmother to both of us originally. However, once I reached elementary school and realized how far from mothering my mother really was, I wanted a new name for the woman who was there for me. So I switched to Nan, and Allyson, in her attempts not to alienate our parents, stuck with Grandmother. Whatever we called her, we both loved her desperately.

When our beautiful and independent Nan left the earth three years ago, she'd set aside enough of an inheritance for the two of us to finally break free from any hold our family of origin ever had on us and, in my eyes, it was just Allyson and me now. Our parents hadn't been physically abusive, but they certainly weren't nurturing and didn't give a single shit about any of our hopes and dreams. Hell, they'd washed their hands of me as a rebellious teen, and I of them. Nan had always done what she wanted, and leaving us her nest egg had been her final snub to my parents. I sent up a high five to her, wherever she was in the great beyond.

With Nan's passing, Allyson had shocked us all and moved from Connecticut to the middle of some cornfields in Illinois when she'd seen a café for sale. I gladly passed on to her the majority of my inheritance when she shared her plan so she'd have enough capital and would be able to leave the shackles of our parents behind, including her position in our dad's business. It had been sucking the life out of her as she tried so hard to comply with what they wanted her to be. I was damn proud of her.

My little sis was finally living for herself, buying the

Sanctuary Café in this small town in Central Illinois, then opening a second location at Highland Woods. And somehow in all of these boss-ass-bitch entrepreneur days, she'd met widower Logan Traub, formed a strong friendship, fallen in love with him, and married the guy last summer. He was a good man, one of the few in my experience, and I was thrilled for her. The two of them *fit* and were having a baby this June.

I'd come to visit last spring to check on her and had met Mr. God of Sexy, as I referred to my brother-in-law back then. Not that I was attracted to Logan, but it made his twin crazy, so I called it a win. I'd been en route to Delaware to visit friends when I called Allyson and learned about her and Logan's change-in-relationship status. My gut started talking after that phone call, letting me know that I needed to be here. I've long believed our ancestors talk to us through our intuitions, so I switched up my plans, and Big Red and I headed west.

That time I stayed for several weeks, working at the café, subbing in for Kate at the yoga studio, and taking the time to get to know my sister's small town for longer than the day or two here and there that I'd managed since she moved. I'd liked my time in Highland Falls, a locale that could star in its own Hallmark movie, but there was part of me deep down that never wanted to be too comfortable. So I'd done what I always do when I felt the itch and hit the road.

Singing along to Swift, I did a mental calculation of how many states I'd been in over the past eight months. Six? Seven? I'd headed to Wisconsin to run a meditation retreat, done some massage work in Alabama, filled in for a friend at a yoga studio in New Hampshire, back to Maryland for a few weeks at another friend's diner in Ohio while a waitress was home with her baby, done some facials and wax appointments for a friend in her resort spa off of Hilton Head, and a few more jobs in between.

I was like a pinball, but as I bounced from place to place, I made time to come back to Allyson as much as I could. In the compass of my life, she was my true north. In the past decade as I'd moved around the country, I hadn't prioritized our relationship enough. That had changed after spending time with her this past spring, and I had only one person to thank for my reset, as much as I hated to admit it. My phone began to vibrate from its spot on the dash, lit up with the name of the caller: Lesser Twin.

Well, well. Apparently I'd summoned the man. Behold the power of a mad woman.

I tapped my phone to accept the call, raising my voice over the wind whipping through the truck. "Greetings, Lesser Twin. What did I do to deserve the honor on this beautiful day?"

Levi's growly voice came through my speakers. "Damn, woman, what is going on? I can barely hear you."

I begrudgingly rolled my windows up. Normally I'd just hang up on his petulant ass, but in case there was anything up with my sis or his brother Logan, I went ahead and relented.

"There, better?"

"Where are you that you can drive around with your windows open in January?"

I thought back to my Google Maps that I had looked at just a bit ago. "Mmm, somewhere just west of Danville, I believe."

"Illinois?"

"No idea if there is another."

"You coming to Highland?"

"I am." I tapped my fingers on my steering wheel, wondering why we were having this conversation. I also cursed the gods that this man and his gravelly voice never failed to make my nether regions sing. Whatever. We all had our crosses to bear.

"And you're driving around with your windows open in January?"

"It's a beautiful day and the air is invigorating."

"Blue skies and sun, sure, Maeve, but it's forty-five out."

"I said what I said. Appreciate what you've got and you'll be happier for it. Life lessons, my sweet." Did I feel bad about the sarcasm dripping at the endearment? Nope. I'd only said it because I knew it would irritate him.

Levi's gorgeous face popped up in my mind, and I fought against the butterflies in my stomach and concentrated on the road. Didn't matter—I could still see the man. Dark hair cut short but longer on top so that it was always a bit disheveled. Long, lean runner's body at a height at least a foot above my five-foot-four curves. A beard I'd like to feel rubbed all over my body, not that I wanted to own that confession to anyone. Yeah, he lived rent free in my mind. It was an issue I was choosing to ignore.

While he might be Logan's twin, I had zero issue telling the two of them apart. So what if the man was mouthwatering? I wasn't here for that. Not for a man who liked to poke the bear, meaning me—not that I was innocent in said poking, I had to admit. My immature, pissed-off inner teenager rose every time I was in his presence. I wasn't proud of it, but that didn't stop me from sinking to his level each and every time.

Logan's twin was a good guy, I knew that deep down. And yet... And yet... I just couldn't help myself. All of his buttons called to me, causing me to work hard to get under his skin. I didn't even know Logan had a twin when I came out last April, but there Levi stood that first day with eyes that twinkled, and I was hypnotized.

He was immediately a no-go, not just because he drove me crazy but also because I was currently off relationships. That had been fine—I was out here for my sister. Attraction was one thing though. What I hadn't counted on was meeting Levi and being jealous of the close relationship he and Logan had.

It was my fault that Allyson and I had drifted apart over the years; there was no one else to blame. I'd bailed on her as soon as I could flee home. While I wished I could have stayed and protected her, it was a get the hell out of there or become a person I didn't recognize vibe, and my survival instinct was too strong to allow that to happen. So was my backbone as Nan had frequently pointed out. At eighteen, I simply couldn't exist in the same space as my parents any longer, so I didn't.

While I'd visit when I could once Ally moved out of our childhood home, she couldn't exactly reciprocate since I was always crashing at a friend's and, frankly, never in one location very long. I didn't have a place to call my own and was fine living that way. Staying in one place made me itchy.

Yet watching the brothers together this past spring, I'd vowed to work to be there for Allyson more, which meant coming to her. I loved her and needed to set aside any guilt over leaving home when I did or any worry about her getting tired of me.

"Yo, earth to the flower child. You there?"

Levi's voice brought me out of my thought spiral. "What do you need, Twin Two?"

"Don't use that tone, Ms. Maeve. Be grateful this is a call and not FaceTime."

"I've told you I don't appreciate video calls without warning. You're messing with my singing time, sir, so let's wrap up whatever this conversation is."

Levi's throaty chuckle did things to me that I didn't want to think about. "My brother wants to plan a surprise party for Allyson's birthday, and I thought you might want to be part of it."

A wave of emotion hit me, and I didn't know what to do with it. I swallowed it down as I ran over my mental calendar. "Does he want it on her actual birthday? Because the twenty-third is coming up."

"Yep, thirteen days away. I think he just came up with this idea last night, but that date is the idea. He said he was telling her about some of the ridiculous parties my parents had for us growing up and Allyson said she'd never had one..."

I brushed a tear off my cheek that had appeared without warning as I thought of the Traub parents, Linnie and Frank, thankful for new reasons that Levi hadn't done a video call. After spending the briefest amount of time with them, I wasn't shocked at all to hear they'd celebrated the hell out of their boys. "My parents didn't see any reason to celebrate birthdays. Waste of time and money according to Patrick and Mona."

I heard Levi clear his throat before speaking. "I'm sorry, Maeve. That's bullshit."

"That it is." Deep inhale, then exhale. I worked to center myself. "I'm in. Let me know how I can help."

Levi was silent for a moment, so I enjoyed the fields as they flew past my window. Interstates were faster, but I often chose state routes when I could. It was a slower pace, and I got to drive through some fascinating towns. While I couldn't truly be out in nature as I drove, it seemed like it was closer somehow.

"Today's the tenth of January, Maeve." Levi's voice brought me back.

"Aware, Levi."

"So you're headed to Highland and are going to stick around for thirteen days in a row?"

Was I irritated at his skeptical tone? Yes. However, I couldn't argue with the man as much as I enjoyed it. I'd stayed three weeks last April, but since then it had been a week or less at a time. I'd come by just last month when Logan and Allyson had a holiday party at their place but had quickly taken off once again.

"Yes, you giant pain in my ass. I planned on spending some time with Allyson for her birthday, so I'm good with helping to plan a surprise party. She deserves to be celebrated." My tone was clipped, but he surely wouldn't even notice. Any thoughts of my parents tended to do that to a girl.

When Levi spoke, he was so quiet I could barely hear him over the radio. "So do you, Maeve."

Yep. Not going to think about his tone and how there was some sympathy laced in it. No need for pity here, thank you very much.

"Okay, I'll be in Highland in the next hour or so. How do you want to plan this? Want to text me what you need?"

"Or we could meet."

"Meet?" My heart skipped a beat, but I was going to chalk that up to a fave from Zach Bryan now flowing out of my speakers. He and Maggie Rogers killed this one. It was clearly not because there was a possibility that Levi was asking me out, right?

"Yeah, you know, talk without a phone between us. Might be faster."

"I like a buffer from your winning personality, Traub."

"Back at you, Ms. Maeve. Logan will be the buffer."

See, I told myself, *not a date*. However, it was harder to ignore the pull of the man in person. Logan's presence would help though.

"Sure. When and where?"

"Tonight? Homestead?"

"Works for me." Homestead was a brewery in Highland Falls owned by some of Allyson's friends, Jake Spencer and Cole Sullivan, otherwise known as Sully. I loved the vibe— it was a refurbished barn right off the downtown area. The food was awesome, and the beer was kick-ass.

"Does Allyson know you're en route? Logan didn't mention it."

"Nope. I was going to call around Champaign and tell her my arrival was imminent."

"Okay. So say around six? I'll meet you two in the bar area, assuming you're crashing with them."

"Yep. I hope Logan has a plan for the two of us to get out of the house without Allyson wanting to join us," I pointed out.

"He'll figure something out."

"Sounds good. See you then." I ended the call before he could say anything else to irritate me.

I hummed along to the music for a few minutes before glancing at my phone's navigation. Noting that I was decently close to Champaign, I tapped Allyson's number.

Her voice filled Big Red, surrounding me like a comforting hug. "Hello, my wandering sis. Where in the USA are you calling from today?"

A warm memory washed over me. "Hey, chickie.

Remember that old game they had at school, *Carmen Sandiego*? Maybe that's been my goal all along, to become Carmen."

"Can we play that online anymore? I found *Oregon Trail* the other day," Allyson mused.

I chuckled, remembering that one from elementary school. Super old-school, but our classroom had still had it. "Did you die of dysentery?"

"Cholera."

"Fair." I paused as I looked at my surroundings, making sure I was still on the correct route. "I'm about a half hour from you."

A shout of joy came through the speakers. "Seriously? I just saw you last month."

"And yet you're having a birthday in a few weeks. Thought I'd come hang with you and the little bean in your belly."

"What?" Her surprise was evident. "You're staying for two weeks?"

My heart thumped as I thought of all the times we were there for each other growing up. I thought of watching Logan and Levi together over the past nine months. Of the stories they had not only of growing up but also as young adults, and I spoke the words my heart told me to.

"Or possibly longer..."

Chapter 2

Grown Men Don't Cry

L*evi*

"Yo, yo," I said, coming up behind Logan and his goldendoodle, Charlie, at the trailhead in Highland Woods. We were headed out on a five miler, and I'd been running late after my call to Maeve. I took a breath, letting the cool air center me as I noted the brilliant blue sky against the bare trees. The woods were quiet today with only the birdsong from a few cardinals to break the silence. Apparently even a relatively warm day in January wasn't enough to bring a crowd to the trails.

Logan rose from where he'd been bent over, loving on his pup, to give an exaggerated look to his Garmin.

"Dude, it's five minutes. Not that late," I said.

"True, just unlike you. Dad's not strict, but on time—"

"Is late, I know." I gave a shake of my head, thinking of my dad's mantra growing up. "I'll explain on the trail. We headed to the bench?"

"Yeah, to start," he said as he and Charlie took off at an easy pace.

I started my watch and headed down the familiar trail

after them. Since I'd moved here officially nine months ago, Logan and I had hit these trails at least once a week. Add that to the runs I did in town with Aidan, another friend, and I was in better cardio shape than I had been for years after falling out of the habit of running on the regular after college.

"So is all well?" he asked as the trail climbed a small hill at the start.

I fell in next to him, Charlie trotting ahead as I watched the ground for spots to avoid. "I was on the phone with Maeve."

Logan let out a huff of laughter. "And you somehow still have your balls? The woman's losing her touch even through a phone."

"Hey, Maeve isn't that bad," I said without thought as I avoided a soggy spot on the trail. It was unseasonably warm for January. No snow and a thawed ground meant muddy conditions. I'd take it over snow and ice, though I'm sure that would arrive all too soon, but it was a bit concerning to see how the climate had been changing since we were young.

"Hmm, defending her now, are we?" The amusement in Logan's voice was clear and made me rethink my original comment, dammit.

"Just don't see a need to disparage Allyson's sister," I shot back.

"You know I have all the respect in the world for her." We weaved through a stretch of the trail. "So you called Maeve," Logan said, getting us back to the topic at hand.

"Yeah." I paused, giving some thought to our conversation. "I wanted to see if she wanted to help plan Allyson's party."

"Allyson will love that you thought of her sister," Logan

said as we caught up to Charlie. The pup watched us, then took off again, bounding down the trail once we'd reached his spot.

"Yeah, Maeve made a comment like Allyson deserved to be celebrated..." My voice trailed off as I thought back to how damn sad she'd sounded when she said that and what it'd done to me.

"Meaning it seemed like she didn't think she did?" Logan said, kicking into another gear and making me dig in.

"Mm-hmm."

"Yeah, their parents did a number on the two of them, though in different ways."

"I'm getting that," I replied as I sent up another moment of gratitude that I was blessed enough to have been born to the parents I had.

We ran alongside each other down the trail for the next few minutes, lost in thought. I wasn't sure what Logan was thinking about, but my brain had Maeve's words stuck on repeat. Before I knew it, we'd reached the small hill that led to Logan's favorite spot in the park, complete with a bench overlooking a bluff over the river.

It was here this past spring that Allyson had conspired with Max, one of our friends who worked for Highland Woods with Logan. They'd planted a sycamore for Logan in honor of his first wife, Nola. It had meant a lot to him, and it helped him find the closure he'd needed to finally scatter Nola's ashes on this bluff.

Charlie was already there, stopped by the bench over-looking the river as he watched us come up the trail, his tail wagging in greeting. He knew the drill. We reached the top of the hill, and Logan walked to the edge overlooking the river for a moment. He needed a moment as he always did here. Hell, so did I.

I moved over to the tree that had grown another six feet since they planted it last spring. I picked a few dead leaves off the plaque Allyson had ordered to commemorate Nola and thought back to the young woman I'd met in college with the twinkle in her eyes and a zest for life that was unmatched. I ran my fingers over the inscription.

In Memory of Nola Traub

Take a look, Take a breath

Bloom where you are planted

Tears pricked my eyes. It had taken five minutes of meeting Nola before I knew she was meant for Logan. I'd introduced the two of them, and that was it. I'd known they were it for each other, and no one was surprised when they ended up married. What I hadn't seen coming was a drunk driver in Boston who put an end to their fairy tale. No one had.

Logan had been a shadow of himself after he lost Nola. He'd locked me out, and it was the first time in our lives I couldn't read him. I was shaken—we all were. He and Nola had planned on moving to Highland after he'd run the marathon that spring, and he went ahead with it even though my parents would have gladly kept him near us. While I was grateful he'd moved to a place that didn't have a memory of his wife everywhere he turned, a selfish part of me had wanted to keep him close too.

Since I couldn't be there for him, I'd bought him Charlie because I needed to know he wasn't alone. Slowly, over the past few years, I'd watched him come back to us, though it wasn't until he and Allyson moved to something deeper than a friendship that he really rebounded. When I met her last spring, the relief I felt was immediate and straight to my core. Just like when I met Nola, I'd know Allyson was perfect for Logan. I didn't know how the afterlife worked, but I wouldn't be shocked at all if I found out when I passed one day that Nola had a hand in putting Allyson in Logan's path. I'd been worried for a bit that he was going to fuck up his chance with Allyson, but he'd pulled his head out of his ass in time and now the two of them were going to be parents.

"Hey, shrimp," I murmured into the air. "Hope you're keeping everyone in line wherever you are." I wouldn't say I was a religious person, more spiritual, but I did believe that something came next, that we went somewhere when we passed. And for whatever reason, I felt my old friend strongly at this place, just as I knew Logan did. I missed the hell out of her, and it didn't escape my notice that I hadn't had a relationship since she passed.

I'd been with Tess at the time, and we'd been together for a year before the accident. One snide comment from her about Logan needing to move on and her desire to set him up with a friend had shown me who she really was. For Christ's sake, it had been less than thirty days after Nola's passing. Before the accident, I'd liked Tess's independence and her forthright nature. After? I wished she had an ounce of compassion for my brother and my family. She'd actually accused me of having feelings for Nola, blaming that as the reason I was grieving someone I "wasn't really related to by blood." Yeah, that had made the end of our relationship a no-brainer. While I'd found some companionship over the past almost four years, nothing for more than a night. Honestly, I hadn't even been that tempted by anyone until recently, which I was choosing to ignore.

With a hand to the trunk of the tree, I let myself feel the centeredness that only came from being outside, at least for me, and moved over to the bench. Charlie, being the best doggo ever, came over and dropped his big ole head right on my knee to stare at me with those soulful brown eyes. Damn. I don't know how Logan ever said no to this pup.

After a few minutes of me sitting by myself, Logan dropped to my side on the bench, stretching his legs and letting out a breath.

"You good, Bro?"

"Yeah," he said. "Sometimes I can't believe how much has changed in a year."

"You said it." I ran my hand over Charlie's fluffy blond head and watched birds soaring above as I sensed Logan's emotions growing closer to the surface.

He was the only sibling I had, so I had zero knowledge if everyone could read their brothers or sisters like we could, but it was something we'd been able to do as far back as I could remember. I could read his expressions, sure, but when something was weighing on him, I could physically feel it. The energy felt different. Sounded woo-woo, but it was there. Thus, when he wanted to run out here today, I knew it was more of a need versus want for him.

"I've got you," I said in a low voice, wanting him to know we could sit here as long as he needed, that he was safe to let it all out. I slid an arm behind him on the bench, near but not suffocating. I was here to hold the space for him.

"I know you do," he said, his voice breaking.

Side by side, shoulder to shoulder, we sat. His shoulders shook, and I brushed away my own tears as I grieved once again for what the world lost, what we all lost. Part of me felt guilty, like I wasn't valuing his new relationship over the first one, but that wasn't it. I loved Allyson for Logan—we all did. Allyson was the first to encourage conversations about Nola, shedding her own tears for the loss of the woman she'd never met. She'd told me one night when we'd stayed up late with a bottle of wine in their early days that there wasn't a competition between who Logan loved more. That Nola had been his wife, that Allyson knew she was amazing, and that his love for Nola even when she was gone didn't diminish his immense love of Allyson. One didn't cancel out the other; there was no competition because our hearts were big enough to love more than one person.

And that was when I fell in love with Allyson for my brother. She got it. Hell, the woman had hung up pictures of Nola through their house since it had been too hard for Logan to do that for years.

Movement above the river caught my eye, and I looked up to see a bald eagle soaring through the open sky.

"Shit, that's impressive," I said with awe in my voice.

Logan sniffed, wiping his face with the bottom of his long-sleeved shirt. "We'll make a birder out of you yet," he said as he rose to his feet.

"Dude, I'm not ready for AARP yet, relax." I grinned as I looked up at him from my spot on the bench. "You good?"

"Yeah, thanks." He stepped over to the tree, running his hand along the trunk. "I've been talking to my therapist a bit more frequently in the past month."

"Do you feel like you're sliding backward?" We hadn't talked about it in any real detail, but depression from his loss had been a deep pit he'd worked out of in the past few years.

His gaze was averted, which made it hard to read. "Not really. It's just... the baby has me rattled."

I played catch-up for a minute. The baby? Their baby? The one coming this summer? I thought about that and then looked his way. "One more person to risk losing?"

"Exactly." Logan grabbed the stick that Charlie was waiting patiently to have tossed and threw it down the hill for the crazy pup to chase and burn off some energy. He watched the dog, still not looking my way. "Sorry I lost it there for a moment."

I stood, moved to stand by him, and leaned my shoulder into his. "Bro, our dad did not raise sons that believe for one single moment that grown men don't cry. You know he doesn't subscribe to that patriarchal bullshit."

Logan snorted in amusement. "Well, if he had, Mom would have cured him of that in a heartbeat."

I smiled, grateful our parents had followed our path and moved here. When I'd decided to relocate to Highland Falls to be closer to Logan, I'd been apprehensive because I didn't want to leave them with neither of their sons close by. Fortunately, they'd decided to journey south as well.

"What does your therapist say about your new worry?" I asked. I mean, I could guess, but if the expert had already weighed in, why not start there?

"That it's okay to feel my feelings. Name them. Breathe through them. Let them go when I can." Logan threw the stick again for Charlie, then turned his head to look at me. I was grateful that his eyes, while watery, weren't giving the vacant stares I'd gotten used to almost four years ago.

"Well then, name that shit." I gave him a smirk. "And how about we do that as we run because as beautiful as it is, I'm getting cold."

"Aww, princess, can't handle it?" He whistled for Charlie, and we started up the trail.

"Princesses are tough, man, no disrespect."

"Good call." He hopped to avoid the muddiest part of the trail, then fell in beside me. "So... worry over a baby that isn't born. Concern that I'll be a shit dad. Fear over something happening to them. And..."

I looked over as his voice trailed off and was thrilled to see a wide smile on his face. "Yeah?"

"And so much fucking excitement. Allyson is glowing now that she's not puking. I cannot wait to see her with our baby."

I shook my head in wonder as we dug in to go up the next elevation. "Damn, you're going to be a dad."

"Sure am."

"And I'm going to be an uncle." I let that soak in, though it had been doing so gradually for months. But with Allyson not really showing yet, it almost didn't seem real. I laughed, then looked at Logan. "At least it's not twins."

"Jesus. Perish the thought. Remember what we were like?"

Our laughter rang out, startling some sparrows as we made our way down the trail. The bright blue sky shone on us as we wound our way through the dormant trees standing sentinel over us, a familiar wind supporting us from the back.

Chapter 3

Birdcage

M*aeve*
The afternoon had flown by. Logan and Allyson's house was amazing—a cabin in the woods with windows that lined the back, letting you feel like you were in a tree house. Not that I was looking for a home of my own, but if I were, a place like that would be high on my list.

I'd made cookies with Allyson, and we'd curled up in the large chair by the wall of windows and caught up. Her morning sickness was, thankfully, a thing of the past. The second trimester was underway, and she was positively glowing. At one point she'd nodded off—it must be tiring to grow a small human—and I'd just watched her, wondering if that was something I'd ever want. I'd always thought not a chance in hell. Patrick and Mona Murphy were the antithesis of what most people would consider decent parents. With the absence of role models in our childhood, I had zero confidence in myself not to screw up my own children. But that fear wasn't holding Allyson back. When I'd asked her about it, she said our parents had shown her what *not* to do. That was true, but it still terrified me. Even the thought of being an aunt worried me. What if I screwed that up?

As evening fell, I entered the Homestead Brewery and waved to Laurie, the hostess. I headed through the dining room and to the bar, shaking my head as I thought of Logan's attempts at subterfuge just an hour ago. He'd hilariously sent me a text from their kitchen when Allyson and I had been catching up in the living room. His theory had been that Allyson wouldn't see us talking and get curious, thus the secrecy. Logan's text said I should tell Allyson I was headed out to meet some of the women I'd gotten to know in town. Once I made my escape, he'd work on his own.

I had my doubts this would work, but time would tell.

The place was hopping for a Sunday evening, though I hadn't found a time when they weren't at least moderately busy. I slid onto a barstool and smiled when I saw Jake Spencer heading in my direction behind the bar. As much as I was hesitant to admit it, I did like coming back to a place where I was known and seeing familiar faces.

"Hey, world traveler," Jake slid a coaster in my direction. "Welcome back to Highland."

"Thanks—how's the baby?" Last month when I'd visited, he and Ivy had just had a baby, little miss Lorelai. I was willing to bet she had joined big sister Addie in wrapping Jake around her little finger.

"Beautiful like her mama," Jake said, whipping out his phone to show me a picture. In it, Ivy grinned at the camera from a spot on a couch. Lorelai was cradled in her arms as five-year-old Addie mugged for the camera from an upside-down position next to her mama.

I gave Addie's outfit a second glance. "Colorful clothes,"

I said with a laugh. She had on rainbow-stripe leggings, one purple sock, one polka-dotted, and some type of T-shirt that appeared to have dinosaurs on it. None of it went together, but the pink tutu on top said she really didn't care. I freaking loved that about the pint-sized dynamo. I also admired the way that Jake and Ivy didn't make her conform to society's standards of what's acceptable in terms of dress. My mom would have died before Allyson and I ever wore a mismatched outfit like that.

"Yep, Addie gives zero fucks, not that she would ever say that."

I smiled, thinking of Ivy. She tended to "curse" with colorful language like *snickerdoodle*. So not only would Addie not curse because she was five, but unless she picked it up from Jake, a real possibility knowing him and his brother, she would be more likely to have creative curses.

"Beer?" Jake asked, gesturing to the taps with rainbow fingernails—also, I was certain, thanks to Addie. I'd had a manicure from her a time or two.

"Black Hole Sun," I said, feeling an IPA tonight.

Jake moved to pour a glass for me as a delicious shiver raced up my spine. Looking to my left, I saw Levi slide onto the barstool. Nice to know that my Levi-radar hadn't abated since I was here last. I wished I could get rid of it, but it seemed to be a permanent condition that I was working hard to ignore.

"Lesser Twin," I murmured.

"Mean Maeve." He gave a nod of his head to Jake. "Evolution." Looking back to me, he asked, "When did you get here?"

"Five minutes ago. Logan is going to follow shortly."

Levi shook his head. "He just called. He'd told Allyson he was going to meet me, and she asked him to think about a night in, something about cuddling up together and watching something because she didn't want to be alone."

Damn. "She told me she'd been feeling more emotional lately with the pregnancy. Maybe I should head back." While we were planning a party for Allyson, I wanted to do more. The first trimester had to have taken a lot out of her, and I hadn't been around to help for more than a week here and there.

In the past year she'd finally gotten some help at the two cafés, but I worried about her when the baby came. It had taken a lot, meaning a push from Logan and a nudge from me, to get her to add more staff in the first place. How were we going to convince her she needed even more? How on earth would she take time off after the baby came?

I had a visual of the baby in a bucket seat on the floor, rocking with a nudge from her foot between her whipping up espresso drinks. She had it in her head that it was only by being a superwoman that she could get our parents to be proud of her. Last year she finally began to let go of some of that. Luckily I'd figured out at an early age that nothing I could do would ever get that from them. I think I'd been five.

Oblivious to my internal struggle, Levi focused on the issue at hand. "Nah. I told Logan we'd do some preliminary planning. I truly don't think it will be too in depth, just need to hear what you think she'd like. Might as well hang out with me for dinner. I promise I don't bite unless you ask nicely." He wagged an eyebrow at me.

Jake placed a glass in front of each of us. Levi picked his up and held it out to me. I reluctantly grabbed mine to tap them together.

This was a terrible idea.

An hour later, I was even more sure of my original

prediction. This man was both attractive and infuriating in equal measure. I couldn't tell you what it was that made him crawl under my skin and make himself at home, I only knew he was there and didn't seem to be going anywhere.

We'd maybe been able to talk about the party for a total of ten minutes in the past sixty. We had a time and food assignments, but whether we'd have any decor or thoughts on gifts, that was up for grabs.

Levi had just moved to Highland this past spring, and yet no less than fifteen people had stopped by to "catch up" with the man. A table of small business owners who were eating together had asked him for some website advice, the head of the Main Street program had dropped by to talk about some video he was making for them, Grace and Aidan—whom I'd met through Allyson—had swung by with baby Mia so that Aidan could check on when they were meeting for a run the next day.

Now, to top it all off, Lou Williams was chatting him up with her husband Verdell. The way Lou was looking in my direction made me nervous. I knew a calculating glance when I saw one, and this woman was trouble. I'd have been able to spot that even if her reputation didn't precede her. Beyond that, I'd gotten coffee a few times with her crew—namely Jeanie and Hattie—and knew she had the pulse of the town under her thumb at all times.

"So"—Lou moved my way, letting Verdell talk to Levi—"how long are you in town for this time, Maeve?" Lou's red glasses framed her curious eyes. Something about her was hypnotizing, and I couldn't pry my eyes from hers even if I wanted.

"Um, at least two weeks?" I stammered. Yep, I *stammered*. That was not something I did. The power of this woman to reduce me to a pile of nerves... She'd never been anything but nice, so there was no explanation other than the certain feeling that she knew all and saw all. Like with one glimpse she could see the secrets you hid within your soul.

"Nothing we could use to entice you to stay longer?" Lou's weathered hand grasped mine as she shot a side look toward Levi, making sure I saw it. Yep. She sure did.

"Well, I don't know about that..."

Lou gave me an assessing glance that was familiar, then apparently decided to switch topics as she twisted my hand in hers to see all my arm. "These tattoos are interesting. I don't think I noticed them last time we talked."

I bit back a sigh. I'd shed my zip hoodie to sit in my sleeveless muscle tank. The brewery was cranking the heat tonight, so I was more comfortable, but that put my tattoos on display. I had two larger ones, then a few small ones tucked here and there, not all visible in a tank. One day I thought I'd work toward a full sleeve, but I wasn't there yet. Lou was in her seventies, easy, and her generation was not known to be a fan of tattoos. At least they hadn't been in any of my past experiences. My mom and dad were younger than her and had been absolutely appalled when they saw my arm with my first one. They couldn't imagine I'd ever be able to find employment because tattoos like mine were only for former and future convicts.

Not that they were judgmental at all. Sure...

"Yes, I have several tattoos."

"What is the meaning behind some of them?" she asked, running a finger over my forearm as she gazed at the flower there with something akin to wonder.

Hmm, maybe not all older folks are anti-tattoo? I knew better than to judge, but when you've heard the negativity over and over, you finally let go of any optimism about a generation.

"Well, that's a peony," I pointed out lamely.

"And is there a reason behind it or do you just like them?"

Emotions washed up inside me, filling my eyes before I knew it. Lou suddenly reminded me of Nan—that's where I'd seen that no-bullshit stare before. They would have been close to the same age. It had been nice to have an adult in my family that believed in me, who saw me. Sometimes I forgot how much we'd lost when she'd passed. The familiar guilt over not being around in her last years welled up again.

"Um, my grandmother, Nan, loved peonies. Her gardener surrounded her house with them. Mainly the pink variety like this one." I gestured at my forearm. "When I was little, I loved cutting them and then shaking them upside down to let the ants out before bringing them inside."

Lou squeezed my forearm. "Beautiful." She looked over the shading, then pointed to the birdcage on my shoulder on my other arm. "And this?"

Yep, a tear escaped. I brushed it away. My throat had constricted, and I couldn't speak. Lou watched, eyes skating over my tattoo, then spoke for me. "The door to the cage is open and one bird is flying away, but another is still inside."

I nodded.

Lou leaned forward and whispered, "Which one are you?"

I worked to clear my throat but still kept my voice quiet. "The one flying away."

Lou sat quietly for a moment before leaning forward to hug me. In my ear, she said, "Young lady, I think we need to spend more time together on this trip of yours."

I soaked in her embrace, relaxing into it. "Sounds good, Lou."

Verdell spoke up from somewhere behind her. "Lou, let's allow these kids to finish their meal."

Lou gave me one last squeeze. "I'll call you tomorrow."

I nodded, not sure I trusted my voice, as I watched her and Verdell walk away.

A clearing of a throat brought me back to the present and, most importantly, to Levi. He was watching me with a look that made me believe he'd heard my conversation with Lou, though his expression didn't give any indication in regard to his feelings about it. Odd.

"What?" I asked, all out of clever conversation for the night. "Do you hate tattoos? Believe women shouldn't have any? One day I will likely have at least one full sleeve. Too much? Hmm?" My fucks had all fled, I was fresh out. Might as well lay down my cards.

Levi raised an eyebrow at me, then let his gaze slowly scan my arm from my shoulder to my fingertips, then back up. His eyes met mine, and I understood what romance books meant when they referred to a hero having a "heated" look, because hot damn, it was suddenly very warm in here.

Still, Levi leaned in so he could speak into my ear. "Turned off by tattoos? Hell no, Ms. Maeve. This"—he ran a finger up the peony on my inner forearm "is sexy as fuck."

I sat back, my eyes not leaving his. Holy. Shit.

Chapter 4

Siren Call

L*evi*

Sweet Lord. The storm brewing around me was named Maeve, and I was not going to survive her.

Verdell had been sharing the ridiculous gossip from the local golf club, which was always something special, but I'd been distracted by Lou's conversation with Maeve. Did I eavesdrop on them? One hundred percent, you bet your ass I did. No regrets. I heard the comments about her tattoos—the peony, which was sweet, but then I'd taken a dagger to the heart when she talked about the birdcage.

For fuck's sake, it didn't take a genius to figure out that the cage was her parents' home. Did that make the bird that remained Allyson? And why would she get a permanent reminder of that on her shoulder? Not that I had an issue with her tattoos—as I'd already said, Maeve's were sexy as hell. My issue lay with what she was being reminded of on a daily basis. What purpose did it serve? What was I missing?

I'd watched Maeve and Lou when they were talking, and as the conversation evolved, Maeve's mask had lowered.

I didn't know if the woman realized she typically had one in place, but I'd noticed it the first weekend we'd met.

That weekend last April was a benchmark in my mind. There was only before Maeve and after Maeve. When Logan, Allyson, and I had pulled up to Allyson's place after a weekend camping with my parents, Allyson clearly hadn't been expecting Maeve to be waiting on her doorstep, but there she was. Logan and I had stood back, watching the sisters rejoice in each other. From all outward appearances, Maeve had been the carefree person that Allyson had described, flitting from one friend to another—one job to another—across the country. No ties, no responsibilities, nothing to bother her.

The vibe Maeve projected was life of the party, crazy hippy chick, afraid of nothing, blunt as hell. Not to mention gorgeous as fuck. She had long blond hair—back then it had been in some type of knot on her head with a scarf, which was how she frequently wore it. But then some nights, like tonight, she left it down like a curtain around her shoulders and *damn*. She dressed often with a boho vibe, but I was a fan of nights where she wore jeans that clung to her hips and a T-shirt that allowed me to see her curves. I'm sure some bullshit out there would say that Maeve was on the heavier end of the weight spectrum. To me she looked exactly as she should. And I fought the visualization of holding on to those curves with a lot less clothing in the way. Nope, not happening.

Maeve had a lot going on, and I didn't think she was ready for anyone to try to sort it out. I also didn't think I was the man for that particular job. That night when we'd hung out at Logan's, I watched from the kitchen as she stared at Allyson and Logan talking on the deck. Those two had been lost in each other, locked in an embrace, deep in their connection and conversation. It was early days for their relationship, but I'd already known watching the two of them that there was something special. Maeve's face, when she'd lost the mask that evening, showed a myriad of emotions. The two that were warring for top billing with each other, however, were joy and longing.

She'd looked over to the kitchen that night and seen my gaze locked on hers, the mask quickly returning as she gave me grief about something or another. Too little, too late because I'd already seen what she wanted to hide. Since then, if I looked deep enough, I noted that Maeve had an element of sadness in her expression despite the smile that was ever present and yet never reached her eyes. And unfortunately for her, I'd realized that she gave me a load of shit anytime she wanted to get the attention away from her, as she was doing now.

"I'm sorry, Lesser Twin, 'sexy as fuck'?" Her current gaze wasn't sad; it said "game on." I mean, not my aim, but I'd take it. Honestly, I wasn't sure what I'd been going for—the words had spilled out with no hope of reining them back in. Anything to get rid of that air of sadness and regret.

Playing into the vibe, I gave her a smirk. "I said what I said, Ms. Maeve. You know you're just out there, enticing all the boys with your sexy ink. A siren song if you will."

The eye roll was immediate and next level. "I'll have you know that my *ink* is for my enjoyment, not for any 'boys.'"

She proceeded to mumble something about "patriarchal bullshit" as she grabbed her empty beer glass and held it up to Jake. Calling out her order to him, she left her glass on the bar, saying something under her breath about being right back and heading in the direction of the bathrooms.

My gaze locked on her retreating form as she pulled on her hoodie and ducked around the corner.

Jake caught my attention as he meandered my way with a shit-eating grin, meaning he'd overheard at least part of our conversation unless body language had told the tale. Add to that the sudden occupant of the chair on my other side being Jake's brother, Drew, and I knew I was in for it.

"Levi, Levi, Levi." Jake shook his head as he took Maeve's glass and filled it up.

"What?" I asked, choosing to go the clueless route. Like hell would I be volunteering any information that he didn't have confirmed. This was not my first interaction with the Spencer brothers. They weren't a whole lot different than Logan and me, though these two had an older sister, Steph, whom I wouldn't piss off for anything. Frankly, how the two of them survived childhood into adulthood without her murdering them was a question for the ages.

Drew clapped my shoulder as he spoke to Jake. "Does my boy here have any game?"

"I'm sorry, I'm your boy?"

Jake ignored my comment. "No, he absolutely doesn't."

I felt the indignation rising inside. "I'll have you know that I have plenty of game when I want it."

Jake smirked at me as he moved to Laurie, who was flagging him down at the end of the bar. He leaned over, then looked back to me with a glance that spoke volumes, though I wasn't sure about what.

Laurie headed back to the hostess stand at the front of the brewery as Jake slowly made his way back to us, wiping down the counter as he did.

Coming to stand in front of Drew and me, he looked at his brother. "Remind me, did young Traub here say he has game?"

"Hey, I'm the oldest sibling—"

Drew snorted, "Didn't Logan say it was by five minutes?"

"Ten. And I'm the same age as you"—I looked at Jake—"and have a few years on this dipshit." I jerked my thumb toward Drew.

"I'll accept that," Drew said. "What did Laurie have to say?"

Jake polished the bar in front of us, an air of relaxation about him. "Oh, not much, just that one Maeve Murphy had given Laurie cash to cover her dinner and drinks when she slid out of this place a few minutes ago."

My head immediately spun to the front door as my hands hit the bar, not that it would do any good. She was long gone. One could only hope that she had just headed home to Allyson and Logan's and not fled town altogether. This was Maeve we were talking about after all.

"Tsk, tsk, tsk." Drew brought me back to the present. "Jake, were we this clueless when we were trying to woo our women?"

"Woo, really?" That was all I had.

"We were, Drew. Sadly, we might have been worse."

"Is there any point in saying I'm not trying to woo Maeve?" I spoke to the ceiling because I just couldn't with these two anymore.

Drew chuckled as he leaned into me. "No point, friend. Your eyes tell the story."

"Yeah. Your eyes didn't leave her ass once as she headed to the bathroom," Jake said with a knowing look.

"She's more than her ass," I grumbled.

"There it is." Drew laughed.

Blake, one of the guys Drew worked with at Highland Woods, stepped up to the bar and drew the Spencer brothers' attention. I took the momentary reprieve in stride and looked down at the party notes I'd sketched out on my phone while Maeve and I had eaten.

We hadn't gotten a ton done, but in talking to her, I had figured out a lot of what we shouldn't do rather than should. Frankly, I had a feeling a lot on this list could apply to Maeve as well. She'd nixed any large parties, saying Allyson would prefer something in their home with friends. That anything that would put Allyson front and center would make her uncomfortable.

I had a feeling most people who met Maeve would assume she'd want to be the center of attention. Allyson clearly avoided it, but Maeve was louder, so I guessed most would assume she was an extrovert. The more time I spent with her, however, I saw that the life-of-the-party persona she projected was to keep people from getting too close to her.

With a tap of my finger, I moved from my notes to Instagram. I'd followed Maeve back in April, and she'd shockingly reciprocated. I found my way to her profile, flipping through her most recent posts. Images from the window of her truck of the barren fields of the Midwest to a blue sky over a city skyline to the ocean—the majority of her pictures didn't have her featured in them, were more like a scrapbook of where she'd been.

I paused at a black-and-white selfie. It was a shot of her eyes in the rearview mirror of her truck, the rare picture with her in it, though barely. You could see that it was raining outside, making the space in the vehicle feel cocooned, and it captured my attention. Something about her expression was lonely, and I couldn't look away. Without thinking, I double-tapped on the picture and a heart floated up.

Shit.

I glanced at the date of that photo. Five months ago. Double shit.

"What's that expression about?"

I looked up to see Jake and Drew had returned their attention to me. Too bad that hadn't happened before my scroll through Maeve's timeline.

Drew looked at my phone and saw the picture I'd liked. "Maeve?"

I slid my phone away. "Yep," I murmured sheepishly.

"What's wrong with that?" Jake said, likely trying to piece my tone together with my actions.

"Hit the Like button on a pic that's five months old."

Both assholes started laughing.

Jake stopped first. "So you're saying Ms. Maeve is going to see that you've been busy stalking her socials?"

"Maybe she doesn't care about notifications?" Drew asked through his laughter.

"One can hope," I said as I picked up my beer, draining what was left in one gulp.

"Another?" Jake asked, holding up a new glass.

"Nah, I'm good."

"I can drive if you want another," Drew said quietly by my side.

Though they didn't make a big thing about it, all our friends here now knew about Nola's death—either through quiet words from Allyson or when Logan had finally opened up. While none of them were irresponsible enough to drive while drunk, they were more conscientious than most. Highland was too small for any type of rideshare, so everyone took turns making sure there was a driver because it was the right thing to do but also as a nod to the loss of Nola.

"It's fine—I walked. But I'll take a water."

Jake filled up a glass and slid it my way as I got my card out to pay.

"You know"—Drew leaned in while Jake slid my card for payment—"we've known you now for almost a year. I haven't seen you show any interest in anyone except Maeve."

I debated protesting once again that I wanted anything with Maeve but then decided there was no use.

"There're a whole lot of reasons not to try anything with her, man."

"Why?" Jake asked, entering the conversation.

"Well, I've avoided relationships for four years," I began. "Still not sure I'm in the mood for one now."

"Because of that woman you were dating when Logan's wife passed?" Drew asked.

I nodded, trying to remember what I'd told them. "Put a lot on the line when you hook yourself to another. Not really in that space."

Jake leaned down across from us. "You told us a little about her at the Christmas party at Logan's."

I thought back to last month's party. I'd been worried about Aidan and his wife Grace, who had been going through a lot. And since I was staying at Logan's that night, I'd had a few more to drink than usual. I vaguely remembered talking to some of the guys around the firepit.

"Yeah?" I said, thinking back to what all I'd told them.

Jake gave me a steady look. "The shit she pulled is not okay, but avoiding any relationship out of fear of ending up with a woman like that is not the call. You know that most people would never have said that shit."

Drew nodded.

Hmm. Apparently I'd laid it all out.

I took a breath, looking up at the soaring barn ceilings. "I know, it's just I judged her so wrong; I wonder if I would get it wrong again."

Drew snorted. "Do you really think Maeve would ever pull any of that bullshit?"

I had to smile as Jake said, "I feel certain Maeve would have words with that woman you dated if they were ever to meet if she knew what had happened."

I decided it was time to show my cards. What was the point in having friends if you couldn't work through the shit that was eating you up with them? "I'm not sure what the point is in talking about it. Maeve Murphy wants nothing to do with me. Whether I'm attracted to her or not doesn't really matter because I stand no chance. Beyond that, she sure isn't sticking around here, so this line of questioning is irrelevant."

I couldn't help but notice the look that Drew and Jake exchanged before they looked back to me.

"Man," Jake began, "if you don't think Maeve is fighting this attraction as much as you are, you aren't paying attention."

My phone lit up with a text notification from Maeve.

Maeve: *Saw you liked my photo from September on Instagram. Stalk much, Lesser Twin?*

My heartbeat increased just reading her message. Yeah, her siren call had me in her snare, and I didn't think there were enough earplugs in the world for me to ignore it.

Chapter 5

Mimosa Mondays

Maeve

I stumbled into Allyson and Logan's kitchen, eyes bleary as I moved toward the coffeepot by locking in on the scent. One cup and I'd feel human again. Well, let's be real—likely it would necessitate at least two.

I grabbed a mug on autopilot, dumped in a spoonful of the hot-chocolate mix that Allyson started using after moving here, and filled the cup to the brim. A swirl of the spoon to mix it all together and I picked up the mug reverently. One deep sip, then another. Heaven.

"Am I interrupting your moment with my mug?" Allyson's amused voice came from somewhere near the fridge.

"Yes," I whispered. Simple, to the point. Frankly, all that needed to be said.

I took another sacred sip. Yep, just as good.

"So, want to tell me who you met up with last night?" Allyson asked as she moved around the kitchen.

I cracked an eye open and analyzed the items in her

arms: Challah bread, an orange, milk, butter. She plopped it all on the counter. French toast was for breakfast it seemed. Sounded good to me.

I slid onto a stool at the island across from her setup and faced down her question with a little trepidation. I knew my sister even if we weren't as close as I wanted. Something about her tone led me to believe she was fishing. Giving her a once-over, I took in the picture of innocence. Her strawberry blonde hair was in a messy bun, and she wore leggings and a graphic T-shirt stretched over her tiny—but growing—baby bump. I decided to start small. "I think I mentioned it when I left—I was meeting up with some of the women in town I've gotten to know." Vague was good, right?

"Ivy? Emma? Grace? Maggie?" She looked at me with an eyebrow raised.

Abort. Abort. The woman knew something was up. I mean, not shocked, but damn. "What do you know?"

She smiled to herself and began to whisk as she talked. "Logan wanted to go out too, and my man is a horrible liar. My guess? He wants to throw me a birthday party."

Interesting. "How bad of a liar is he?"

She snorted and met my eyes; hers were twinkling. "I mean, I'm not trying to make that sound worse than he is. Logan isn't a *liar,* but when he's trying to keep something from me—a gift he bought, a surprise he has—he can't meet my eyes. When I ask any question to clarify what's up? Forget it. He gets this creepy grin as he tries to reassure me that he's not hiding anything. It's comical."

I joined her laughter because I could absolutely picture that. "Do you think it's a twin thing? Would Levi do that too?"

"Wouldn't you want to know?" She wagged her eyebrows at me with an assessing glance. "So, sister of mine, who did you meet last night and is my husband, in fact, trying to throw me a birthday party?"

I dropped my head into my arms on the counter. "Yes?"

"Is that a question?"

I picked my head back up to meet her eyes. "How did you guess it was a birthday party?"

Her gaze softened, and she put down the whisk to squeeze my arm. "Because I know the man. We talked about his childhood birthday parties the other night. Get this, when the two of them were four, it was pirate themed. He and Levi dressed up in pirate gear, as did all of their friends. They had a gangplank across an inflatable pool, a treasure chest, pirate music, et cetera. At six, they had a Jedi party, complete with homemade robes and lightsabers. Frank was the Jedi master and led them all in Jedi moves. It's insane."

I listened, not at all surprised by any of it. Linnie and Frank Traub were like winning the parent lottery.

Ally continued. "When he asked what kind of parties we had and I said Mona and Patrick didn't do birthday parties, well, the man looked at once like he might crumble with sadness *and* that he wanted to change that immediately."

I nodded. Seemed on par for Logan. "And so he wants to rewrite our crappy childhood?"

"I mean, I'm not really there for a pirate or Jedi party, but I have a feeling I'll never spend another year without having my birthday celebrated."

"Hmm, a pirate party wouldn't be terrible. I'd like to tell Levi to walk a plank anyway. Besides, there are worse things..." I picked up my coffee mug to have another shot of joy.

"True story."

We sat in companionable silence for a bit, me drinking my coffee, Ally making breakfast. I appreciated that she could even take this moment for us when last year she would have been running herself ragged, managing both cafés on her own, both understaffed. Logan had helped her change that. And since she'd gotten pregnant with their little one, she'd started going in later in the morning at least three days a week. The shadows that had lived under her eyes had disappeared almost completely, and I was here for it. Now, did Logan and I still want her to add another employee or two? We sure did. But we were taking things as they came with the goal of convincing her before June.

"So who did you really meet last night since Logan stayed here?" She looked from the griddle where she was melting butter to me.

"Levi." I braced, knowing there would be follow-up.

She moved the melted butter around, nodding to herself before looking back my way. "So the lesser twin was willing to be alone with you?"

"I mean, we really weren't alone. Heck, Lou and Verdell were there."

Allyson looked quickly back to me from the bread she was dipping in the egg mixture. "Lou saw you with Levi?"

"Yep, sitting at the bar." I had a feeling I knew where this was going.

Allyson tossed her head back in laughter before catching her breath to look back my way. "Oh, Mae, you are going to be the talk of the town. Lou does love her gossip."

I shook my head at her. "Chickie, tell me something I didn't know. She's already called this morning to arrange a coffee date." With that, I drained my mug. Moving to the pot to get a refill, I asked the pertinent question: "Are we telling Logan that you know about the party?"

Ally flipped a piece of toast on the griddle. "And ruin his fun? Absolutely not."

I looked over the stack of challah bread. Hmm. "Um, you know I'm not here to judge, but that's a lot of French toast even if some is for Logan. How hungry is this bambino making you?"

She looked up at me, a guilty expression that immediately had me on edge. "Umm, so we might be having some company?"

"Might? And who can just drop by for breakfast on a Monday morning?" Was my heart beating faster? Sure was.

"People that are retired and/or self-employed." She flipped another piece of toast before turning the oven to warm.

My throat was dry. "Let me guess—Frank, Linnie, and Levi?"

"Got it in one." She leaned over, pulling a baking sheet out of a cabinet. Cooked French toast went on the sheet, it went in the warm oven. As she prepared for the next batch, she glanced my way. "Are you okay with joining the family breakfast?"

My brain ever so helpfully flashed back to standing next to Levi the night before at the bar. The goose bumps that arose when he ran his fingers up and down my arms as he said my tattoos were sexy as fuck. Damn. The panic I felt initially that caused me to flee the brewery, but the excitement when I realized he had liked an Instagram post. Scratch that, an old Instagram post. I'd sent him a text to tease him about stalking me. His reply was on par for his usual comments that left me reeling as much as I'd like to deny it.

Lesser Twin: *When I turn my attention to you, you'll know, Ms. Maeve.*

My internal angel reminded me that I wanted to avoid relationships, including one with Levi Traub. The devil inside told me to climb the man like a tree.

I was rooting for the angel. She was more powerful than she realized. I worried the devil would win because I was a weak woman in regard to that man.

"Earth to Mae," Ally called to me from her spot at the stove. "Are you cool with Logan's family descending on us?"

"Do I have the option not to be?" I'll admit it, I sounded a bit like a petulant teen even to myself. But pulling up my defenses to stave off any attraction to Levi Traub at the hour of eight in the morning on a Monday seemed like a big ask.

Allyson laid down her tools and gave me a serious look. "While you're visiting, this is your home too. If you need time without anyone, I'll text Linnie and call off breakfast this morning."

Remorse hit me swiftly and without hesitation. "No, no. I'm sorry. I'm being a bitch. I like the Traubs, and they're welcome here of course." I ducked my head to take a drink and not look at Ally for a minute. To be honest, she made me face my bullshit, and I wasn't ready for that so early in the morning.

A spatula tapped the counter in my line of sight. I looked across the counter to Ally.

"If you need to flee and go for a drive or just get out of here, that's fine."

My heart squeezed. How often in our adulthood had she covered for me, staying to face our parents and allowing me to get away from their judgmental eyes? Hell, she did it when we were kids too. While I was the oldest, I felt like she'd tried to take on the role of protector from an early age. Though I had for her too. However, even as the youngest, she worked hard to be what they wanted and keep the focus off me. I was a disappointment to them in so many ways it wasn't even worthwhile to count them.

Nope. It was a new day. I wasn't hiding anymore. To be fair, Logan and Levi's parents were light-years from ours, so nothing to fear there. Just Levi, and with his family here, there shouldn't be any concerns.

"I'm good, Sis, but thanks. Now, how can I help?"

"I think we've got it. Logan is making the bacon; I've got the French toast. Linnie is on mimosas, not that I'll have one, and Levi is bringing fruit." She flipped another piece of toast.

So many things for my mind to cling to, where to begin? "Logan is on bacon?"

Ally pointed behind me, and I looked through their living room to their deck. Ah. Mother Nature continued to show off this January morning. Instead of the typical gray skies of winter in Illinois, there was a brilliant blue. And judging by Logan's fleece jacket that he wore with joggers, it wasn't too chilly. The man stood by a Blackstone griddle, spatula in hand, talking to their dog Charlie who was sitting by his feet.

"He's been out there the whole time?" I asked as I watched Logan in amusement. The conversation he was having with Charlie was met with a head tilt from the pup, like he was trying to understand what Logan was saying.

"Yep, although he and Charlie might have been in the yard when you first came in." She glanced with fondness at the two of them. "Should be done soon."

I turned back to the issue at hand. "Mimosas on a Monday morning?"

Ally laughed as she slid the last pieces of French toast on the cookie sheet and put it back in the warm oven. I moved around the counter to hip check her away from the sink. Maybe I didn't have a breakfast assignment, but I could damn well do the dishes.

"Linnie loves a mimosa. She's not a big drinker, but one beverage per gathering brings her some kind of joy. And champagne? Forget about it. She's giddy."

"Will the guys have one?" Mimosas shouldn't be gendered, but I racked my brain, trying to think of a time I'd seen men gravitating toward the beverage.

She shrugged as she leaned her hip against the counter, watching me clean the dishes. "I mean, maybe? Linnie doesn't need anyone else to join her to find joy with a mimosa. Frank will, likely. Levi and Logan are a question mark."

"I volunteer as tribute." I scrubbed a stubborn spot on the still-warm griddle.

"Hey." Ally's voice pulled me out of my mission to degrease the dish. I looked to my left and saw her soft expression.

"Hey," I whispered.

"I know what you're doing."

I looked from the soapy water back to my baby sis. "Um, the dishes?"

She slowly shook her head. "No, I mean the multiple visits last year. The one right now even though you were just here three weeks ago."

My heart clenched. "Am I too much? Should I grab an Airbnb? Want me to hit the road?" My stomach rolled.

Dismay washed over her face. "Too much? How can you ask that? Mae, if you want to live here in this house for the rest of our days, that still wouldn't be too much. I meant I know you're trying. I wanted you to know that I see it and appreciate it." She took a step toward me. "I appreciate you."

I wiped my hands on a towel on the counter before stepping into her arms. "I appreciate you too," I said into her shoulder. We squeezed each other tight, her tiny baby bump pressing into me to remind me that there was someone else with us right now.

The door opened, and I heard Linnie cry, "I've got Mimosas!"

We didn't move as we swayed together.

I whispered, "You weren't kidding about her love of the drink."

Ally snorted. "She just likes anytime her family is together. It's unreal."

Linnie and Frank came around the corner into the kitchen, Levi trailing them. Shockingly, I barely noted him because upon seeing the two of us, Linnie's easy expression grew to one of joy. "My girls!"

Tears sprang to my eyes. Logan and Levi's parents had not only swept Allyson into their family once she and Logan started dating but included me in that special group. Allyson left my arms to give Linnie a squeeze, and then I stepped up to do the same. Looking from her to Frank with their welcoming expressions, I wondered if there was a time in my life that my parents had made me feel as welcome.

But really, I knew the answer was no.

Chapter 6

Gender Reveal, Anyone?

L*evi*

Maeve was killing me this morning, and I didn't even think it was intentional. She wasn't her snarky, confident self that I'd grown to know. She was quiet, her eyes stormy and watchful. I'd seen her face moments ago when my mom busted in the kitchen and hugged first Allyson, then Maeve. There was a look of confusion and wonder before she fought it back. I mean, Mom could be a whirlwind, but I had a feeling it had more to do with a maternal figure showing affection.

If I ever met her parents... Well, I had no idea what I would say, but it wouldn't be good.

And let's back up to the hug the Murphy sisters were sharing when we walked in. My nature to want to ensure everyone was okay was screaming to find out what was going on. Was Maeve all right? Was Allyson? Did I need to kill someone? I mean, a bit extreme, sure, but you didn't mess with the people I cared about.

We weren't going to look too closely at that line of thinking.

"Bacon's done," Logan crowed as he entered the house via the porch. Charlie trailed closely behind, likely looking for a leftover piece of bacon or two. The golden retriever in him was strong, making the pup a true scavenger.

"How much did you make?" I asked, ignoring the draw of Maeve and heading in the direction my nose wanted to follow. I mean, bacon. It's all that needs to be said.

"Two pounds, you carnivore. Think that's enough?" Logan kicked the door shut behind him while still being able to bat my hand away as I reached for a piece.

"Just checking to make sure it's okay for consumption," I grumbled.

"Charlie already did that; no worries." Logan shot me a grin before heading into the kitchen, stopping to kiss Allyson on the cheek, then Mom.

Mom patted Logan on the cheek, then raised her bottle of champagne. "This needs to be opened, boys. Let's go."

"On it, Mama Bear," I grabbed it out of her hand and headed to the counter with my bowl of fruit and the bottle and got to work. In minutes, I had some champagne in a glass for her with a splash of mango juice instead of orange, just the way she liked it.

I slid the glass toward Mom and looked around the kitchen. Dad was feeding Charlie treats I was sure he didn't need. Mom and Maeve were talking as Maeve pulled down some plates for our crew. Logan was swaying with Allyson in his arms as he rested a hand on her belly. I held the bottle up to the group in the kitchen. "Anyone else?"

Dad, Logan, and Maeve quickly voiced their drink orders. Logan grabbed a sparkling water for Allyson. Once we all had our drinks, Mom raised hers in a toast.

"Let's celebrate all of us being together for breakfast on a random Monday. And we even get to have Maeve with us." Mom put her arm around Maeve's waist, squeezing their sides together, which she clearly wasn't expecting.

As I raised my glass up for a drink, Logan spoke. "Wait just a second."

Lowering my mimosa, I looked from Logan to Allyson, who was still locked in my brother's arms. They shared similar cat-that-ate-the-canary smiles, and I began to get a pulse of energy from my brother. I gave Logan a glance that said *what is going on?*

Patience, grasshopper. He shot a look back at me.

"You two are doing that weird twinspeak, aren't you," Maeve said in my direction.

I shrugged and looked back to Logan, wanting to get the show on the road. Logan leaned down to Allyson, speaking into her ear, "You want to take this?"

"Sure," Allyson said, then looked up to us. "So we had an ultrasound last week."

My mom began to dance around with her hands, including the mimosa, raised up over her head. "Oh my gosh, oh my gosh, oh my gosh."

"Linnie," Dad called, reaching out a hand to pull her against his chest. "At least act like you're cool."

"Why?" she asked, reclining her neck to look up at him.

Dad shook his head, giving her an affectionate glance, then looked back to Logan and Allyson. "Go ahead, kids."

I watched the two of them share a secret smile as I tried to predict what Logan was going to say but got nothing. We already knew it wasn't twins, something about numbers in some blood test when Allyson had first found out. I knew they were excited to have a singleton, and while I got that, I thought it would be hilarious for Logan to have to deal with two kids who were similar to us.

Allyson leaned her head on one of Logan's arms. "Well,

first of all, the most important news is that the baby is healthy."

"Excellent," Dad murmured.

"As for the gender…" Allyson began.

"You're not doing some big reveal?" Maeve asked.

"Like…" Allyson looked at her sister with a raised brow.

"You know, shooting colored powder out of some type of cannon, cutting a cake, fireworks, and the like," Maeve said, shooting a wink in my direction. She knew, as I did, that those were the exact opposite of anything Allyson, or Logan for that matter, would want to do.

"One, still pissed you know how to wink and I don't," Allyson grumbled. "Two, no big reveal, just telling you all. And"—she looked around our little circle—"it looks like I will continue to be outnumbered in this household."

"It's a boy!" Mom threw her arms up once again, knocking my dad's glasses askew as she squealed and danced in a circle before throwing herself into Allyson's arms.

I crossed to Logan and pulled him in for a hug. "Congrats, Bro. A baby boy."

"Yeah, surely one will be easier than the two of us were," he said into my ear.

"One can hope." I stepped back so that Dad could pull him in and looked over to Ms. Maeve, standing on her own as she watched the scene unfold. I stepped over next to her and tapped my hip into hers to pull her back to the present.

"You ready to be the best aunt ever?" I asked, making sure to inject some humor into my tone.

Didn't work though because she still seemed lost in her thoughts. "Hope so."

Before I could say anything to lighten the mood, Allyson had stepped up to pull her sister into her arms.

Maeve whispered to her, "I'm so happy for you" as they rocked back and forth.

As the brunch marched on, there was a lot of family togetherness combined with missed chances to talk to the woman currently occupying my thoughts. I wanted to pinpoint what it was that made Maeve Claire Murphy occupy so much of my brain space. Did I want to change my stance on relationships? Nope. Did I think I should break my self-imposed rules for her? Not a chance. And yet I was already plotting another time she and I could meet up to plan this birthday party for her sister. Would we address the likely mutual attraction that I had foolishly given voice to at the brewery last night? Probably not. None of it made a lick of sense.

Her mood lightened as the morning went on. She, Mom, and Allyson were talking about Mom's new gardening group and some gossip about the town. Charlie whined at the back door, so I headed over to let him out and decided to take a few moments for myself on the back deck.

Charlie bounded off the steps toward the tree line just a ways off that made up one of the borders of Highland Woods. I knew he'd do his business and then head back, so I stood, leaning against the railing, as I took a deep breath.

"Centering yourself? Kate would be proud." Logan's voice brought me back with the mention of Drew's wife, who was a yoga teacher in town.

"Something like that." I continued to stare at the trees. An eagle soared above against the brilliant blue sky. The cool temps didn't bother me—I knew we were blessed not to have temps below zero right now.

Logan stepped up against the rail next to me. "I can feel your mind churning. What is it about Maeve that's getting to you?"

There were a lot of people I might try to bullshit. My brother wasn't one.

"Not sure, and that's the honest truth." I searched to separate the waves of feelings that hit me with this woman. Irritation, protection, attraction were the first three that came to mind, but not at all the only ones. "It's like she fascinates me but also pushes my buttons. And, frustratingly, the more I learn about her, the more I want to make her life easier. I have a feeling she'd have me by the balls if she heard that, however."

Logan laughed. "Um, yeah, you might be right there. She is rather fiercely independent." He whistled to Charlie, then turned to face me. "You know you've got a savior thing, right?"

I swiveled my head in his direction. "What?"

"Nothing toxic, but you like to help. Hell"—he patted Charlie's head once the pup reached him—"this guy is a perfect example of it. I mean, you couldn't control the fact that I'd lost my wife or that I was taking a job three hours away, so you bought me a dog so that I wouldn't be alone." He raised a brow in my direction. "That's you, fixing what you can."

"So you're saying I should buy her a dog." I cracked a smile.

"Yeah, that might not work with her nomadic tendencies."

My smile disappeared at the reminder that she was only here temporarily. Damn.

Logan must have sensed my need for a topic change. "So almost a year in, how are you feeling about your move to Highland Falls? You used to this place yet?"

I thought about the differences between Aurora, where I'd lived near my parents, and Highland Falls. It wasn't just the city versus small town. And if we're being honest, there were a lot fewer options for food here, or hell, shopping in general. No food delivery unless the restaurant offered it themselves. And it was hard to get used to walking into an establishment, like the Homestead, and having everyone turn their head your way to see who just came in. There were downsides, sure.

But anytime I found myself standing in Logan's backyard at night, I would stare at the night sky, getting lost in the stars. There were so many it was breathtaking. Even my place in town allowed you to see more than I ever had.

Traffic? Nonexistent. The only issue that'd stopped traffic since I moved here was a lost cow from a nearby farm, wandering the roads into town, looking for home. Heck, my house off of downtown meant I could walk to the majority of spots I visited daily. It was a different way of life for sure.

Finding a new place to live was a piece of cake because Logan knew everyone. And small-town people were nosy, sure, but so nice. Heck, when I'd been struck down with a nasty virus this fall, I'd had soup, casseroles, and more show up on my doorstep.

It was cliché but true—Highland Falls was a place where neighbors looked after each other. And even though my parents had been miles from my place in Aurora, I'd missed my twin. Being only minutes away made something inside me settle. Having our parents move down was just the icing on the cake.

"Feeling pretty good," I answered. "It's an adjustment, but I'm getting there."

"And you have enough editing business? I know you were worried when you moved away from Chicago, but I figured when you hired Aidan, you must be doing well." He clapped a hand to my shoulder, somehow oblivious to my inner turmoil.

Freelance editing hadn't been my original plan, but working for a company that gave zero fucks about their employees had made jumping ship pretty appealing. When they'd balked at my taking any time off to be there for Logan when Nola passed, I knew I had to get out of there.

My first jobs kind of fell in my lap and allowed me to get my name out there. Now the work was steady, but being your own boss had stressors of its own. Add to that I no longer had a salary to depend on and the money that came in was contingent on the hours I put in—well, that was a recipe for becoming a workaholic.

That didn't even touch hiring our friend Aidan a month back, though he was part time for now. I needed the help and was sure it would work out, but I couldn't help the anxiety that it produced, telling me I wasn't making enough to keep us all afloat.

But this wasn't anything to stress Logan out with. "Yeah, everything is good."

He scanned my expression, likely trying to ascertain if I was telling the truth. Deciding to let it go, he moved from the railing. "Maybe think more about that one." Logan inclined his head to the windows lining the back of his house.

Just beyond them, I could see Maeve and Allyson, arms wrapped around each other, Maeve's head thrown back in laughter at something my dad was saying. "She's under your skin, Levi. Might want to think some more on why that is and what you're going to do about it."

With that truth bomb, Logan headed back into the house, leaving me to watch the birds soar over the trees as I pondered questions I didn't have answers to.

Chapter 7

Girls' Night Out

M*aeve*
For the umpteenth time that night, I questioned why I had decided to stay for a few weeks instead of stopping in this town for a weekend and then coming back for Allyson's birthday. Hell, I'd even considered staying longer. Sometimes I felt like Highland Falls and the people in it were quicksand, and the more I fought, the more I sank down into their suffocating embrace. A little dark, possibly, but accurate.

In the days since brunch at Logan and Allyson's, I'd tried to distance myself from everyone, to find some time to re-center myself. Was I successful? That would be a solid no—it was next to impossible here. Instead, I'd worked a few shifts for Allyson when I clocked Logan watching her on Monday night with a worried expression as he asked her to get some more rest. She'd refused to call in for reinforcements even though I *knew* she had so many employees who would have jumped at the chance. So I did what any sister would do and mandated she take a few days off and stepped up in her place.

Heck, my shifts at the café in town hadn't even felt like work. Allyson's right hand, Andy, rocked her job. Sidenote —I was green with envy over her tattoo sleeve. One day mine would be there. Bonus points awarded to her, Andy made certain the environment at the café was fun, even—or especially—for the employees.

This week I'd worked with some of the new hires— Gabe and Henry. You know, people say teens don't have a work ethic, but those two sure did. We took turns picking songs for a playlist and had a blast cranking out some food for the patrons.

If anyone had been looking for peace and quiet, the Sanctuary in town wouldn't typically fit the bill, but that was all right. The vibe at the café at the park was a little more chill. The one in town? It was always abuzz with energy, and the past few days were more of the same. That might have something to do with Lou and her crew, who typically circled up around a table and discussed what was happening in town while calling out across the space to anyone entering that they knew. I'd joined them for a few minutes each day, and my abs hurt from laughing from the stories they'd shared.

From there I'd worked a few shifts at the yoga studio. Kate's business partner, Kristine, was out with the flu, so that was the least I could do. I'd subbed an afternoon for Ivy at the bookstore when she needed to pick Addie up early from school with a bug of her own. And between it all, I'd exchanged texts with an increasingly infuriating man. Levi said he wanted more of my input on this party, but we hadn't gotten together again since the brunch. Instead, he'd started a group text with Logan and me, ironing out most of the details there. It was almost like I wasn't the only one trying to avoid people around here. Hmm.

But tonight I was setting those concerns aside. It was a Friday night, and I was meeting a few women in town for a drink or, in Allyson's case, a water and letting all my worries go.

Allyson and Logan had finally given into my cajoling and were headed to a getaway cabin in the woods the next morning, just a few hours' drive from here. Logan promised he was going to put Allyson to bed and not let her out of it until the dark circles were completely gone.

I was on Charlie duty, though Logan said Levi was happy to run back up if needed. As if I couldn't take care of a dog for the weekend. Whatever—I was sure he'd continue to stay far away from me, which was just fine.

"What are we singing along to tonight?" Ivy squeezed past the crowd to join Allyson and me at the bar.

Allyson was deep in conversation with the woman on her other side—I think she'd said she was retired from the school. Ms. T? At any rate, I focused on Ivy. "I don't think there's karaoke here tonight..."

"Who needs karaoke, I just like to sing," she said, arms up, dancing in place.

Jake appeared in front of her on the other side of the bar. "Behave, mama," he positively growled as he gave her a look that made my panties want to melt right off. Damn.

I looked from Ivy to Jake, then back to my friend, choosing to ignore the sexual energy between the two, who had been married for almost a year. "How's Miss Addie feeling today?"

Ivy looked at me with a bright smile. "She's good. Looks like it was a twenty-four-hour bug. Noah has her tonight with her sister Lorelai since I wanted to come out to visit for a bit."

I racked my brain for a moment—there were a lot of people to keep track of in this group. "Noah?"

Jake slid my requested IPA in front of me. "Noah is Addie's dad."

That's right. "Your ex?" I asked, working on the Highland Friends and Family Tree in my head.

Ivy shrugged like it was no big deal. "I mean, I guess? We dated in college and Addie was not planned. We grew up with each other, so I think of him more like a childhood friend than an ex."

I glanced to Jake. To be honest, I hadn't hung around with the Spencers a ton, just a few times here and there as I passed through. Jake was Addie's dad in my mind, though even I knew he wasn't her birth father. I hadn't realized this Noah guy was in the picture though. Surely Jake wasn't as relaxed as Ivy.

Once again, the people of this quaint Hallmark town proved me wrong.

Jake shot me an easy smile of reassurance. "I know, it isn't your usual story. And honestly, at first I was jealous. But Noah wasn't part of Addie's life for her first few years, or not as much as he wanted to be due to where he was living. He's moved to the area to change that and has proven again and again that he's a good guy and here for us in any way he can be. Hence him taking both kids for a few hours tonight so that Ivy can get a break." He shrugged and went to help the next customer at the bar.

Ivy pulled up a vacant stool and looked at me with an amused expression. "Is it really that weird?"

I nodded toward Allyson. "Hell, our parents aren't civil to each other most of the time, and they're married. So in our world"—I held my thumb and pointer finger in a pinch about an inch apart—"it's a little strange."

She shrugged, unconcerned. "I like weird."

Jake passed her a glass across the bar.

"Me too," I said as I tapped my glass to hers.

We sat in silence as we nodded along to the music for a beat or two before Allyson joined into our circle, done with her earlier conversation, with a question aimed to Ivy. "Who all is meeting us tonight?"

Ivy tilted her head to the side, clearly considering the answer. "Let's see." She ticked people off on her fingers. "Emma is hibernating because she said she's sleeping for two."

"I hear that," Allyson murmured. Emma was just a few weeks ahead of Allyson on the pregnancy timeline.

Ivy, undeterred, continued. "Maggie said if she could get her mother-in-law to watch El, she'd be here."

Made sense. I saw Maggie's husband Sully running around, changing kegs.

"And the library crew—Elle, Nate, Tim, and Grace—have a book club tonight but might swing by after. And finally, our yoga contingent, Kate and Kristine, are coming after their Friday-night wind-down class."

Sounded like Kristine was feeling better, which was great. At a shout from across the bar, our heads swiveled. Tim was leading the group from the Ryan Library through the brewery. Seemed book club was over.

"High steps, friends," Tim said to the procession behind him. He called over to Sully, "Cole Sullivan, I'm going to need you to switch this music to Ms. Swift." He pursed his lips as he thought about a song. "I'm feeling like marching on the patriarchy. How about 'The Smallest Man Who Ever Lived'?"

"I live to serve." Sully tapped on a screen to switch the songs.

"Maggie is a lucky woman," Tim said over the crowd, coming to a stop with the group in front of us.

"Yes, I am," Maggie said, laughter in her voice as she came in from the side door.

I looked around this group that had welcomed me with open arms once I started visiting Allyson, glanced to Tim, and said the only thing I could think of. "So, shall we march?"

His beaming smile answered me back.

Two hours later, a sheen of sweat covered my face. It was hard to dance when there wasn't really a dance floor, but no worries, we prevailed. We'd shaken our bodies to the greatest hits from Swift, Cyrus, Nicks, and more. At one point Lou and the woman Allyson had been talking to joined us, albeit at a much slower pace.

Allyson was on her two millionth or, more accurately, fifth glass of water. I'd had several IPAs but was just feeling a nice buzz, and she'd be driving my butt home. I briefly thought of checking on Ally to see if she was ready to head. Ivy and Maggie had both ducked out a song ago. But before I could find her, Tim caught my attention.

It wasn't hard to see why he'd catch anyone's attention. The man was over six foot and had a flair that was uniquely his own. I always loved to see what T-shirt he chose for any given day. Today's had a unicorn sporting a rainbow mane swinging on a stripper pole, as one does.

He ducked his head to talk directly into my ear. "Marvelous Maeve, isn't that the man you love to hate walking into this fine establishment?"

I glanced from him to the front of the brewery. Sure enough, one Levi Traub was walking in, and I had enough alcohol in me to admit he looked like one of my dreams sprang to life. His hair was mussed just so, making it look like he'd rolled out of bed. He wore a thick flannel open over a Henley and jeans that I just knew hugged his ass. My heart fluttered. Logan would have told him we were coming here if he'd asked. Were we finally done ignoring each other? Did I want to be? Jury was still out.

My eyes locked on him, watching him laugh as he talked to a group and then left their table, scanning the room as he clearly looked for someone. I told myself to look away, but that was a futile endeavor even when I heard Tim murmur *oh girlie* and then walk away.

Before I could give myself another pep talk, duck behind someone, walk to the bathroom, *anything*, the man looked up and locked his gaze with mine. The surprise on his face was evident, which told me he hadn't realized we'd be here or I hadn't factored into his visit. Well, I told myself, that was neither here nor there—maybe we could still touch base. And while talking, I could continue to sort out these confusing feelings.

I raised my hand to wave and started to take a step toward him when I heard someone else shout his name. Levi's head swiveled to the side as he said something, and I watched the hostess from when we entered tonight, Laurie, walk right up to him and wrap him in a tight hug.

What in the ever-loving fuck? My stomach dropped.

Levi took a step back and looked my way with a strange expression on his face, gave me a wave, then nodded at Laurie and turned to walk out of the Homestead with her by his side.

Without my knowing it was possible, my tender heart shattered into a million pieces. I looked back to my friend group only to see that they'd witnessed it, and their looks of sympathy for me made me want to hop in Big Red and get as far as possible from this little town.

Tim gave me a once-over, then said in a loud voice, "There isn't much I enjoy straight, but a shot of tequila is one. Let's go."

Allyson stepped up to my side. "I'm sure it's nothing, Mae. That's Laurie—you've met her, right? She's a single mom here in town, and all of us help her out. I'm certain that's what Levi was doing. Let me just call Logan and..."

I raised a hand. "No, absolutely not. Levi and I aren't anything to each other. What he's doing with"—I sucked in a huge breath—"Laurie is not my business." Looking at Tim, I called out, "I'll take one of those shots."

Tim high-fived me, and I worked to do what I've always done—shove down what threatened to break me and move the fuck along.

Chapter 8

This Ain't It, Baby

Levi

I couldn't get the look on Maeve's face at the brewery last night out of my mind. It played, over and over on repeat, reminding me of how badly I'd screwed up, though I couldn't figure out what on earth I'd done.

Logan and I went online to play *Warzone* while he had his place to himself since Allyson and Maeve had gone out with some women in town. My place being empty, I could easily swing a night of gaming without anyone wanting me to be productive or anything. We'd multitasked like pros, talking over our headsets while keeping up a group text with Sully, who was working at the brewery and filling us in on the night's shenanigans as we attempted to not embarrass ourselves in the game. Sully had joined our chats between changing kegs and being an extra set of hands at the brewery, and our text thread slowly filled up with next week's lunch plans, which days we had free, and we all did a bit of trash-talking on who was the rustier player between Logan and me since Sully didn't play much. While trying to best another squad of likely preteens who were better than the two of us, Sully messaged that he'd have to catch us later. It seemed that Laurie, the brewery's hostess, had a dead car that wasn't responding to a jump and he had to figure out a way to get her home.

I hadn't thought anything of it. We all knew Laurie, and she was one of the kindest people with the worst luck imaginable. Her ex, however, was the biggest piece of shit to ever draw breath. Our entire friend group helped her out when we could. Heck, anyone in Highland Falls would, except she hated asking for help. Besides, Logan and I were getting our asses handed to us. I was glad to take a break.

I hadn't counted on seeing Maeve there looking like she *belonged* in Highland Falls. I'd clocked her when I walked in—she'd been in conversation with Tim from the library, and her face had been filled with happiness. I knew she was only in town for the moment, but my brain was playing tricks on me. It made me want what I knew wasn't possible. So when Laurie had called my name, I'd turned to give her a ride home rather than do what my soul was urging me to do —walk across the bar and kiss the living daylights out of Maeve, nosy townspeople be damned.

Realistically, I knew if I tried that the woman would knee me in the balls. Didn't stop the desire. What was it Logan had called his dick when he was lusting over Allyson way back when? I thought about that for a moment. Ah, Benedict Arnold, which I'd shortened to BA. Damn cock was a traitor. For Logan, it was having feelings when he wasn't ready for a girlfriend. For me? Looking at someone who'd been irritated with me from day one. That being said, my lower brain was all in. No survival instinct, I guess.

And yet, right before I turned to Laurie last night, I could have sworn Maeve's expression switched from something that looked like interest to one that was almost heartbroken. I was sure I must be wrong, but that didn't stop the feeling in the pit of my stomach that somehow I'd fucked up.

That sense of foreboding had followed me outside to check that Laurie's car really wouldn't start with a jump. And, just as she'd said, no dice. I drove Laurie home to relieve her neighbor who was babysitting her kids. She was, as always, appreciative and offered me a meal on her at the Homestead. I reminded her that we all knew how tight funds were when she was doing it all on her own and told her to let us know if she needed help getting a new battery.

The drive home was consumed with thinking about what could have possibly upset Maeve, what I was missing. I'd known the woman for nine months. True, she drove me crazy a lot of the time, but less so lately. I felt like we had a good friendship even if we pushed each other's buttons. I respected her, and unless I was mistaken, she respected me. There was the small matter of being attracted to her. Totally normal, right? At any rate, it didn't sit well with me that I'd done something to upset her, even inadvertently.

Pulling myself back into the present, I stared at the two monitors in front of me. I couldn't even remember the first thing I needed to do, which didn't bode well. It was Saturday, so it wasn't like I needed to be working. Funny thing when you were your own boss though. It was all too easy to work far more than you should. I glanced at the action list that Aidan and I had mapped out for last week and next. We were on track, but I always felt like I should be doing more.

I scanned the list for something I could do mindlessly to get us ahead to start the week, but the vibrations from my phone brought me back to present. I looked at the screen to see a text from Logan.

Baby Bro: *You really fucked up now.*

Had to be about Maeve, right? That didn't sound great even if it was in line with what I'd been thinking.

Me: *Care to elaborate?*

Baby Bro: *Just leaving our place with Allyson to head to that cabin until Monday. Let's just say the other Murphy sister is pissed, and according to my beautiful bride, she's pissed at you.*

Damn, I knew it. My gut had been right, but I was still at a loss.

Me: *Thoughts on why?*

I mean, I'd helped Laurie with her car. Did Maeve have something against Laurie? Not possible—that would be like disliking Bambi. Everyone loved Laurie.

I looked at my phone screen. Logan's message showed he was typing. Fuck it, I left my desk and headed to my kitchen to get something to eat. Ignoring my phone, I grabbed a bag of chips and sank down onto my couch, intent on doing some damage to this bag, but his incoming text made me pause.

Baby Bro: *Allyson isn't sure because Maeve is being Maeve, which means she's trying to act like she's fine. But you might want to try to talk to her.*

That made me snort.

Me: *Yeah, Maeve doesn't love talking to me at the best of times. She certainly isn't going to want to have a convo if she's pissed at me even if I did nothing wrong.*

Baby Bro: *All I'm saying is try to fix this. We're supposed to be having a birthday party for Allyson a week from today, and I don't want bullshit between you two to ruin it. Allyson is headed back this way from the café, so you're going to have to figure this out on your own. We're off.*

Shit. One week?

Me: *On it. Enjoy your time and tell Ally to rest up and grow that baby.*

Baby Bro: *That's the idea. Thanks.*

I looked at the chips on the table in front of me. They weren't calling my name as they had been. To be honest, I'd lost my appetite. How in the hell did you fix something when you didn't know how you'd broken it? Part of this reminded me of dating Tess, how I often felt like I was making up for bullshit I didn't know I'd done. In hindsight, that was just Tess working to control me. If that was the way Maeve was, I had no interest in that.

I paused, thinking it over. I really hadn't done anything wrong. Why not just operate from that standpoint? Unless I'd completely read her wrong, Maeve wasn't about manipulative bullshit. If Maeve had a problem with me, she was going to need to let me know. For now we had a birthday party to plan.

Picking up my phone, I texted the woman who wouldn't leave my mind.

Me: *Coming your way in ten. We have one week until Allyson's party and still a few plans to finalize.*

I put away the chips and grabbed my keys. As I was headed to my 4Runner, her text came in.

Flower Child: *Bring coffee.*

Well, I guess that was better than expected. I turned out of my drive and headed to the Sanctuary.

Twenty minutes later, I pulled up outside Logan and Allyson's. As I approached the door with two coffees, I had the internal debate—knock or head straight in. If I was just coming over to see Logan and Allyson, I'd never knock if they knew I was en route. But with Maeve, I hesitated.

Snap out of it, I told myself. Balancing the two drinks, I pushed the door open and called out as I entered, "Coffee is here."

"In here." Maeve's voice came from the kitchen.

I headed in that direction, a strong aroma making my mouth water.

"What is that deliciousness?" I asked, coming around the corner and locking on Maeve with her back to me, leaning over to pull something out of the oven.

"Brownies," she said as she placed a hot pan on the top of the stove.

"For me?" I cracked as I slid a coffee onto the counter for her.

"Hardly," she said as she placed the potholder on the counter, still facing away from me.

I couldn't help but notice her body was tense and went back and forth on if I should just keep talking or if I should address it. That hesitation lasted just a moment as my mom popped up in my subconscious to remind me that it was the rare problem that didn't get better with communication.

I could almost *feel* her slapping me upside my head. Yeah, yeah, Mom. Got it. Deep breaths and dive in.

"Want to talk about why you're pissed at me?" My heart threatened to beat out of my chest. I worked on appearing calm even if I wasn't on the inside. I knew I hadn't done anything to feel bad about, but I still felt guilty nonetheless. Maeve was clearly upset, and if I'd been the one to make her that way, I wanted to fix it.

Maeve grabbed her coffee and slowly turned, putting the counter at her back as she looked up. Her eyes were troubled, far from the fiery ones I was used to. That didn't sit right with me.

True to form, Ms. Maeve didn't bullshit but dove on in. "I'm pissed at myself for being pissed at you."

I nodded, taking a sip of my coffee like this made all the sense in the world.

"I don't get jealous..." She faltered.

I perked up. Jealous? I tried to appear supportive and willing to listen while that heart that had been beating out of my chest threatened to jackhammer its way out.

She set the coffee aside for a moment as she began jabbing the air with her finger. "And you're welcome to hook up with anyone you want. I don't shame people for their sex lives." Maeve's cheeks were rosy, and she looked decidedly away from me.

I did an internal double take before wading in to this conversation, because clearly we had some miscommunication going on. "Um, sorry. Hook up? Sex life? Unless you're referring to my hand, which is a solid date and shouldn't be disparaged, there hasn't been anyone to speak of since last spring."

Maeve's surprised expression swiveled my way. "What?"

I shrugged. "Small towns. I moved here and realized that the whole 'don't shit where you live' phrase could apply to hookups here. Not that I wouldn't necessarily, but it would have to be worth the risk of pissing off some local, you know?"

"But the hostess last night? I saw you leave with her." Now Ms. Maeve looked positively squirmy, like it cost a lot for her to admit that.

I didn't want to acknowledge how much I loved this conversation because I knew she'd fortify those walls in a heartbeat. "Did you?" I grinned. Couldn't help it.

Maeve gave me an assessing glance, then threw a pot holder at my head. "Don't look so smug, you asshat."

I laughed as I leaned down to pick up the poor pot

holder—it had never harmed anyone. "The hostess is Laurie. She's a single mom with a deadbeat ex. We all help her out when we can."

Maeve muttered under her breath, "I bet you do."

"Now, now." I couldn't lie, there was a large part of me that was enjoying this. "I've done a lot since you've met me that you have valid reasons to be pissed about. But last night? That ain't it, baby."

"Baby?" She raised an eyebrow at me.

I continued, undeterred. "One, nothing has ever happened between Laurie and me. Nothing will either. Last night she told Sully her car was dead. Logan and I were texting with him, and he mentioned it. I knew she needed to head out to relieve her babysitter, so I came up to take her home, which is what I did." I stepped around the island to get closer to Maeve just as my body was singing for me to do. "Does that clear it all up so you can be done being pissed at me?"

Maeve looked down at her bare feet. "I don't know that I'll ever have a time when I'm not at least a little pissed at you."

I tapped her toe with my sneaker. "But we're good?"

She looked at me with clear eyes that were closer to her norm. "We're good."

I felt my body leaning toward hers and wondered if this was the stupidest idea I'd ever had or the greatest. But to be honest, I didn't feel super in control of my actions right now anyway and was just going to go with it.

I slid a hand to her hip, and she didn't seem to protest but stepped closer. Right as I began to lower my lips to hers, a loud bark came from below. We both jumped back to look down to see Charlie happily sitting between both of us, a bag at his feet.

"What the fuck, Charlie," I grumbled.

Maeve, however, gasped, which seemed like an extreme reaction. She leaned over and picked up the bag by his feet and then held it up to me. "Shit, shit, shit," she whispered, her face becoming pale.

I was beyond confused at this point. "What?"

She shook the yellow plastic bag at me again. "I got out chocolate chips because I was toying with putting them in the brownie batter, but then I decided to stick with my original recipe."

"And...?"

"And this bag was half full." She shook it again.

"So...?" I looked at her before it clicked, then back to the smiling dog. I glanced up to Maeve. "Are you saying the dog ate the chocolate chips?"

She nodded grimly.

"Dogs aren't supposed to eat chocolate."

"No, they aren't," she said, remorseful, as we both turned to look at Charlie, whose tail sped up with happy wags.

Shit.

Chapter 9

Charlie the Wonder Pup

M *aeve*

This was not good. This was so beyond not good. I put a hand to my chest, wanting reassurance that I was breathing, but it was the hand holding the offensive yellow bag, so I punched the air in frustration.

"What are we going to do?" I shrieked. Was I hyperventilating? I was hyperventilating.

"You're not hyperventilating," Levi called, rubbing Charlie's fluffy golden head.

Did I say that out loud? "How are you just sitting there calmly?" I asked, beginning to pace.

"Hmm, I would have pegged you for being excellent in a crisis," the asshat said, still petting the pup. How on earth had I ever considered kissing this man? I mean, the nerve. My ancestors had apparently led my gut astray. They could no longer be trusted.

"One, I'll have you know I'm excellent in a crisis," I muttered.

"Clearly." He had the nerve to smile at me.

"Two, there will be no pegging, mister. Of anyone." I resumed pacing.

"Spicy, I like it," he said as he pulled his phone out.

Charlie continued to look unaffected. I, on the other hand, thought I might come unglued.

"What are you doing?" My irritation levels rose. Why in the world would he consider *now* a good time to make a phone call? He was probably calling Laurie.

My inner conscience rose up. *They are just friends, and it isn't any of your business who he calls.*

Shut it, I thought in reply.

"Hi, Vet Med?" Levi said, and I spun to face him. "Yeah, I'm house-sitting a goldendoodle who got into a bag of chocolate chips." Pause. "Yep, not a great choice on his part." He looked at the bag and then Charlie, who lay down on the floor and gave us big eyes. "I'd say about a cup's worth, two on the outside. Mm-hmm, semisweet. Yep, sounds good. Just give me that number. Hold on." He grabbed a notepad from the counter and wrote something down. "Okay, thanks!"

"What did they...?"

He held a finger up for me to wait as he dialed a new number.

My gut was clenching like I wanted to vomit or run to the toilet—I wasn't sure which. I couldn't have killed Allyson and Logan's dog. Surely he'd be fine, right?

Sitting on his phone, Levi looked my way. "I'm on hold, but they told me to call the ASPCA's poison control line. That's what I'm doing."

I looked at Charlie, who glanced my way and gave what could only be described as a smile—the dog looked like he was having his best day ever. Damn pup. I still loved him to pieces, but I sure as shit didn't need this kind of stress in my life. Who knew dogs took food off counters? Probably someone who had owned one before.

"Hi." Levi was pulling out his wallet. "Yes, I heard about the charge." He rattled off his credit card information, then put his card away as he once again summarized Charlie's exploits.

"Okay, let me repeat this all to make sure I've got it." He handed me a pen and the notepad, I was guessing to write down what we needed to do. "Charlie will likely be fine, but just in case, we're going to induce vomiting. We need to give him a handful of food because that will help. Then we need to smear some peanut butter in a bowl and then put a table-spoon and a half of hydrogen peroxide on top of that to let him lap it up before he gets to the peanut butter."

He nodded at me, making sure I had all of that. I nodded back. Sure did. This sounded awful.

"After that, we are to put him on a leash and walk him around until he vomits." He paused, and I scanned my scribbled directions. Yep, we were still good so far. Levi resumed the conversation. "Once he does, pick up his water until he hasn't gotten sick for an hour. If the first round of peroxide doesn't work, try a second. Do I have all that?"

I looked up to see his eyes were on me, waiting to see if I needed anything repeated.

I nodded, reading over what I've written for a final time. I think I had it. Jesus. I couldn't harm Logan's dog; Allyson would kill me, and I would never forgive myself. Why on earth hadn't I put the chocolate chips away? My parents always said I was irresponsible. Clearly they were right.

"Hey."

I looked up to see Levi staring at me, apparently done with the phone call.

"Charlie is going to be fine. Dogs are resilient." He

nodded toward the pup, and Charlie started wagging his whole body as he got up to sit right by Levi's legs, giving us a bark in reply.

"I should have put the chocolate chips up." I could hear my voice quiver.

"Sure, but then he could have dive-bombed the brownies, eaten the trash, devoured a roll of toilet paper, who knows what else? You do the best you can and when something goes awry, you figure out what the next steps are." He tapped my notepad. "These are next steps, so let's see if we can get this adorable pup to upchuck some chocolate."

"Yay?" I looked at him skeptically, then glanced to Charlie. He was fine for the moment, but we should probably get the show on the road. We reread the directions and got to work.

Levi took off for the bathroom, where he thought the peroxide would be. I grabbed a small bowl and the peanut butter. Charlie leaned into my side, as if to ask what I was doing.

I leaned down, grabbing the soft curls of his head with both hands. "We're going to get you to puke this stuff up so you don't get super sick. You got that, Charlie?"

He leaned forward and licked my nose. I got a whiff of his chocolate-chip-scented breath and gave the dog a hug before standing back up. He was not a small dog, but he leaned into the hug like he was giving me comfort instead of the reverse. I sent up a prayer to the goddess, ancestors, or anyone who'd listen to look after this pup.

Levi came back in and grabbed a measuring spoon. We worked together to get the concoction ready, giving Charlie a little food before setting the bowl down in front of him with the stuff he needed to drink.

"Do you think he'll go for it," I whispered.

Levi shrugged. "Time will tell."

Charlie looked from Levi to me, to his bowl, then back to us.

"Come on, pup," I whispered.

Levi placed a hand on my lower back. I chose to ignore the electricity that cascaded down, telling myself that it was not the time. "Relax, he's part golden retriever. No way is he leaving peanut butter around."

Sure enough, Charlie took a tentative lick at the bowl. He didn't look thrilled but then did another and another. Sure enough, within minutes all the peroxide and peanut butter were a thing of a past and the bowl was licked clean.

"Now what?" I asked.

"We put him on a leash and head out. Bundle up—it's not exactly warm," he said, grabbing his fleece and Charlie's leash.

Gear on, the three of us headed out the door and into the yard. I looked out toward the road. Logan and Allyson's driveway was a gravel road that went over a creek bed that was currently dry. Beyond that was a country road and barren fields for as far as the eye could see with a few farms dotted in for good measure. The home backed up to Highland Woods.

"Woods or road?" I asked. Charlie turned toward the road. "Guess that answers that."

"As long as the roads are clear, I know Logan walks him daily on the road. He only walks along the woods when snow and ice make the roads too slick." Levi slowed down as we traversed the small creek bed.

"Why's that?" I asked, taking my time on the rocks and waving away Levi's proffered hand. I had enough to deal with waiting for this pup to puke, all tingles this man made me feel or not feel were moving to the back burner of my conscious for now.

Levi shook his head at my refusal, but we soldiered on. "Few reasons, I'd imagine. One, it's a hell of a lot easier to walk. Now if it's icy, you stick to the grass and you won't wipe out. Otherwise, hard surfaces are faster. Two, Logan and Allyson ran that marathon last spring and they stuck to the roads, so that's what Charlie is used to."

I nodded, remembering the stress Logan had associated with racing. It had been a victory when he and Allyson finished.

"And three, there are small animals in the woods, and the smells make it really hard for Charlie the wonder pup to just walk. He wants to check everything out." He looked at the pup with a smile.

"Ah, and we just need him to walk right now."

"And get on with evacuating his stomach," Levi agreed.

We hit the country road and walked along the shoulder. Charlie, thus far, showed zero effects from the chocolate or the peroxide concoction.

I shivered as the wind picked up. The gray skies all around were not inspiring any thoughts of warmth.

"Need to go back?" Levi asked. Apparently I hadn't been subtle with my reaction.

"No, but how long do we think it takes this to work?" I asked, hopefully not unkindly. It wasn't that I wanted the dog to be sick, but I wanted that chocolate to exit his body so I could stop stressing about it.

"The people on the phone said anywhere from fifteen minutes to half an hour and"—he glanced at his watch—"we're just past fifteen minutes now."

As if on cue, Charlie came to a halt and started to make a terrible sound that I'd only heard when my friend's cat tried to yak up a fur ball. He had his back arched, head down, heaving.

"Here we go." Levi put his hand on Charlie's back, rubbing it and talking to him.

I stood, frozen, unsure as to my role here. "What do I do?" I whispered to Levi.

He looked up at me. "You don't have to do anything, Charlie has it. But if it makes you feel better to do something, you can pet him or talk to him."

I nodded, crouching down by Charlie's other side. "You've got this, Charlie. Puke that crap up." I rubbed my hand along his neck.

As if he'd needed my words, an avalanche came out of the pup's mouth with a pool of chocolate plopping down on the road along with some kibble. I wrinkled my nose at the visual while also cheering on the inside.

Looking at Levi, I asked, "What next?"

Levi was watching Charlie. "She said on the phone that he might get sick more than once, but we can take our cues from him."

I looked back to Charlie who, other than some drool hanging out of his mouth, looked like he was living his best life.

I shrugged and stood up, Levi following me, and Charlie tugged us back onto the road.

"Whoa, pup," Levi said. "I think we can head back so we can get you rested and I can call poison control back."

"Why are we calling back," I asked, falling into step with the two of them.

"They said to let them know when he got sick and they would advise any aftercare."

I took a deep breath, grateful that the chocolate was out of his system, and said a quick prayer that he was truly fine now. "Do we need to call Allyson and Logan?" I asked, hoping we didn't but knowing we did.

Levi turned his head slightly and gave me a small smile. "You really don't want to, do you?"

"I mean, I'm not jumping for joy about telling them I tried to kill their dog," I grumbled.

"Flair for the dramatic, hmm, Ms. Maeve?" Levi said lightly. "Charlie is fine. I can let Logan know, but he won't be upset. He knows his dog."

Charlie froze, did the hacking thing again, and puked up another pool. This one was smaller than the last. Still...

"I don't know if I can have chocolate ever again," I said with a groan.

"I'll eat the brownies then," Levi said as we resumed walking.

Charlie hardly even seemed fazed.

"Blah." I shuddered, thinking of that brown liquid. No, thanks.

"So while we head back, do we want to talk about what happened in the kitchen earlier?" Levi asked with a lilt of amusement in his voice.

"You mean when the dog ate chocolate?" I asked, choosing to go the clueless route.

"No."

I could see his wide smile in my peripheral.

"When you explained to me that you weren't actually hooking up with anyone last night?" I asked, heading back over the dry creek bed and up the drive to the cabin.

"Warmer." Levi unsnapped Charlie's leash before opening the door and letting us in.

"Hmm." I unwound my scarf and put my winter gear on the hooks by the door. "You must be referring to our close proximity in the kitchen before Charlie announced his poor decision-making skills."

"Bingo," Levi shed his coat and came to stand in front of me.

"Hmm." I looked up at him, wondering what the right call was here. I didn't know where I'd be in a month; he lived here. Our siblings were married. I didn't want a relationship; I had no idea if he did. However, would I mind getting cozy together? Yes, no, yes, no. Maybe? Ahhh.

A sound pulled me back to the present. I stopped my thought spiral and looked at Levi in alarm. "Were we supposed to let Charlie drink water?"

"What?" he asked, then likely clocked the lapping sound coming from the direction of the water bowl. "Shit. Charlie!"

We both raced into the kitchen, only to see Charlie turn from the bowl and then puke up another puddle of brown liquid right on the kitchen floor.

"Damn." He skirted the puddle and grabbed the water bowl to put it on the counter.

"I've got the paper towels," I called, heading his way.

Looked like it was going to be quite the evening. At least I could put off the should we or shouldn't we conversation for a little bit because, frankly, I had no idea how to say no at this point, and that was more than a little concerning.

Chapter 10

Charlie, My Wingman

Levi

I woke up in stages, first registering the dawn coming up and hitting me in the eyes, then the fact that I wasn't in my bedroom, and finally that I had a body pressed against me. I cracked one eye and looked down to see the blond riot of waves that belonged to Maeve spreading out over my outstretched arm and the pillow. She nestled back against me, clearly still asleep.

On her other side, I saw her arm wrapped around Charlie, who was stretched out facing the two of us on her other side, making Maeve the filling in this bizarre sandwich. Charlie gave me a look that told me he knew exactly where my mind was, firmly in the gutter, and to get myself together.

I thought back to last night and Charlie's fun explosions. Maeve had been a wreck, but I figured it was likely par for the course. However, I did finally manage to call back the ASPCA's poison control. They'd suggested we call Charlie's vet when they opened on Monday just to be safe but said he would likely be fine and to "monitor" him overnight.

I'd taken one look at the hesitation and nerves on Maeve's face and offered to spend the night. Had I thought that meant we'd be spending hours pressed up against each other? Hell, no. That was stuff reserved for my fantasies. I figured Maeve would head to the guest room where she was staying, and Charlie and I would camp out on the couch. And yet when she'd made the suggestion so we'd both be able to monitor him all night, I hadn't paused one bit in my rush to say yes.

Charlie hadn't shown any more ill effects from the chocolate or the peroxide, but the hotline had suggested taking him off any food and drink until the morning, then reintroduce gradually. We'd texted Logan, leaving Allyson off the chat, where I was straightforward and gave him the lowdown. Maeve, however, had apologized profusely, clearly worried Logan would be upset.

If you had asked me last April if a puking dog would shake the woman I'd met outside Allyson's place, I'd have said hell no. I would also have been dead wrong. Logan and Allyson's opinion of her clearly mattered more than I'd realized.

Logan had texted back that Charlie had clearly kept the DNA of a golden retriever that liked to eat anything and, not shockingly, this hadn't been his first foray into the world of chocolate. Logan even told us that the first time it happened, he'd done the peroxide route. From there on out, he'd tried to keep anything with chocolate away from Charlie, but if he got into some, he didn't stress too much.

Would have been good intel to have, but I let that go as it seemed to reassure Maeve.

We'd gone to bed, and it had only been a little awkward. I had on basketball shorts of Logan's and a T-shirt. Maeve was wearing an outfit designed to drive me to madness. There was some type of floral bottoms that looked like harem pants, but the material was sheer. The top had the same flowers going on, also sheer because fuck my life, but it was sleeveless and the hem went up above her belly button in the front. She'd looked at me and appeared mortified by the whole thing, like she hadn't thought through what she was wearing until she had to come out and see me, her luscious curves on full display. Clearly, I knew this hadn't been designed to get the reaction my body was wanting to offer up, but Jesus. I had forced myself to look away.

Getting into that bed had been some kind of tightrope walk of temptation. When we'd started out last night, Charlie had been in the middle, creating a barrier between the two of us. What point of the night had he migrated to the other side of Maeve? I gave the pup another glance, wondering if I should thank or punish him.

Maeve shifted back again, rocking her hips until her ass was snuggled right against my cock. Damn it. The bastard wanted to rally, and I worked on talking him down. Not the time, dude.

Attempting to move carefully without shifting my bed companions, I reached behind me for my phone on the bedside table. Turning it on, I saw the notifications and opened the texts that had come in from Logan.

Baby Bro: *How is my pup? Proof of life?*

Without thinking, I took a pic of Charlie watching me with his big brown eyes and shot it off to Logan. It was only when I saw his three dots for a reply that I examined the picture again and realized it was clear that Maeve was in bed with Charlie, and that I, by nature of taking the pic from the angle I had, was on the other side of her in the same bed. Shit. I tried for the quick exit.

Me: *He's good. Hope you all have a restful day. I'll keep you posted about Charlie.*

Baby Bro: *Nice try. Rewind. And you took that picture how? Just passing by our guest room and thought you'd snap a pic?*

Me: *Would you believe me if I said yes?*

Baby Bro: *Hell no.*

Me: *I don't know what to say without pissing off the woman who is currently in this bed. I like my balls where they are.*

I wasn't sure what made me more nervous, sharing this with Logan or the fact that he didn't reply right away. I watched the screen, almost willing the dots to appear. Finally, after what felt like ten minutes, but in reality was probably two, his reply came through.

Baby Bro: *I hope you know what you're doing. The Murphy girls have had a shit time of it and deserve nothing but the best. Maeve likes to put on a front that nothing can bother her and she doesn't need anyone, but if you're paying attention, I think she needs us a whole lot.*

I looked over to Maeve peacefully sleeping next to me. I couldn't see her face, and a deep well inside me wanted to lie in a bed with her for hours, days, reassuring her that someone was there. What the hell was that bullshit? Time to examine that later, I guessed.

Me: *I think you're right. But don't worry, we both lay in here last night to watch Charlie. Nothing has happened with me and Maeve.*

Baby Bro: *But you want something to, right? I mean, Charlie can be a hell of a wingman.*

I looked at his text and debated lying, but that wasn't

what we were about. Hell, if I tried, he'd call me out anyway.

Me: *I'm not sure, but I think so and it scares the shit out of me.*

Maeve chose that moment to wake up. She rolled to her back and opened her eyes, looking up at the ceiling.

"How did Charlie get on the other side of me?" Her voice was gravelly with sleep.

I fought the urge to lean over and kiss her nose. "Not sure."

"At least my boobs stayed contained," she grumbled, closing her eyes and rubbing a hand over her face.

"I'm sorry, what?" Contained? The tank did little to hide her breasts, which were not small and not hindered by a bra at the moment. I felt like I should win some type of award for trying not to stare, but now she was just drawing attention to them. What to do?

"These tops are all well and good until you roll around in your sleep and wake up with one breast out of the neckline, one out of the armpit. It's a look," she said, eyes to the side, a hint of a blush on her cheeks.

"Not sure what it is that you're seeing, but my vision is filled with pure sex appeal." I didn't know how to hold my cards close this morning apparently.

She stared up at me, her beautiful eyes wide, a smattering of freckles I hadn't noticed across the bridge of her nose and cheeks. From this viewpoint, I could also see a slight scar on the upper corner of her lip.

Before I could stop myself, I reached out and traced my finger over it while she gave a small gasp. Boundaries were apparently vacant before eight in the morning. "What happened here?"

Her eyes didn't leave mine. "Hit the corner of the kitchen counter when I was making dinner for Allyson."

"How old were you?"

"Nine."

I could see emotion swimming in her eyes. "Why were you making her dinner?"

She shrugged and broke eye contact to look away. "My parents were at a dinner function for my dad's work."

"And they couldn't afford a babysitter?" I knew they had money, so I was trying to match what I knew with this reality.

Charlie, apparently sensing Maeve's emotions, sat up and put a paw on her stomach. She reached up to pet him. Being the dog he was, he lay down on her side and tucked his head into the nape of her neck. Lucky dog. The smile that she had in reaction to the pup brightened the room, though it was short-lived. "Once I turned eight, they told me I was responsible for Allyson when they went out. They didn't have full-time help and said it was ridiculous to pay someone else for what I was perfectly capable of doing."

I fought back a growl. She had been a child, for Christ's sake. "What did you do?"

I watched a tear roll over her cheek and wondered if I should drive to Connecticut right now to give those people a piece of my mind. "I finished making dinner and then called my grandmother—"

"Not your parents?"

Maeve whispered, "I knew they wouldn't come. My grandmother, Nan, did and took Allyson and me to the ER where they gave me stitches, and then she brought us home."

"Did Nan say something to your parents?"

Her blue eyes locked on mine. "I'm sure she did, but they wouldn't have cared what she said."

I took a breath, trying to get ahold of the emotions coursing through me. "Babe, I hate your parents."

"Babe?" An amused expression washed over her face, taking us out of the heavy.

Leaning into it, I whispered, "Yeah, *babe*."

Her gaze raked over my face before she gave me a smirk. "You have morning breath."

"So do you."

"Do you care?"

"Fuck no." I leaned down, sliding her away from Charlie as I lowered my mouth to hers, giving her the chance to stop me before this went over the cliff.

Thank God she didn't. Her lips were soft and parted immediately. I tilted my head, working for a better angle while sensations roared through me, telling me to wrap her in my arms and never let her go, which seemed a bit caveman-like.

I slid my hand to her stomach and was relishing her soft curves when Charlie decided to announce his presence once again with a loud bark. The sound reverberated through the room as a moan of protest came from Maeve or me. Truthfully, maybe both of us.

Just as I was about to say *fuck it* and lock the dog out of the room, Maeve's phone chimed with a text.

She immediately sat up. "That's Allyson. I have her notification on bypass so that I always hear them." She reached over and glanced at her phone screen, then shot a worried look my way. "Shit. Logan told her about Charlie." She looked around the room, then unplugged her phone and headed to the door.

"Where are you going?"

"I can't talk to my sister from a bed I'm sharing with you," she said, sounding aghast.

With that, she was out the door and headed down the stairs. I fell back against the pillows and looked at Charlie as he tried to cuddle up next to me.

"Cockblockers. All of you. Ughhhhhh." I looked up at the ceiling as the dog laid his big fluffy head on my belly. Just when I'd thought I might be getting somewhere.

Chapter 11

Denial Isn't Just a River in Egypt

Maeve

I'd had better days. Temptation, thy name is Levi Traub and all.

Just eight or so hours ago, Allyson had called while the man was melting me into the mattress with a kiss that rewired my brain. I mean, just the memory threatened to light up my body.

I'd raced out of that bedroom like I was on fire with the convenient excuse that I couldn't talk to my sister while lying in bed. The truth was I needed some distance stat. I had zero idea what we were doing and needed to figure that out, which absolutely couldn't be done in Levi's presence. The reality was that I wanted to straddle him and just see where things went, but still, I needed to calm myself and sort out how I was feeling.

A large part of me said fuck it, it didn't matter what we were doing, the only thing that mattered was doing it again. The common sense part of me said to slow down and figure out a way to protect myself. If I was being real here, pursuing anything with Levi would likely only end in heartache for me, and I wasn't here for that.

After a brief phone conversation with Allyson where I tried like hell to reassure her that she didn't need to race home for her pup, I'd fled the house. It was a cowardly move, but what else was a girl to do? T. Swift might be able to do everything with a broken heart, but I didn't want to chance it, and mine was still currently in one piece. So off I ran.

Well, scratch that. First I'd changed, checked on Charlie again, and told Levi I was running to the grocery store. But in reality, it was all a lie to get me to my baby. Big Red and I needed some solid road time that involved loud music, windows down as much as I could tolerate—damn the January temps—and the horizon in front of us.

In truth, I felt itchy. Everything inside me begged for more distance between Highland Falls and me, to find some open roads. I wanted to hop on a state highway and head in any direction without thought. But something kept me local. A voice that sounded suspiciously like Nan kept telling me to be here for Allyson for her birthday. Surely I could make it one more week.

So I stayed, but I did spend an hour driving around, singing at the top of my lungs and following the country roads in front of me. In Central Illinois they were, typically, laid out in a grid, so getting lost was next to impossible and they allowed me the space I needed.

Arriving back at Logan and Allyson's that afternoon, I learned that my baby sis had ignored my suggestion to stay for another night at their getaway. Fortunately, seeing that Charlie was doing just fine, Levi had headed to his place as well, so the only person I had to avoid now was my sister. Lord knew she'd be able to sense my turmoil at five paces.

Apparently the peace was to be short-lived.

"So, big sis"—Allyson was curled up in the media chair by the windows that overlooked the backyard—"want to come chat?"

I looked at Logan, who was making his infamous pork stir-fry. "She sounds like she's up to no good. Any idea?"

The man wouldn't meet my eye. "Nope. I, uh... just need to get these onions cut up and we'll be cooking."

Um-hmm. That wasn't suspicious. Nope. Not at all.

There was no avoiding it, so I took my glass of rosé, which was going to be necessary, and went to sit down next to Ally.

"Yes, my devious sibling," I said, sinking back in the chair and kicking my legs out in front of me as I placed my drink on the table to the side. My maxiskirt settled, and I tossed the end of the blanket that Allyson had draped across her lap over my bare feet.

"You know, there's a great invention called socks." She grinned. "Been around for a while."

"You don't say." I wiggled my toes under the blanket. "You know I prefer bare feet whenever possible." I looked over her way. "So..."

"So... Levi sent Logan a pic this morning."

I had zero idea where this was going, but it wasn't starting where I thought it would be. "And?"

She picked up her phone, tapped the screen a few times, and turned it toward me. I looked over to see my bed, Charlie's fluffy blond head looking straight at the camera. And I could just see my waves and the top of my shoulder along the bottom of the picture. Which meant that only one person could be behind the camera.

"Hmm, I feel like I should sue Levi for taking a photo of

me while I slept," I murmured. "Invasion of privacy and all."

Allyson snorted. "You know it wasn't."

I did, but I was working any distraction I could find. Should have known she was too smart for that.

"Logan asked for a proof-of-life pic of the pup this morning. I think, to be fair, Levi just shot a picture and sent it to him without thinking." She put her phone down and gave me a serious look. "So, want to share what's up with you and... what do you call him? Lesser Twin? Evil Twin?"

"Did I ever call him evil?" I kept my gaze straight out the windows into the backyard. Every fiber of my being was calling me to deny, deny, deny.

"Let's try a different tack. How do you feel about Levi Traub?" She stared at me. "And, Maeve Claire, look in my eyes while you tell me."

Damn her. It wasn't that I didn't want to talk to her about Levi, more that I didn't want to own any of what I was feeling. That made it all too real, and what did it even matter? I was leaving in less than a week, feelings be damned. I took a breath and met her gaze. "Levi Traub is a perfectly nice guy, I'm sure, even if he doesn't always show it."

The snort from the kitchen told me that whether he wanted to or not, Logan could hear our conversation. I mean, their place wasn't huge even if it was gorgeous.

"Sorry," he called.

"Nothing I wouldn't tell you," I said back, ignoring Ally's arched brow. The woman might be shit at winking, but she was the queen of an impervious look.

She squeezed my arm and said, "Denial isn't just a river in Egypt, Mae. If you're not going to be honest with me, I hope you are at least being honest with yourself."

Guilt ate away at my insides. Here I'd spent over the past nine months wishing I had a closer relationship to Allyson, especially when I looked at siblings like Logan and Levi, and yet when I was presented with the opportunity to open up, I didn't take it.

I grabbed some courage and Ally's hand and squeezed it, rushing the words out. "I'm attracted to him." I felt heat course up my chest and neck, I'm sure making my cheeks flush as well. Super.

Allyson squeezed my hand back. "Was that so difficult?"

I pulled my legs up to my chest, straightening my skirt over them. "Yes," I mumbled into my knee.

She scooted next to me, wrapping an arm around my shoulder. "Why?" she asked, her voice filled with kindness.

I thought about it, trying to figure out how to give words to my feelings. Clearing my throat, I worked to push the words out. A whisper was as loud as I could manage. "It makes me feel vulnerable to own my feelings." I gathered some more courage before spitting the rest out. "What if he doesn't feel the same?"

Ally dropped her head on my shoulder. "That makes sense."

My breathing settled. "It does?" It helped to voice this insecurity into the air instead of her understanding gaze. That made it too much.

Her arm tightened across my shoulders. "Sure. One, it's always scary to put yourself out there. But, more than that, when did Patrick or Mona ever have any desire to know how we were feeling? When did they ever have a real conversation with us about our needs or wants?" Her voice was clipped. "Never, that's when. It was about how we looked to everyone outside the house. *Those* were the feelings that mattered, God knows it wasn't ours."

I nodded in silence.

Allyson picked up my hand and put it on her ever-growing belly. "I refuse to repeat their mistakes." Her voice was fierce. Mama Bear was representing even when her cub wasn't here yet.

I rubbed the taut surface and spoke the truth. "You would never."

Her hand rested on mine. "I hope you're right."

A tear rolled down my cheek. Then another. Memories of growing up in that oppressive house assaulted me. I'd been invisible until they wanted to remind me of my failings, and then I was all too seen. As the memories flashed like a carousel in my mind, I spoke up. "I am right. You've always accepted me."

"Of course, Mae. You're amazing."

Allyson had always believed that. So had Nan. It was only as an adult that I began to internalize it. Something I was still working on.

"Ally, whoever this is growing in your belly, I know you will celebrate them. No matter their size, sexuality, or how they express their individuality, they will be treasured. I can see no way in this world where you won't cheer them on for being who they are, unabashedly. This child will be loved." The tears were now rolling down my cheeks without abating.

Allyson squeezed my hand harder. "I hate what they did to you."

I snuggled closer to her. "And I hate what they did to you." A memory, one of many, of my mom telling me I was too fat to wear an outfit popped in my mind. I remembered being fourteen, standing in front of a mirror, looking at myself with confusion because before I had run into my mother, I'd felt beautiful. One interaction with Mona and I was searching for what was wrong with me.

Allyson had come up behind me, wrapped her arms around my waist, and whispered how gorgeous I looked, trying so hard in her what must have been thirteen-year-old body to reverse the poison of our mother. Who knew it would be a lifetime job.

"I hate that I still let her voice whisper in my head," I said, knowing she would get it.

"I hate that I do that too, but I think we're doing good work to beat it back. It'll just take time." She turned and kissed my temple. "I understand why you left, and I know you struggle with that."

My heart cracked in two. "How do you know that?"

She gave a watery laugh. "Babe, you shouldn't ever play poker. Your feelings are pretty clear... Ohh." She moved my hand to the right side of her small bump. "Can you feel that?"

We sat there with my hand on her belly.

"There it is again," she said.

"Nope, nothing yet." I patted her belly and then scooted back and stretched my legs out again before facing her.

"Logan has been trying to feel the baby kicking too, but no dice. Apparently it's easier for me to feel it at first, but as this little nugget gets bigger, you all will too." She moved her legs to rest her feet on my lap.

"Comfortable?" I asked, rubbing the arch of her foot.

"Yes, but maybe get the right foot too?" She grinned at me. "Anyway, as I was saying, in case I haven't made it clear, I prayed you'd leave home when you graduated high school. Nan and I were both grateful when you did. So don't you ever feel guilty about putting yourself first. I know it took me a while to follow your lead, but the reason I was finally able to was because you showed me the way."

Her tears now bathed her cheeks as well. I squeezed her foot in my hand. "Thanks, babe. I needed to hear that."

She wiped her cheeks while watching me, then gave me a cat-that-ate-the-canary look. "So... back to Levi?"

"Thank God," Logan called from the kitchen. "This is a lot of emotion, and I want you both to know that the only reason I'm crying is because of the onions I'm cutting."

We both laughed and I called out, "Sorry not sorry."

Allyson nudged my stomach with her toe. "Spill, girlie."

I shrugged. "Not sure what there is to say. Like, the man drives me crazy, but I also think about him a lot. And, well, we've been growing closer..."

Allyson squealed and bounced in her seat. "Tell me everything!"

"This is about my brother, I don't think we need to hear *everything*," Logan called.

"Hush. Put on music if you don't want to hear," Allyson replied. "And remember, Logan Traub, you are a vault."

Within seconds, the sounds of the Avett Brothers came from the speakers around the kitchen and living room.

Allyson gave me an expectant look with that damn raised eyebrow again. I knew that look—it meant *get on with it*.

I shrugged. "There's not a ton to say. We've texted since the first time we met. Mostly to annoy each other."

"Sexual tension building..." Allyson rubbed her hands together.

"Whatever. At any rate, he called when I was headed back this time." I looked to the kitchen, then to Ally to mouth, *To plan your party.*

Got it, she mouthed back. I loved that this surprise party was really just a surprise to keep Logan happy.

"So we've seen each other a few times and, as much as he drives me to madness, I also feel comfortable with him. Like conversations fly by."

"And he isn't bad to look at, right?" She shot me a terrible wink. Bless her.

"I mean, he's no god of sexy over there, but he'll do." I raised my eyebrows at her.

"They're identical."

"Doesn't seem like it."

"I know."

We sat there for a moment, listening to the Avett Brothers sing "Murder in the City." Allyson had told me about the Traub twins singing this past spring at karaoke. How that was when she began to see a future with Logan. I thought of all Logan and Allyson had been through over the past year and how much they had ahead of them.

"Levi and I kissed." I slapped my hand over my mouth. It was like my body gave permission to speak before my brain.

"Well, now we're getting somewhere. And how was it?" Allyson rubbed her hands together like an evil genius.

I sighed. Might as well get it all out. "It was great, and we were already horizontal in a bed..."

"And?" she asked expectantly.

I gave her a look. "And then you called."

She threw her head back in laughter as I joined her. I mean, what else was there to say?

Chapter 12

Sinkhole, Anyone?

Levi

It had been forty-nine hours and eleven minutes since I'd last seen the very fine ass of Maeve Claire Murphy, not that I was counting. I'd brought my work to the Sanctuary Café in town, thinking the background noise would distract me, but no luck so far. I was sufficiently caffeinated and had enough chocolate muffins to necessitate adding some miles to this week's workouts, but my brain still couldn't focus. I glanced at my phone screen again, praying that it would tell me a new story.

No new messages. Well, that wasn't entirely true—no new messages that I was waiting for. It looked like the group text I had with several guys in town was just as healthy as ever. According to my notification screen, there were thirty-one new messages. That might worry someone else, assuming that surely there was a problem if these men were texting that much. Nope. Opening it, I saw that we were texting today about...

Ridiculous bird names and beers. Jesus. These people. I had no idea how they got anything done at work.

Last spring Jake and Sully had created a new beer, as they often did for their brewery. This one was released in conjunction with bird hikes that Drew was leading at Highland Woods. They'd tossed around some names for it before settling on *Learn to Fly*. However, in a quest for the perfect beer name, we'd all learned that the people responsible for naming birds must have a weird sense of humor. I liked to joke that I was too young to pick up the hobby of birding, but we were all learning at least a little. Whether I'd ever be able to pick one out in nature, that was questionable. And yet we'd been educated on important bird names such as the tufted titmouse, dickcissel, red-breasted nuthatch, and—I looked at Drew's newest addition—a fluffy-backed tit babbler.

Where the ever-loving fuck had these names come from?

These guys were a lot, but I was so damn glad I was here and could count them among my closest friends. Living up north in Aurora had gotten lonely even before everything imploded with Tess. College had been the opposite; I'd been surrounded with friends and my brother twenty-four seven. Graduating felt like I'd been set adrift. Meeting people wasn't as easy. For the first few years, I'd worked my ass off for a company I hated. Everyone there had been a decade older, easy. I had nothing against that, but they were all at different stages of life than me and didn't want to go out after work because they needed to get home to their partners.

I'd met Tess and felt like everything was finally clicking and took the risk to start my own business even if it took me off the straight path I'd thought I wanted—job security, relationship, eventual marriage, kids, the whole deal. Even working for myself, I hadn't been lonely because I'd felt like

I was where I should be. Then it was all shot to shit with the loss of Nola, and my entirely family was unmoored. It hadn't helped that Logan had moved three hours away when I wanted to be able to set eyes on him daily and make sure he was okay.

Moving to Highland was the first time anything had felt right in over three years, or hell, maybe since college. Even looking back at the time with Tess, I was beginning to wonder if I had ignored some red flags because I wanted so badly to have what Logan and Nola did, to be closer to where I thought I should be. Last winter I'd become concerned, I'd felt down more often than not. Nothing alarming, but a path I needed to switch, so I made the move here.

Small towns got a bad rap for being hard to make friends, and I knew some likely closed ranks, but I'd had the opposite experience in Highland Falls. I was likely benefiting from Logan being here ahead of me, but that was just fine—I'd take it.

So yeah, their text thread was unmatched lunacy, but I was grateful to be included. Most days I would have done some googling online and popped in with my own—I mean, rough-faced shag anyone? But that wasn't in the cards today. I needed Maeve to text me.

Why didn't I text her? Because I was a fucking coward. The king of all the cowards. I could own that fact to myself even if I couldn't say it to anyone else, namely my brother, who'd apparently overheard enough of a conversation that he knew "something" had happened even if he wouldn't tell me exactly what had been said. He mumbled some bullshit about being a vault and how Allyson would kill him if he said anymore.

Ahhhhhh.

I mean, did she like the kiss? Did she think I was too forward? Had she wanted more? Did she only look at me as an extension of my brother and, in a sense, like a sibling? *Shudder*. What did it mean that the bluntest person I'd ever met had yet to give me any shit and had fled my vicinity like she was on fire?

It couldn't be good.

I opened my thread with her multiple times a day, trying to get the courage to text her, but this was Schrödinger's cat, and I didn't know if I wanted to find out what was inside. Right now I could pretend we were still friends, that nothing had changed. Not ideal but better than learning she wanted nothing to do with me. All I'd been able to get from Logan was she was still in town, which I'd been grateful to hear because I would have put money on her taking off for places unknown.

We were hosting a party in four days, and I didn't want to go into it not knowing how she would react, but I also wasn't sure the best course of action here.

I looked over the party checklist for what was possibly the millionth time in the past hour since I couldn't focus worth a damn.

Someone cleared their throat behind me, and I turned to see Aidan—my friend, running partner, and new employee—standing there with a baby in a sling on his chest. "You planning on keeping up with those sighs or are you going to share with the class?"

I kicked a chair out from the spot across from me. "You and Mia want to join me for a minute?" There were plenty of spots at the café, the morning rush had long gone, and we were coming up on lunchtime, so the next wave would be soon.

"Yep." He nodded to the counter. "Let me grab my coffee and we'll be right over."

I pushed my computer back, patting the spot in front of me. "Pass me that baby."

Aidan shook his head with an indulgent look. Mia was a constant companion of his, especially since Grace had gone back to work two months ago. He'd taken paternity leave from the sheriff's department, but that became permanent when their daycare fell through. It just so happened that I needed some part-time help, which allowed him to stay home with the baby, and they had daycare set up to start this summer. At that point we'd look to see if I needed someone full time, which seemed like a huge step for me but possibly necessary.

So Aidan and Mia were a matched set, but every time I saw him out, the same thing happened—someone wanted to hold that baby. She was adorable and super chill—who could blame the citizens of Highland for wanting to snuggle up?

He handed Mia to me in her adorable fleece one-piece. I tugged her hood down and took in those rosy cheeks, pressing a kiss to the small thatch of dark hair on her head.

Mia clapped her hands onto my cheeks, rubbing my beard. Her dad had one as well. She began an impressive combination of nonstop babbling accompanied by an impressive amount of drool.

"Is that a fact?" I asked when she finally took a breath. Her brown eyes were wide and locked on mine with a look of seriousness.

Aidan sat down next to me instead of across, I assumed to allow Mia to see he was back. His coffee was placed out of reach as he gave his daughter a look filled with humor. "She talking your ear off?"

"She sure has something to say," I said to him, but then Mia tapped my face to get my attention again with another stream of sounds.

Aidan leaned over and pulled out a bottle he had already prepared. Shaking it quickly, he popped the lid off, and Mia quickly turned in his direction at the sound. He took her back as she settled into the crook of his arm, happily drinking from the bottle he had propped against his chest.

"So"—he glanced at my computer—"what's the source of the sighs? Do you need more from me?"

"No, no, you've been a great help. I'm just hoping I'll have enough business to make you full time this summer."

Aidan shot me a look. "We've talked about this. If you don't, that's not on you. We will figure it out."

"I know, I know." It was a weird kind of stress, employing a friend, knowing his family was depending on a salary. My client list had grown, but I absolutely worried at times about keeping them all happy, ensuring I didn't lose business.

"If it isn't work, what's stressing you?"

"Well, work is always a stress, but..." I thought about whether I really wanted to talk to someone. Maybe it would help. "How long have you been with Grace?"

"Me and Grace?" Aidan ran a hand over his face. "Seems like forever, but really we met in college. So over ten years." He gave me a knowing look. "Is there something you want to share about you and one Ms. Maeve Murphy?"

I gave him a look of surprise. "Why would you say something about Maeve?"

Aidan's smile was wide. "Levi, it is apparent to anyone who's around the two of you for any length of time that there is enough sexual tension between you to heat up a room. We're all just waiting on you both to finally act on it."

Jesus. If Aidan had noticed, it was guaranteed we were a discussion point at least among his wife and her friends, if not more. Hell, Lou Williams had given me some shit after Maeve first got back in town and then ditched me at the brewery. When I'd seen Lou out the next week, she kept asking if I needed some advice on how to snag a girlfriend since, in her words, my game was a mess.

Stalling as I decided what I really wanted to reveal, I took another drink of my coffee. I could trust Aidan, right? "So this goes no further than this table, right?"

"Want me to plug Mia's ears? She is quite the gossip." He moved to cover one, which I nudged him away from.

"Don't be ridiculous. And I'm aware that telling you is telling Grace."

"Ehh." He gave a gesture with his hand to indicate that was a maybe. "True but not always. Depends on if it comes up." He tapped Mia on the nose as her gaze locked on him. "Right, baby? We are a vault." Looking back to me, he said, "So Maeve."

"Yeah. Well, I feel like we've been circling each other since we met."

"True statement."

"But also, in being around her for the past nine months or so, I realized that she's fascinating."

"Another true statement." Aidan smiled at me and nodded for me to continue.

I tapped the worn wood table and thought about how to lay this all out in the most concise way possible. I mean, Mia's bottle was almost gone, so time was limited. "Forgoing any bullshit in the interest of getting this out before this place fills up again, I'm attracted to her but have been off relationships for years and I'm not sure I have any desire to go there again." I wiped my hands on my jeans. "And yet when we found ourselves watching Logan and Allyson's dog a few days ago, we ended up spending the night in the same bed, I kissed her in the morning, and she took off when she got a call from her sister." There. Concise and hit the main issues. I looked up and met his steady gaze. "Haven't heard from her since."

Aidan nodded as he took that all in, not in a hurry to fill the silence, which I respected. Mia polished off her bottle, and he put it on the table before lifting her to his shoulder to get out any air. As he smoothed her back, he looked my way. "So you don't want to ask her sister?" He tipped his head toward the kitchen where Allyson could be seen rushing around.

"Hell no. That smacks a little too close to elementary school and asking a friend to ask someone out for you."

"Elementary school? You were quite the player."

"Maybe it was middle school." I raked my fingers through my hair again, feeling frustrated. "Do you have any actual advice?"

Aidan sat quietly for a moment before saying something that made my heart skip a beat. "Sorry, Levi. I hadn't realized how much you liked her."

Mia let out an applause-worthy burp.

I backtracked because this was getting too real. "I mean, I'm attracted to her, I just worry that I pushed the kiss, it wasn't good, or I pissed her off."

Aidan started to speak before someone cleared their throat behind us. *Surely not...*

"You didn't push me, Lesser Twin. No worries there."

Yep, that was Maeve. Luck was not on my side today.

Turning around, I took in the blond beauty standing in

some kind of wrap that was layered over a cream thermal and slim jeans that hugged every damn delicious curve, threatening to make me lose my mind. However, I couldn't dwell on that because flanking her on either side was Lou and her posse, Jeanie and Hattie. Judging by their matching cat-that-ate-the-canary expressions, they'd heard every word as well.

With a look to Aidan, I murmured, "What do I have to do to get a sinkhole right here, right now?"

Aidan tossed his head back with a booming laugh as Mia patted his beard.

Maeve hadn't looked away, the amusement apparent in her gaze. "Looks like you're going to have to deal with me."

Great. Just great.

Chapter 13

Cards on the Table

M*aeve*

If I wasn't mistaken, there was a hint of a blush working its way up Levi Traub's neck, likely through his beard, and staining his cheeks. The man looked positively sheepish, and I was *here for it*.

He sat with my comment for a moment and then grew taller, as if his spine lengthened, and said, "You mean like how you dealt with me on Sunday morning at Logan's?"

"Oooh, what is it that the kids are saying these days? Burn?" Lou was positively cackling.

"Behave," I murmured to my right.

"Behaving is no fun," Jeanie said from my left.

"And we do like to have fun," Hattie, otherwise known as Trouble Number Three, piped in from just past Jeanie.

Aidan was apparently a wise man and decided it was time to head out after the commentary from the peanut gallery. With goodbyes said from all, my three companions then looked my way, waiting to see what was going to happen next.

Hell if I knew.

Levi cleared his throat, drawing our attention back to him. "Maeve, would I be able to borrow you for a moment?"

"Feel free to talk in front of us," Lou said with what I was sure she thought was an appearance of innocence.

I worked on a stern look that spoke volumes if Lou cared to try to decode the meaning. "No, you all go grab us a table. I'll be over in a few." The unspoken message of "mind your own business" being one that Lou was not a fan of and would likely ignore.

"Want us to get you a coffee?" Hattie asked.

I glanced toward the counter and was not the least bit surprised to see my sister headed my way with a coffee. "Nope, Ally's got me."

The three troublemakers headed to the counter with glances my way telling me we'd chat about this later. Before I could re-center myself, Allyson reached me and passed me my drink that I hadn't ordered but she knew was needed. "Lavender latte."

"Thanks."

I took it from her and moved to sit down at Levi's table, but before I could, she placed a hand on my arm, leaned in, and whispered in my ear, "This is your shot. Relax and have some fun. It doesn't have to be forever, but why not try for something for now?"

With that, she gave me a half hug, moved to Levi to give him the same, and sauntered on back to the kitchen. I'd hate her for being rational if I didn't love her so damn much.

Levi pushed a chair out from the table with his foot and gestured for me to sit down. I did, eyeing him with more than a little apprehension if I was being honest.

"So what all did you overhear?" He eyed me warily. Apparently we were both uneasy today.

I didn't love it. I wanted us to be as we always were—

full of a little sexual tension and a whole lot of sarcasm. "Just that you love me and want to marry me," I sang, going for some lightheartedness to cover my anxiousness.

"I *did not* say that." Oh, that blush of his was working its way back. Yessssss.

Karma wasn't my friend though, because I could tell from the warmth of my neck that now *my* face was on fire. The question was why? Was it his vehement denial? Or was it that my singsong comment actually didn't sound like the worst thing in the world? Nah, we weren't going to examine that too closely.

Instead, I went with the banter that was the basis of our relationship. "Screwing with you, Lesser Twin." I took a centering breath and continued, choosing honesty. "I heard that you do like me and are worried you pushed that kiss on me."

Levi ran his hands through his hair and looked vaguely ill. I had to put him out of his misery because as much as I liked to mess with the guy, I couldn't have him worrying about consent. Hell, if anything, my complaint was that we stopped at a kiss. This was not something to think about in detail while the gorgeous man was in my vicinity though.

I leaned across the table, and grabbed one of his forearms, tugging him toward me so that the entire café didn't listen in. The conversations around us were, hopefully, enough cover. "Levi, cards on the table—you didn't push anything on me that I didn't want to happen if you catch my drift."

I leaned back, leaving my hand on his arm. Tingles were shooting between us, at least on my end, and I fought the urge to crawl over the table and into his lap. That would really give the trio of gossips to my left something to share.

His warm eyes met mine, and the concern was present. "Maeve, are you sure?"

"Absolutely."

"Then why did you leave?" His voice cracked on the last word.

I squeezed the arm I hadn't been able to let go of as I felt my cheeks heat again. Time for some more bravery. "If I'm being honest..." There was a pause that went on for far too long. "...because you scare me."

His eyes widened, and he gave me a look of horror. "Jesus, do you think I'd hurt you?"

Yikes. I was a train wreck in my attempts to reassure the man today. Damn. I needed to straighten this out, but how? "No, that's not what I mean. As much as you've driven me crazy over the past what? Eight or nine months? I've never had any fear of you hurting me physically..."

"What then?"

I bit my lip, trying to think of what to say to get my point across instead of barreling ahead to try to rush the conversation. Clearly that approach had been a disaster so far. After a moment, Levi leaned over and pushed gently down on my chin to free my lip. He sat quietly, waiting for me to go on while I fought the moan that wanted to bubble out of me.

Refocusing, I looked around the café. There was a small line at the counter, folks coming in for lunch. We were garnering attention from two parties—Allyson at the counter, who hadn't stopped watching us with concern etched on her face, and then Lou at her table with her posse. Their expressions were positively gleeful because of course they were. Lou waved her cell phone at me and then mouthed, *Kiss that hottie.*

Sweet Jesus. She was likely taking pictures.

Levi cleared his throat. "Spill, sweetheart."

I arched a brow. "Sweetheart?"

He shrugged, and I again wanted to shove the table aside and climb the man like a tree. Instead, I crooked my finger at him. His eyes were wide and locked on mine, but he leaned forward and we met halfway across the table where I whispered my truth into his ear: "You scare me, Levi Traub, because you make me feel things I'm not ready to examine."

I started to lower back down, but it was Levi's turn to place a warm hand on my forearm to stop me.

He whispered back, "Maeve Murphy, I could say the same thing to you."

We both sat down with some force. They say the truth will set you free, but I didn't know if that was true for us. Where did we go from here?

Levi spoke first. "So to wrap up my concern, you didn't leave because I forced you or because you didn't like the kiss."

"Nope." I went for lightness even though my heart was hammering in my chest and gave him my best sultry grin. "It was a damn fine kiss, Traub."

"*Levi*, Maeve. *Levi*." He took a breath, glancing up at the ceiling as if to gather some strength, then looked back to me. "If it was a damn fine kiss, I think it bears repeating, don't you?"

Those words made the butterflies in my stomach begin to dance. Still, I played it off to see how serious he really was. "Here? Should we just lie down on the floor and go for it? Will we be stopping at a kiss, or were you going to angle for more in front of the espresso machine?"

"You're saying you'd like more?" Apparently we were both choosing to be blunt today.

I blinked, looked at my latte as the tingles that had been due to the connection between us moved into my core and spoke of good things. The heat was no longer confined to my neck and face. In fact, I wondered if I was having a very early hot flash. "I'm not saying I'm opposed."

"Can you say that while looking at me, Maeve? I don't want there to be any misunderstanding here."

I looked up and took a deep breath. "I absolutely would be down for more with you, Levi, but what I said before holds true. You do scare me. And I don't want to misrepresent what's going on here. I'm not staying."

My gut churned. Was that a deal-breaker? I mean, he already knew I didn't live here, but would that reminder be more than he could handle? Allyson said to relax and have fun—maybe this could be some fun?

Instead of reacting badly, he reached over and squeezed my hand. It was like he was trying to comfort me without setting off the entirety of this café to spread some gossip far and wide in Highland. Hell, just this conversation had probably already started tongues wagging. If Lou hadn't snapped a few photos of us to place on the town's social media pages, I'd be shocked.

"Maeve..." Levi sounded like he was confessing something that was weighing on him as well. "I'm scared too. It's been a while for me and trust is a hard one, so I appreciate your being up-front. I'm also not asking you to change who you are. How long are you staying?"

My gut clenched. I loved that he accepted me while a childish part wished he'd ask me to stay. "Well, the party is on Saturday and today is Tuesday. My plan was to leave Sunday morning."

Guilt swamped me as I remembered telling Allyson I might stay longer. I knew all too well that she'd understand if I needed to go, but part of me felt like I'd be disappointing her. Hell, maybe I'd be disappointing me. Something to examine later when I wasn't sitting with this gorgeous yet confounding man.

Levi nodded for a moment, processing my upcoming departure. "Okay, so does that give us a few days to see how this goes? Maybe we try hanging out and not pissing each other off on purpose?"

I fought a smile. "I have no idea what you're talking about."

"Maeve," he said, drawing out my name.

I winked and held out my hand. "Deal."

He slid his hand into mine to shake. "Deal."

"Kiss the girl, for Pete's sake!" Lou yelled from across the café, making heads turn as Allyson admonished her.

I looked at Lou and the crew and burst into peals of laughter. God, I loved this place. I didn't like settling down, but if anywhere felt like a place I could, Highland Falls was it.

Levi slid from his seat across from me to the chair on my right. Reaching out, he gently turned my chin toward him and said softly, "She is the town matriarch—maybe we should listen?" His warm eyes watched mine, and I slowly nodded my agreement. "Before anything happens that we can't take back, I should ask if you want to keep the next few days secret from everyone or if you're more the out-in-the-open type?"

He asked the perfect questions.

"I hate secrets with every fiber of my being and prefer to live my life out loud." My gaze never left his.

He looked thoughtful and nodded at my words. "That you do, Ms. Maeve. That you do." With that, he leaned over and pressed his lips to mine in a gentle kiss that was both appropriate for the setting and made a promise of good things to come.

In the background I heard Lou's whistle, Jeanie and Hattie cheering, the sounds of coffee being made, the murmur of conversations, but they all were so much less important than the man in front of me.

Levi pulled away, and I immediately missed his mouth on mine. "Dinner? Tonight?"

"Yes please," I breathed out.

"For now your crew awaits," he said, nodding toward my septuagenarian friends.

I looked their way, then back at him. His hair was tousled. The concert tee he wore proclaiming him a fan of Nathaniel Rateliff & the Night Sweats was stretched across his chest. I really didn't want to go sit with my three trouble-makers and debrief on this encounter. I wanted to go find a horizontal surface with Levi and soak up all that I could before Sunday.

"Nope." His smile made me want to shave off the beard for a moment to see if he had a dimple. However, I also wanted to run my hands over his jaw again and feel that scruff. Decisions, decisions.

"*Maeve...*"

Oohhh, that felt like I was in trouble.

"What?" I tried for a wide-eyed, innocent look. To be honest, it wasn't one I was very familiar with.

"Your face doesn't hide much, and I can't play hooky from work with you—I need to get some stuff done." He gestured at his computer. "So go sit with that crew. Try to keep them out of trouble."

I sighed, indicating my thoughts about this suggestion. While it wasn't what I *wanted* to do, I needed a hot second or two to get my thoughts in order. I stood to head over to

Lou and company. "So, dinner?" I hated that I sounded uncertain.

"Dinner." Levi gave a delicious glance down my body and back up. "In case I only thought it and didn't say it earlier, I love those jeans on you, Maeve."

I looked down at my skinny jeans and tan booties. Some would likely say they were too snug. I don't have thin legs; I have strong ones, Sturdy, as my mom liked to say with some disgust in her tone. Whatever. I attributed it to my Irish ancestry. Somehow I could see my ancestors, out in nature, standing strong on the ground in some Irish countryside, looking out to sea. That had helped me accept myself when my mother tried to teach me to despise my body.

And, for what it's worth, bless American Eagle for their inclusion of a lot of stretch in these jeggings. That made them my favorite, and having someone clearly appreciate my denim as well as the curves they covered was, well, arousing.

"Thanks."

"I'll text you this afternoon about what time I'll pick you up."

"Looking forward to it." I started to step away but thought better of it. Two steps brought me to his side and I bent down, gave him a swift kiss filled with promise, and then walked away.

"That's my girl," Lou called as Jeanie did a wolf whistle that would produce a cab in a New York minute.

I kept walking, shaking my head at the menaces in front of me as I heard Levi give a throaty chuckle behind me that made me shiver with desire.

What had I gotten myself into?

Chapter 14

Unexpected Guests

L*evi*

After watching Maeve's sexy-as-hell ass walk away from me at the café, I thought long and hard about where to take her for dinner. Clearly, the Homestead was an option—we both loved the brewery. I even debated some of the pubs in town or the Italian restaurant, Giuseppe's. But the reality was, wherever we went, we'd be on display. The blessings of a small town. Hell, the café proved that this morning.

So right or wrong, I made an unusual choice for a first official date and grabbed groceries to make her dinner at my place all while firing off a text to have her come over at six instead of picking her up.

Sure, we could drive thirty miles—or more—each way and go to Champaign, Decatur, or Bloomington-Normal. All of those cities would have more options and more privacy than Highland Falls afforded. That being said, I didn't want to sit in a car for over an hour when I could be sitting on a couch with the woman who drove me to thoughts I should absolutely not be having.

In other words, dinner at my place it was.

I was slicing an onion when I heard my front door open. Logan, without a doubt, I figured, not turning around from my spot near the stove.

"In here, Logan," I called over the Zach Bryan song coming out of my speaker.

"Not Logan," Allyson said, startling me as she dropped her coat on my couch and came over to kiss me on the cheek. "Whatcha making?"

"Fajitas," I said with a raised eyebrow in her direction. I mean, Allyson had been to my place since I'd bought it this summer, but only with Logan. I had zero complaints about hanging out with my sister-in-law, but something was up. "Are we going to be graced with my brother's presence as well?"

"Nope, you're going to have to survive with only me." Allyson moved around the island and pulled out a stool, sliding in. "Can I get a drink?"

"Of course." I moved to the fridge to grab a LaCroix for her, her favorite pregnancy drink. I also grabbed a few peppers for me. Passing Ally the drink, I moved my cutting board to the island across from her. Might as well get this conversation going while finishing dinner prep.

"So, not that I don't love you stopping by without a heads-up, but want to share what brings you here?" I sliced up the yellow pepper, pushing it to the side of the cutting board before beginning on the red one. "I have to assume this impromptu visit has something to do with my dinner companion tonight?"

Allyson tipped back the seltzer, taking a long drink before setting it down. "Ahh. It's not the same as a glass of rosé, but I'm starting to actually enjoy it." She glanced down, spreading out her fingers before clasping her hands together. When her eyes met mine, she seemed troubled. For the first time since she walked in, I got nervous.

I laid down my knife. Maybe this wasn't a conversation to have while cutting vegetables. "What's up, Ally? You're starting to worry me."

She leaned her head back and took a deep breath, gathering strength it seemed. "It's like this," she said to the ceiling but then looked my way again. "I'm worried about you and Maeve."

"Can I ask why?" I hated the idea that Ally might think I'd be bad for her sister.

She focused on the LaCroix in her hand, rotating it so that she could run her thumb up and down the can as if trying to calm herself. "I encouraged Maeve to try to make something work with you, thinking you two could have some fun together, but I'm wondering if that was the right move."

"Because you think I'd be the wrong person for her?" I braced, wondering how I'd feel if she agreed with that statement. Zach Bryan was singing about love being brought home and finding your way back, but I was feeling pretty low as I waited for her to tell me where she was.

"No." Ally looked up at me, her eyes watery. "Because I worry you're going to get your heart broken."

Oof. Punch to the gut. "You don't have the same concern for Maeve?"

Allyson hopped off the counter stool to begin pacing through my kitchen and living room, her hands flying as she talked. "Of course I worry about Maeve. That is my baseline. But now I'm adding you to that." She stood at my window for a moment, looking out on the quiet street, and growled in apparent frustration.

I wiped my hands on a towel and headed her way. "Ally, Maeve and I are adults, and this is just dinner."

She glanced over her shoulder at me. "And do you really think this is going to stop at dinner?" Her expression told me what she thought about that.

"Ummm, I plead the Fifth?" I mean, we only had a week. I sure as hell didn't want to stop at dinner. Where that led—well, would be up to Maeve.

Turning to face me, she grabbed my hands and squeezed. "At first I thought the two of you were a great idea. You drive each other crazy, but we all know that's just repressed sexual tension."

I coughed, covering my sudden unease at the direction this conversation was taking. Allyson didn't notice but picked back up on her pacing and ranting.

"But then I realized Maeve isn't here long. And you could get attached to her and get your heart broken. Or"— she spun and looked at me, speaking with emphasis—"*so could she!* I mean it, Levi." She headed back toward the kitchen. "This has disaster written all over it."

My front door opened to my right, and Logan slid into my living room, Charlie by his side. They came to stand next to me as we watched Ally go. Logan's wound-up wife was doing laps around my kitchen as she spoke to the air about all of her concerns, which had now morphed to concerns about the world, global warming, the patriarchy, school boards, and more.

He looked my way, then nodded toward the kitchen and whispered, "So how long has this been going on?"

I looked at my watch. "Um, maybe five minutes?"

He nodded as Allyson continued, oblivious to her husband walking in. Now she was looking in my fridge, murmuring to herself.

"I'm assuming this started with her concerns about your date tonight?"

"Pretty much." I gestured at Ally, who was now furiously scribbling on a notepad on the counter. "Though now it seems to be her concerns for the planet. Do you share those concerns?"

He shrugged. "The concerns for the planet or for you and Maeve?"

I raised an eyebrow at him. "Maeve and me. Concerns for the planet I'm sure we all share."

He nodded. "Truth. As for the two of you? I mean, could this thing you're doing crash and burn? Sure. But what if it doesn't?"

"Let's not get ahead of ourselves," I said. "Maeve leaves this weekend."

"And you know she'll be back..."

"Yeah, she'll be back," I mulled that over for a moment. He was right—it wasn't like Maeve would leave Sunday and I'd never see her again. So did that mean if we were spending time with each other this week, it was done on Sunday? Or was it something that could be casual and continue when she was here? Did I even want that? Would she?

"Logan, what are you doing here?" Allyson had looked to the two of us when Charlie crossed to the kitchen to sit by her feet.

Logan walked over, wrapping her up in his arms as he pressed a kiss to her head. "Hey baby, you just had to come warn Levi?"

She leaned back, and I could see that her eyes were watery. "I just love them both so much—what if they get their hearts broken?"

Her head dropped back to his chest as he rubbed his

hands up and down her back. "I know, sweetheart, but we need to let them live their own lives and be here if they need us."

When he looked my way, I mouthed, *Pregnancy hormones?*

He shook his head at me and mouthed back, *Don't even suggest it.*

Ah. So in other words, yes, but not to be discussed. Got it.

"It's so hard to see your babies grow up," Allyson said into Logan's chest.

I pointed to myself. *Am I a baby?*

Logan nodded with a smirk, but he kept rubbing Allyson's back. "I think Maeve and Levi are both older than you, sweetheart."

Allyson made a noise of agreement. "But it's still hard."

"Raising adult children, yes, I'm sure it is hard." Logan agreed with her and kept his eyes on me.

I rolled my eyes and shook my head. Unreal.

"Luckily, we have years before we need to worry about that with our baby," he said as he rocked back and forth with her in his arms.

"But what if I screw them up? What if I'm a terrible mom? What if I don't prepare them?" Allyson looked like she was trying to burrow into Logan's chest.

My heart broke for her. How had Logan known that she had more concerns going on below her purported worry about Maeve and me?

"Babe, I have zero concerns about you as a mom," Logan whispered as they swayed.

I looked from them to Charlie, wondering if we should escape and give them some privacy. I glanced at Logan and nodded toward the bedrooms. *Should I go?*

He shook his head. *Stay. It's good.*

I shrugged and dropped down on the couch, giving Charlie the pats that he deserved as the best doggo.

"Really?" Allyson's voice was skeptical.

"Really." Logan gently kissed the top of her head. "Now, do you want to tell Levi what has you so worked up?"

Allyson spun out of his arms to look at me. "Oh, Levi, I'm so sorry that I came in here like this."

Logan tugged her over to my giant leather chair and pulled her down to sit with him.

"You're good, Allyson. Really." I rubbed Charlie's head, which was now propped on my knee as he begged with his eyes.

Allyson snuggled back into Logan's arms, tucking her head into the crook of his neck. She played with his hands as she said in a soft voice, "You know a little about Maeve and my parents, right?"

I met her gaze and nodded.

"To say they weren't people to use as role models for parenting would be an understatement. I think sometimes I worry about being a mom because it isn't like I had a good one." She looked up at me. "And I always worry about Maeve getting hurt. And now that you're part of my family, that worry extends to you." She shrugged and looked at Logan, then back to me. "Today... somehow those worries got tied together." Taking a breath, she threaded her fingers with Logan's. "Maybe that was some of my pregnancy hormones?"

I gasped theatrically.

"You don't say," Logan said with awe in his voice.

"Hey." She sat up, pushing at Logan's shoulder. "Not nice, babe."

He laughed and I smiled at her.

"I appreciate the concern, Ally. And I know it was from a place of love."

She nodded with a serious expression. "It really was."

"And excuse the language, but I fucking hope to not run into your parents anytime soon, because I have a lot to say to them." I fought to keep the irritation out of my voice.

"They are deserving of all the fucks in the world thrown at them," Ally said, anger dripping from her words.

"That they are," Logan piped in.

"Levi..." Ally looked like she was debating how to say something. "Be careful with Maeve. Her heart is more tender than I think even she knows."

I looked up and met Allyson's eyes, trying to convey with everything in me the seriousness of what I was about to say. "I will guard it as the treasure it is."

She watched me for a moment before turning to Logan and saying in a whisper, but one I could still hear, "He'll do."

Chapter 15

Are You Ready for It?

M *aeve*

I had to own the fact that the butterflies in my stomach had taken flight. Nerves flooded my system, which was not something I was used to. I was grateful he'd decided to have me over for dinner—I certainly hadn't been looking forward to the town gossiping about how our date went. But coming over to his place added a level of intimacy that I didn't know how to deal with. Add to that the fact that Levi seemed to see things I'd rather hide, and this evening was one that I was looking forward to with some apprehension.

As I headed up the curved walk, I admired Levi's place. He had a cute cream cottage with empty flower boxes under the windows facing the road. I imagined them with colorful flowers come summer. Geraniums? Maybe. Blue shutters flanked a few windows, and a chimney rose on the right. Quite frankly, far more adorable than I would have thought he'd pick. It didn't scream bachelor pad. The lights were on inside, giving the windows a warm glow that looked welcoming as I held tightly to my jacket against the rapidly chilling January night.

Stepping up to the wooden door, I knocked and glanced over my shoulder, looking for imaginary neighbors staring at me from their front porches. God knew if Ms. Lou or her crew saw me headed into Levi's house, they'd have something to say. Lou had certainly been full of energy that morning at the café.

It had been hard work to sit back with Lou, Jeanie, and Hattie and *not* spill the beans that Levi and I had a date. Not that I wanted to keep this secret, mind you. I was being honest when I told Levi I liked to live my life out loud.

Living with my parents and trying to fit into the narrow version of what they found acceptable had taught me that. But I'd like a day between deciding to go out with Levi and the wave of commentary I knew would be headed my way.

Though if I wanted that, maybe we shouldn't have kissed in the café. Ah well, worth it. Even if it had been too brief and made others feel invested in whatever this was between us. It was a sign of good things to come.

Before I could let my concerns get the best of me, the door opened and I found my sister on the other side. Well, that was interesting and unexpected. Upon closer inspection, it looked like she'd been crying.

"Ally?" The concern in my voice was obvious, though I hadn't even tried to mask it. I stepped inside and immediately pulled her in for a hug. She wrapped her arms around me, mumbling something incoherent into my shoulder. While we rocked in our locked embrace, I scanned the room.

One, I was just as impressed by the inside of Levi's house as I'd been by the exterior, but I'd get back to that later. My sister took priority. Logan stood behind Allyson, fatigue obvious around his eyes. Levi stood just behind him; however, his eyes were crinkled with some amusement. We locked on each other while I absorbed the message he was sending my way—whatever was going on with my sister, it wasn't dire. I felt my body relax even in a small way and sent a small smile back his direction.

"Hmm, interesting." Logan spoke up, looking from Levi to me.

"What?" I asked in a soft voice, not wanting to do anything to pull Allyson away.

Logan pointed between Levi and me. "You two are working on your own language. Impressive."

Levi came behind me and slid my coat off, hanging it up before leaving me back to my sister.

I rolled my eyes at him, and then Allyson pulled back, looking up at me. "Sorry I crashed your date. I meant to be out of here before you arrived."

"We'll get back to that in a second. Are you okay?" I looked up and down, scanning for anything visible that would explain her emotional state.

"Ehhh." She shrugged, looking down at her feet. "There is a small possibility that my hormones might be a bit much right now."

"No way," I said, working to sound surprised.

"Hey." She elbowed me. "You sound like these two fools. Pregnancy is no joke."

I kissed her cheek and pulled her to Levi's sectional. Ally picked the chaise portion, stretching her legs out as she sighed with contentment. "Levi has the best couch," she said to herself as she nestled back into the cushions.

There was a cream throw draped just beyond her feet. I snagged it and passed it her way.

"Thanks," she said, giving me a tired smile before reaching out and tugging me down next to her.

I noted that the Traub brothers were headed toward the kitchen, likely to give us a semblance of privacy. Levi looked my way, and I nodded to tell him I had this.

"Want to tell me what's on your mind?" I asked, stretching out to sit with her and laying my head back. The night was not starting out as I had anticipated, but clearly I was where I needed to be. My libido could wait, as could the little part of my heart that was begging me to open up for once. Silencing it all, I focused on my sister, who was running her hands over the blanket and studiously avoiding my gaze.

Allyson sat quietly for a few beats, but I continued to wait, wondering what she was struggling with here. Knowing our childhood, there could be a laundry list of choices. I couldn't imagine the weight of becoming a mom. I hadn't had a burning desire to try that role out, but if—and that was one hell of a big if—I ever gave it a whirl, I knew I'd need to process a whole host of childhood trauma first.

Finally, Allyson laid her head back on the cushions as I had and let out a sigh worthy of all the built-up bullshit we all deal with. "What doesn't have me upset lately?"

I nudged her foot with mine, indicating that she needed to continue, and she held up her hand and began ticking off grievances.

"Well, today I was upset because I somehow ordered cake flour and not all-purpose for this week's bakery order. I seem to be"—she glanced toward the kitchen and then leaned over to whisper in my ear—"constipated more often than not." She sat back up and continued, "I cried at work when Andy made the schedule—"

I wrinkled my brow in confusion. "What? Why?"

She hung her head. "Because my brain is in a fog, and she did it better than I did."

I slung an arm around her shoulders to pull her in. "Ally, ignoring the likely pregnancy-induced brain fog, if Andy rocks at making the schedule, why not just have her make it? I mean, she could actually make it now *and* when you return from having the bambino. You know, one thing off your plate?" I faked a gasp. "Shocking idea, right?"

She let out a large sigh filled with all the emotions of a little sister and knocked her shoulder into mine. "I know. My reactions aren't making a whole lot of sense right now." Another big sigh. "And then I got worried about you and Levi dating and somehow that morphed into my concerns that I'll be a shitty mom."

Yep. Saw this one coming.

"I already talked about it with Logan and, by default, Levi, right before you came. I know that this is likely some anxiety coming up from our childhood. Well, the mom stuff. The worries over the two of you are because I love you both and can't help but worry."

"I feel that. But Ally..." I shifted so I could meet her gaze. "Levi and are adults. If we try this and it bombs, that's on us, not you." My gut clenched a little at that statement. Not that I thought we'd be together forever—or hell, that we were even "together." I'd given up on those pipe dreams for myself.

I figured Levi and I'd use this week to get this attraction out of our systems, possibly have some excellent horizontal moments, and when that was done, because I couldn't imagine him wanting more than a few days with me no matter what I might dream, it would be time to move on.

Hopefully we were both adult enough that there would be no hurt feelings. Honestly, I thought we could do that, or I wouldn't even be trying anything with him.

"Can you really just be that relaxed about this?" she asked me with a heavy dose of skepticism evident in her tone.

"You bet," I replied, wondering what percentage of truth was present in that answer.

Ally narrowed her eyes, her expression telling me what she thought of that answer. Then her face relaxed and she reached out to grab my hand. "I made a decision today. Well, I've been thinking about it for a while, but today I decided to go for it." She glanced toward the kitchen where Levi and Logan were working to ignore us and having Charlie do tricks. Looking back to me, she whispered, "And after this afternoon, I know it will be the right call."

"What's that?" I asked, squeezing her hand. "Adding more fiber to your diet?"

"Maeve." She used a tone of voice that told me she didn't find me as amusing as I did. "I'm going to start therapy."

A sense of ease flooded me. That was a huge step for her. "Tell me more."

She shrugged, letting go of my hand and shifting back against the arm of the couch, pulling her legs up to her chest. "I think I always thought of therapy as only necessary for what Logan has taught me is big T trauma, like his loss of Nola. What I was less aware of was little t trauma, like our childhood. I don't know, I'm wondering if it would be good to work through that before this little bean joins the world this summer." She rubbed her small baby bump and looked up at me like she was waiting for my approval.

"I hope you know that you don't need me to agree with this idea."

She shrugged. "No, I don't think you need to agree, but..."

"Yeah?"

"I'm wondering if, sometime in the future, you might want to go with me?" Her voice had trailed off at the end, so she sounded almost unsure.

Well, shit. Did I want to go unpack all of the bullshit in our childhood that bubbled up at times to make me feel insecure? Um, that would be a hell to the no. This was a great step for Allyson, but not one I was prepared for. However, would I for my little sis? More than likely, though I prayed it wouldn't come to that.

I was certain Nan was somewhere in the great beyond, positively cackling. She'd think it would be good for me and would love that I felt I had to do it. I mentally scowled in response and refocused on Ally. "Are you wanting me to come with you at the beginning?" I asked, working to sound open to anything.

Allyson gave me a knowing look. "No, and I know you're not crazy about the idea. I likely have some work to do on my own, I just want to know that you're open to it and not just telling me what you think I want to hear and then taking off to avoid disappointing me to my face."

I gave a theatrical gasp, hand to chest. "Moi? Try to avoid disappointing you?"

She shook her head at me. "Someday maybe you could work out your little *t* trauma too."

I gave her a look. "Not sure I'm ready to unpack all of that quite yet, Sis. Might need a pack mule for all my baggage."

Ally shook her head, "You have no more baggage that anyone else; you just need to realize you aren't to blame for it." She gave me a small smile before we were invaded by the pup and Charlie hopped up to lean his fluffy head in for a hug. She rubbed her face against his head.

I worked to lighten the mood. "This dog doesn't understand what it means to be the correct size for a lapdog."

"I don't think doodles do, as a rule." Ally's face was more relaxed than when I'd arrived, which I'd take.

"Allyson Murphy, can I borrow you for a moment," Logan called as Levi headed toward our spot on the couch.

"Sure." Ally squeezed my hand. "Thanks," she whispered.

"Anytime, babe." I grinned at her and then gave an assessing glance to Levi, who plopped down in the spot she'd just vacated.

"So I hope I haven't misjudged here," he began.

Well, didn't that make my nerves return with a vengeance. "What's up?" I worked for cool and unaffected. I didn't think it landed quite right.

He nodded toward Allyson and Logan in the kitchen. Logan had pulled her in for a hug, and the two of them were swaying to the music coming out of the speakers as Ally threw her head back at something he said and laughed. It was a beautiful sound.

"I asked Logan if they wanted to stay for dinner, but then I realized you might think I didn't want to spend the evening alone with you when that wasn't my intention at all—"

My heart swelled. I mean, if the man wanted me to fall for him, this was the way in. However, I knew that wasn't what his aim was, so I worked to temper my feelings. "No, I get it, you wanted to reassure Allyson."

"Yeah, she was stressed when she got here. I thought maybe if she saw the two of us together, friends who were just a little closer, it might put some of her fears to rest." He shrugged like he wasn't completely sold on his own idea.

I gave him a heated smirk. "Maybe if we engage in a little PDA, it will help her see that we can be casual and it won't impact our dynamic."

"You're a giver, Maeve Murphy." Levi shook his head at me.

I shrugged and worked to look innocent. "What can I say? I'm willing to take one for the team."

Levi leaned over, his breath heating my neck as he whispered in my ear. "Plan on staying after they leave. I need to express my appreciation of this pair of jeans again."

I bit back my grin. He'd mentioned how much he liked them earlier, so who was I to change what was working? "I can work with that."

"You two, get over here and let's get this dinner on," Logan called.

Levi pulled me off the couch and didn't let go of my hand as we moved to the kitchen. The heat racing up my arm brought me back to my bedroom a few days ago when I woke up next to the man. And that kiss that I'd wanted to go on for hours.

Yeah, this train of thought needed to change or my face was going to be flushed and Allyson would know exactly why that was.

Levi leaned in just before we reached the kitchen. "Maeve, you're going to need to find a way not to look at me like that until these guys take off or I can't be held accountable for my actions."

Playing with fire, I looked him up and down. "Hmm, I

can think of worse things, Mr. Traub." I raised one brow at him and grinned. "Let the games begin."

He shook his head at me, scanning me with a positively scalding stare. "Oh, babe, are you ready for it?"

Yowza. Every part of me tingled. Maybe I could convince Allyson to take off now.

Well played, Levi Traub, well played.

Chapter 16

My Siren

L*evi*

Maeve Murphy was under my skin, and there was only one way I was going to work her out. I leaned against my front door, having just said good night to Logan and Allyson, and glared at the woman who had driven me to the point of madness.

She gave me an innocent look from twenty feet away as she wiped down the kitchen counter. "Doing okay over there, Lesser Twin?"

"Maeve," I growled. I was a good person, I really was. I believed women were in charge of their own bodies. I always stopped at a lemonade stand, and believe me, there were a lot of kids in this small town who were banking on people like me. I did what was right and voted to make our world a better place.

As I reached the kitchen, Maeve gave me an impish look. "Did you just growl at me?" she asked while looking at me and blinking those beautiful blue eyes.

"I am not one of those alpha assholes," I growled again.

Maeve looked up at me. "I mean, Grace has shared

some fabulous romance books from the library with those alpha assholes, as you call them. Some of them are surprisingly feminist." She shrugged, then lowered her voice like this was a secret between the two of us, though no one else was around to hear. "I think it's kind of hot."

I worked to fight the caveman urge to toss this pint-sized dynamo over my shoulder and head to my bedroom. Or hell, the kitchen counter looked good. Flat. Free of clutter. Waist high. I shook my head, trying to clear those thoughts.

Our dinner with Logan and Allyson had been delicious food, good conversation, and lots of touching on Maeve's part. Small moments when she brushed past me on the way to get something. A foot rubbed against mine at the table. And washing the dishes after dinner? Forget about it.

Not only had Maeve slid between me and the counter anytime she could, at one point she "accidentally" splashed water on the front of her white shirt while standing at the sink. She'd given me an innocent look with an "oops" and then headed to my room to borrow one of my shirts. Which, of course, was far too big on her, so she'd tied it in a knot at her stomach. I could see a strip of her belly and had immediately wanted to drop to my knees and press my mouth against her skin, devouring her curves.

Allyson and Logan had noticed and, unfortunately for me, been highly amused. I was certain my phone would be flooded with texts filled with commentary from my brother anytime now. And yet I'd held myself in check and hadn't thrown those two out before dinner was over no matter how much I wanted to. I deserved a damn medal.

"What are you trying to do to me?" I said from my spot on the other side of the island, holding on with white knuckles and praying for willpower I didn't have. If I got to her side, we were going to be horizontal somewhere in a matter of minutes, and that felt like moving a tad too fast. Did I care? Yes? No? I couldn't even think coherently anymore. My veins thrummed with desire.

Maeve left the towel she'd been using to dry the dishes on the counter and began to walk around the island toward me. I took a step back, heading in the opposite direction.

"Levi." She took another step toward me.

I raised a hand at her, and she came to a stop. "Maeve, I'm going to need you to stay there." I was now on the other side of the island as she gave me a skeptical look.

"Why?" She took a breath, then laid it out in her trademark bluntness. "Levi, it's Tuesday. I leave on Sunday." She held up her hand, fingers spread. "That means we have five nights to see how we are together. I already know we have chemistry; you know it too. And, quite frankly, at some point tonight I decided I wanted to see what would have happened if Allyson's phone call hadn't interrupted us last weekend."

"Was this decision made before you began finding any moment to press yourself up against me?" I took some deep breaths. That should help, right?

"Maybe?" She bit the corner of her lip. A flush was working its way up her neck and to her cheeks. She was breathing deep, like that had taken some courage to spill out those words.

And while I might have hoped this was where our night might take us, I hadn't thought it would happen without a whole lot more conversation. I didn't want to rush her and didn't want her to think this was the only thing I wanted from her. The woman was leaving in five days, dammit. And I knew she looked at this as an itch to scratch.

The truth that I wasn't telling her was I saw more potential than that. However, knowing Maeve, if I shared those thoughts, she and her red truck would have tires squealing as she left town. So slow and steady it was, which also meant listening to the woman and what she wanted.

"Okay," I said.

She looked up at me with wide eyes. "You aren't going to have a long conversation with me about if I'm sure, if I want to wait, or try to convince me we need more time?"

I stepped toward her around the island, and now she started stepping back. "No."

"That's it?" she asked as we continued our dance around the island.

"That's it. You're an adult and I trust you to know what you want, Maeve." And while I did want more from her, the idea that I trusted Maeve to know what she wanted was the absolute unvarnished truth. Hell, she needed more people in her life who recognized that.

She stopped. "Damn, that is ridiculously sexy. You know that, right?"

I stopped too, confused. "What? Why is that sexy?"

She worried her lip between her teeth for a minute before she took a breath, and then the words just spilled out. "I don't know—it seems like a bunch of people question if I know my own mind at times." She took a second, peering through the windows that looked out over the sink into my darkened backyard. "Always have."

Her voice was quiet, but I heard her. You know, meeting Maeve nine months ago, I would have thought she was confident and lived her life out loud. And sure, part of that was true. But it was also just as true that her fucking parents did a hell of a number on the woman. I knew that, but reminders were also helpful. We might be trying this out, and I might not get my way. This might end up being a moment in time. But whatever we were, I wanted to be her friend. I wanted to help her put the past in the past and take charge of the future she wanted.

Looking at her blond waves tumbling over her shoulders, down my concert T-shirt for Disturbed—a show I saw last fall with several of the guys here in town—to her jeans that hugged those curves, I made a decision.

Eyes locked on her the whole time, I took three steps and came to her side, then tilted her face from the window to lock eyes with me. "Whatever else we are, Maeve, I will promise to always trust you to know your own mind."

Watery eyes looked back at me, searching for the truth of my words. After a few scans, she nodded, deciding something. Maeve rose, brushing her lips across mine.

Lowering herself back down, she whispered, "Take me to your bedroom, Levi."

I nodded, pressing another light kiss against her lips, and led her out of the kitchen and down the hall. Each step built up anticipation. Every foot closer to my bedroom set fire to the feeling in my gut that begged me to toss Maeve on the bed and never let her leave.

My bedroom was only thirty feet or so from the main area of the house, but every step felt akin to torture. In seconds that felt like hours, we made it. I tugged her through the door and shut it behind me. I mean, no one was left in my house, but Allyson and Logan had a key, and I wasn't taking any chances.

Maeve took a step toward the bed and paused, taking in the room. I wasn't a teenager and hadn't been one for years, so there weren't clothes tossed everywhere. The room wasn't huge—hell, the whole house was on the smaller end. But I liked this room. My mom had taken charge here and bought a shit ton of pillows and several blankets. I'd been confused by what I considered excess, but when you put it all together, it gave the room a hell of a cozy vibe. And as winter was upon us, I was a big fan of lounging in my bed and watching something on the television as the outside temps hit the single digits.

But that was for later. Could I imagine lazy Sunday mornings where Maeve was stretched out over my bed, naked as the day she was born? Hell, yeah. But there was work to do before we ever got there.

"I love your room, Levi." Her voice was breathy as she ran her hand over the tasseled cream blanket at the end of my bed. She passed the dresser and peered into the bathroom, flipping on the light. "Your shower rocks too."

It did indeed. Redid that beast when I moved in. The tile in there had been straight from the early eighties. Now there was subway tile, glass doors, and a bench in the shower that I'd love to have Maeve sit on while I—

"Levi, you with me?" Maeve was looking at me from the bathroom door.

I shook my head. "Sorry—I've had more than one fantasy of you in that place over the past year."

Maeve stepped closer, skimming a hand over my chest. "You have, have you?"

I ran a hand through her hair, twirling it into a ponytail and tugging until she was looking up at me. "Too many times to count." With a brush of my lips to hers, I stepped back. "You are wearing entirely too many clothes."

She snorted as a smile spread across her face. "The same could be said for you, Evil Twin."

"Evil, am I?" I asked as I tugged my T-shirt up and off, dropping it to the side. My hands unbuttoned my jeans and began to tug the zipper down as I tipped my head in her direction.

Her shirt, borrowed from me, found its way to the floor

first. Then her jeans made their descent. She grinned my way as she kicked them to the side. "I'm good with a little bit of evil."

I took in her glorious body. I was no poet, but I was sure I could come up with a poem—hell, maybe an ode?—to her glorious curves. I wanted to run my tongue up and down those thighs, make her legs tremble. She stood proudly in her bra and underwear, which were made out of some kind of sheer pink fabric that left absolutely nothing to the imagination. My mouth watered and I shoved my jeans down, stepping out of them as I moved toward Maeve. I toed off my socks and drank my fill of the fantasy standing in front of me. Down to my boxer briefs, I took a final step forward, compelled by the need that had taken over.

"Maeve," I whispered, my hands finding her hips and pulling her flush against me.

"Did you want to go over plans for Allyson's party on Saturday?" she asked breathlessly, tilting her head to the side so that I could run my tongue along her neck.

I feasted on the spot on her neck by her collarbone, noting that tracing it with my tongue caused a hitch in her breath. Running my nose back up, I pressed my mouth to her ear. "Now? You want to party plan now?"

She let out a low laugh. "I mean, we are together. We should use this time wisely..." Her hands were on the move, one going into my hair, the other landing on my ass and squeezing.

"Maeve," I growled, holding her to me and stepping toward my bed.

"Levi." She mimicked my growl. "So that's a no on the party planning?"

Reaching the bed, I gave her a light push, and she fell back with a laugh and bounced on my mattress. My eyes devoured the sight in front of me. A soft light came from the bathroom, bathing Maeve in the glow. Her face was relaxed and filled with amusement and more than a bit of arousal. Her curves were stretched out against the blanket on the bed, and I wanted to tear off her underwear and sink into this woman. My siren. I couldn't turn away. A nagging voice told me that five days would not be enough.

Tell me something I didn't already know.

Chapter 17

Fireworks

Maeve

Levi Traub was making my mouth water, and I wasn't complaining about it one bit. I mean, the man stood at the edge of his gorgeously layered bed—who knew the man gave a damn about bedding—his gaze caressing my entire body and heating me up from the inside out. Had I ever felt this desired? That would be a resounding no. It wasn't his actions, his words, or his looks that made me feel this way—it was all of it. Levi's actions backed up what he'd said—the man found me attractive and didn't hold back. Quite frankly, that didn't suck in the least.

What I wasn't fond of was the physical distance between us right now. Sure, it was a matter of feet, but I was ready for it to be an inch or less. In other words, let's get the show on the road.

A goal in mind, I sat up and reached behind me to unclasp my bra. With a glance at Levi, I clocked his eyes locked on mine. I wanted to get back to feeling his mouth on me. Anywhere. I wasn't picky at this point; I just needed him. Selfishly, I would also like him to continue that earlier trip down my neck to continue to map my body with his tongue, but I did interrupt him with a conversation about birthday parties. Where that had come from, I had no idea. It was just Levi and what he brought out of me. This moment between us was hot as hell, but it was also *fun*. I liked being around him. I liked sitting on the couch and talking to him. I loved giving the man shit, having him dish it back. And the fact that he respected and listened to me? I couldn't even put words to what that did to my mind.

I didn't know if I'd survive sex with this man, but I was willing to try. I was a giver like that.

I slid my bra straps down my arms, going slow because if I sped this situation up, it was going to become a rush to the finish and I wanted to enjoy it. Who knew how many opportunities I would have with Levi? I wanted to soak them all in.

"Babe, I really like this bra and underwear," Levi said, his voice gravelly.

I tossed it to the side and sent a smirk in his direction. "That's because they are, for all intents and purposes, see-through."

He raised an eyebrow at me. "Exactly." He looked at my bare chest, then back up to my face. "Your breasts are as beautiful as you are."

I mirrored his raised brow back at him. "Planning to come over here anytime soon and check them out for yourself?"

He gave me an upward head nod. "You've still got some underwear to take off."

I snorted. "As do you."

"Enjoying the show, sweetheart. I'll shed these in just a minute." He scanned my body, and I could see the arousal in his expression in the light from the bathroom. "I need this layer between us so I don't just rush us."

I licked my lower lip and gave his body a passing glance of its own. He had dark hair lightly dusting his pecs, and then it almost formed a line that ended at the waistband of his briefs like the path on a treasure map. I wanted to follow it with my mouth and do some discovery of my own, but I looked back up at him and spoke words that made me feel vulnerable, though after his comment I felt like I wasn't alone in this. "I don't want to rush either."

"Might not be able to help it, Maeve, so let's get this show on the road." He crossed his arms as if he was trying to hold himself back.

I slid my thumbs into the sides of my underwear, lifting up to get them over my ass, then shedding them as quickly as possible. I lay back, the soft white blanket seeming to let me sink into it. Words didn't come as I watched Levi drink in my naked body spread out on the bed in front of him. I was a fairly confident person, but even I was surprised that I had zero desire to cover up in front of his obvious perusal. He ran a hand over his beard as he searched for words. I wondered if I'd end up with skin raw from beard burn. More pulses of desire through my body at that idea. Interesting.

His voice, when he finally found it, was hushed and reverent. "Maeve Claire Murphy, do you have any idea how sexy you are?"

I ran my hands up my sides, over my breasts, to lie above my head. On the one hand, it felt like a submissive position. On the other hand, I knew I was in control and could tell Levi what I wanted, and he'd do whatever he could to fulfill my desires. Had I ever felt as safe with a person as I did with Levi Traub? Nope, sure hadn't. This man made me want to lie in this bed and have all my mail forwarded. I never wanted to leave.

"Why don't you show me?" I asked, my voice doing its best to mimic Stevie Nicks.

There was no time to contemplate my breathy nature because in a matter of seconds, Levi had shoved his briefs to the floor and was lowering himself onto the bed. He came to lie on top of me with his arms braced on either side, keeping most of his weight off me.

His lips brushed mine. "Is this what you have in mind?"

I lifted my head to nip his lower lip before lying back. Rocking my hips back and forth, I could feel his hard cock against my core. "Somewhat?"

He let loose a chuckle. "Okay, princess, what is it you need?"

I tilted my head, pretending to think about it when what I really wanted to do was beg him to insert tab A in slot B. Tapping my finger on my lips, I said, "I think a certain part of you"—hip swivel again, grinding against his hardness—"needs to be inside me."

"Is that so?" More laughter from him. His chest and stomach were pressed against me, and the vibrations passed between us like a secret.

I nodded decisively.

"Well..." He lowered his mouth to my neck, his lips and tongue causing goose bumps to rise in his wake. Sliding down to pull a nipple in his mouth, he tugged on it and met my eyes. "We'll get to that, princess. Promise." He lowered his head once again, moving to my other breast after he'd tortured the first to the point that my body was unable to lie still.

A moan filled the room, and I had a vague realization that it was from me.

"What do you need, babe," Levi asked as he moved from one breast to the next with pit stops in between to press kisses all over my stomach.

"More" was all I could verbalize.

Before I could even begin to wonder where he was going next, Levi's face was in front of me. My heart began to sink. Was this where he was going to say we should take it slower or only go this far tonight? Was his promise that he was listening to me all talk?

"Maeve." He lowered his mouth to mine, placed a swift but decisive kiss, then pulled back. "I want to make sure we're on the same page."

"Okay..." Arousal was clouding my brain, and I was trying to follow where this was going.

"When you say 'more,' my plan to satisfy that request is to continue to worship this beautiful body of yours, put my mouth between your legs and drive you mad. Then, when I get you to orgasm, I want to have sex for the first of what I hope will be many times tonight. Is that what you were visualizing?"

I mean, yes, sign me up. I hadn't missed the "first of many" comment, and I was down with that. Hell, I'd be fine with spending every moment until I left town in this bed save for the break for Allyson's birthday party. Maybe we could FaceTime in?

"Sounds great, where do I sign," I said, running my hands down his back.

Levi smiled as he continued to press kisses all over my face and chest. I reached up when I could and got my mouth on his neck but then would pull back to look at him, mesmerized.

He whispered in my ear, "I don't think I've ever had more fun while having sex."

I shook my head at the man. "Point of order, there has been no sex of any kind yet."

He smirked back. "Point taken, ma'am. I'll get to work."

I lightly smacked his ass. "You do that."

"Kinky," he said, wiggling his eyebrows at me, then lowered his mouth and began moving south, kissing everywhere he could as he went, his soft beard causing friction and building up sensations on my skin in his wake.

My inner critic tried to ruin the moment, to point out my far-from-flat stomach, telling me my curves were far from attractive. I kicked that voice right on out. It was the same as always, the criticisms my mom had lobbed at me for far too long from my childhood. For the most part I loved my curves and thought I looked good. But the negative comments, even banished, were insidious. Levi was doing damn fine work to drive them out. His clear attraction was helping to bolster my confidence right now because the man was not making a secret of the fact that he was drawn to me and my voluptuousness was a positive to him, not a negative.

Before my thoughts could completely derail me, Levi's mouth found my vulva and my body threatened to levitate off the bed. Levi's arm across my stomach kept me in place. Any denial from earlier was gone—the whimpers and moans filling the room were absolutely from me. There wasn't even a question at this point.

"So, fan of oral sex. Good to know," Levi said before licking me from bottom to top once again.

"Who the hell isn't a fan?" I asked, not even trying to sound unaffected.

Levi used his shoulders to push my legs farther apart. "I mean, I've heard of a few."

"Mythical creatures and they're missing out."

"Noted."

Before this banter could continue, Levi parted my lips and found my clit. Oh. My. God. I was in heaven. My hips were moving on their own, my thoughts in the clouds, and energy was thrumming in my body and shooting down to one pulsing point where everything began and ended.

He found a rhythm, and I called his name over and over as the sensations built up like I was going up the track on a roller coaster until I was hovering on the top of that ramp, unable to tip over, and suddenly I couldn't hold back a moment longer.

I shattered.

The whoosh of feeling that flooded my senses was intense. My body pulsed over and over, and I lost any sense of what was happening until Levi was right there, his cock at the opening to my vagina.

"Ready?" he said, his voice so deep.

I hooked my legs around his waist and pulled him in. "Yes," I breathed out in relief as I was finally filled. We were connected.

"Holy shit," I whispered as he began moving in me. My body was still on the edge, the earlier avalanche of sensations threatening that it wasn't done.

"Hold on," he growled as he lowered himself against me, slid an arm under my back to hold us together, and rolled until I was on top.

Damn. That was hot. We held for a moment, making sure we were still connected, and then I sat up and moved.

There was that feeling inside me, just out of reach, that I chased. Rocking back and forth, I felt it build again, which didn't seem possible. Levi's hands were everywhere, sliding up and down my thighs, over my stomach, to my breasts. As he pinched a nipple, I was suddenly there again, fireworks shooting though my body as I gasped, looking down at him.

He shot me a grin as my hips slowed down, my vagina tightening around his cock. As I absorbed the electricity flying through my body, his hands clamped onto my hips and he thrust up a few times before finding his own release.

Magic.

As his body relaxed, I lowered to his chest and went limp against him, my energy completely spent. He wrapped his arms around me and pressed a kiss to the top of my head.

I found my voice first. "So that didn't suck."

His chest vibrated with his laughter. "That it didn't." He ran a hand over my back and my ass. "I'm guessing you'd be up for a repeat at some point?"

I nodded against his pecs, kissing them between words. "As many repeats as possible."

"Ah yes. The ticking clock."

"Hmm?" I was feeling sleepy.

"Nothing." He paused, his voice sounding a little funny as I felt him slip out of me. "Want me to get a washcloth for you, or do you want to do it yourself?"

I swallowed. It did something to me that he took care of me. Didn't want to examine that too closely.

"I got it." I slid off him and out of the bed.

He grabbed my hand before I could take a step away. "Stay tonight?"

My heartbeat sped up. I should say no. I was not a fan of sleepovers, and the one when Charlie had been sick was still playing through my brain. A naked sleepover was much more dangerous. And yet my mouth moved of its own accord. "Yes."

He nodded. "I'm going to deal with the condom and get the house closed up."

He slid out of the bed and padded out of the room as I watched his fine ass walk away.

Stepping into his bathroom, I took in the beauty of the area once again. I'd only peeked in earlier, but I'd still clocked the space. It wasn't large, but at the end of the room was a glass-enclosed shower with black metal joints, white tile, a giant waterfall showerhead, and a bench. On the right was a freestanding dresser with a sink on top, a toilet tucked to the side when you walked in. The space was well thought out and fit the vibe of Levi's home.

He had just moved here when I met him last spring, after living in the Chicago area most of his life. I wondered what made someone realize they wanted to settle somewhere. I'd never had that feeling, though I had been coming back to Highland Falls a lot this year. And it felt comfortable, like if I gave it a chance I could want to stay here more. But to stay somewhere permanently? I didn't know if I had it in me to ever do that.

It would be easier if I could. Was it something broken in me? Did my parents cause that? Was it something I'd done? My parents sure thought it was—my mom told me I needed to grow up and become an adult. But nothing I ever did was good enough for them, so I'd stopped looking for their approval around elementary school.

I looked in the mirror, and my reflection met my gaze through a watery vision. All I wanted was to find peace. I felt like I'd been looking for it all my life, but it was just out of reach. Even my time with Levi felt like it was filled with potential, but if I took a step back, it slipped from my grasp, a constant reminder that something permanent wasn't for me, wasn't mine to keep.

I shook my head, re-centering. Five days and then I was off again. Reminding myself that this was for now and then I could leave didn't bring me the relief that it usually did, and I had no idea what to do with that.

Chapter 18

It Was Legendary

Levi

As I opened my eyes on Friday morning, I was met with the same sight that I'd woken to for the past three days, Maeve Claire Murphy in my bed. She lay on her stomach, face buried in the pillow, her blond waves spilling over the white sheets and down her bare back. I listened as she made adorable sounds in her sleep, something akin to a content sign as she burrowed, completely unaware of the effect she was having on me.

I'd been curved against her until a few moments ago, as I had been on Wednesday and Thursday morning as well. She'd come over Tuesday night for dinner and hadn't really left since then. Well, that wasn't true. She'd worked a few shifts for Allyson at the café, taught a yoga class for Kate and Kristine, and gone out to coffee with Lou. But staying at Logan and Allyson's? That seemed to be something she'd set aside for her remaining days in Highland, and for that I was fucking thrilled.

Don't get me wrong, the woman was still skittish as hell. However, any drought I'd had in terms of my sex life was gone, and we were currently residing in something akin to a monsoon season. It was legendary. I sure as hell wasn't complaining about it. The two of us had chemistry, that was clear. And when we were in bed, I felt like we were making progress toward what we could be. Her barriers would lower for the moment, but they were less a wall and more like a damn drawbridge that she yanked up as soon as she realized it was down, which happened as soon as we were done.

I wished I could figure out what I could say to make her realize she could trust me, that she could trust this place where we'd found ourselves. I'd even tried to talk to Allyson in a moment of desperation. I hadn't wanted her to betray any of Maeve's secrets, but I was flying blind and needed to know what I was up against.

It did no good. Allyson didn't want to speak behind her back either, but I felt like she at least knew where I was coming from. We both wanted what was best for Maeve, the question was whether that meshed with what I wanted for the two of us and how on earth I should approach the conversation. I couldn't ask for what I wanted because it would likely scare her off. And as much as I wanted more, could I risk that again? Allyson had encouraged me to give Maeve time, reminding me that she'd been coming to visit far more now than ever before.

Questions were racing through my mind. Would Maeve want something more? Was I ready? Would she trust a person in her life regularly beyond her sister? I wasn't so sure, and I didn't know if I blamed her. I mean Logan and my parents were amazing. They could drive me crazy, but their intentions were always the best. What did it do to a person to have the foundation that was supposed to be established by your parents built on a sand dune?

Between Maeve, Logan, and Allyson, I'd heard the horror stories about the Murphy girls' upbringing over the past year, filing them away as each fleshed out who Maeve was just a little bit more: birthday parties that never happened, accidents while babysitting, hurtful words, lowered expectations, negligence, an absence of love.

Maeve felt invisible in her family, and it was obvious why—she didn't measure up in their eyes, so she wasn't deemed worthy. She avoided vulnerability at all costs, but who wouldn't when you couldn't count on the people you should be able to?

I wanted to shout from the rooftops that I saw her, that she could lay down her weapons, we weren't battling. But that would mean very little. I had to show her, and one of the ways I could do that was to let her go in two short days. It might kill me, but I planned on doing it. And while I was pretty sure I wanted to try to explore something more with Maeve, I wanted her to feel seen not just because I wanted to date but because she was a friend and deserved to feel the worthiness of herself deep down in her soul.

Before I could dwell on my current dilemma any longer, the beautiful woman next to me rolled in my direction and opened those cerulean-blue eyes that made me want to dive in.

"Hey," she whispered, snuggling closer and pressing a kiss to the beard on the underside of my chin.

"Hey." I wrapped my arm around her waist, pulling her flush against me as I kissed the top of her head. "What's your plan for today?"

She took a deep breath like she was centering herself before a hectic schedule. "Big Red and I are headed to Highland Woods."

"Working in the café?"

Her head bobbed up and down against my chest before she spoke. "Logan texted; they have a prenatal appointment today. I volunteered to do Allyson's afternoon shift." She ran a hand up and down my arm, over my shoulder, down my back. "Then I'm confirming the party details we went over last night."

I inhaled her scent, almost a whiff of the ocean with something earthy, and said a silent prayer that I had many more days ahead with this woman in my arms. "I'm texting everyone the reminders today, right?"

"Yep."

"Anything else we need to take care of before tomorrow night?" I asked as I stroked her back.

"Nope, I think we're good."

I paused, then asked what I'd suspected for some time. "How long has Allyson know about it?"

Her eyes shot up to me, merriment dancing there. "You knew?"

I kissed the tip of her nose. "Princess, you two should never play poker."

She looked disappointed. "Damn, you think Logan knows? Allyson wanted to let him continue to have fun with this."

"Nah, his vision is clouded by love," I said, shaking my head. Only these women would take a party for one of them as a way to give back to someone else.

That seemed to be enough of an answer for her, and we lay there for a few minutes in comfortable silence. I couldn't say what was on Maeve's mind, but I was soaking up the moment. I felt completely at peace and didn't know what to do with it. Two days. In all reality, I was really going to have to let her go in two days. Damn.

To distract myself, I asked a question I'd wondered

about for some time. "So what's your origin story for Big Red?"

Maeve's laughter was unexpected and light as she leaned back and looked up at me. "How long have you wanted to ask that?"

I brushed her hair away from her forehead. "Shortly after meeting you and clocking that truck at Allyson's."

"It was my grandmother's gardener's truck, but Nan loved it. She said she loved the brashness of it, the lack of frills but reliable nature. The loud muffler." She rolled into me, putting her back to my chest and nuzzling her ass against my cock. It wasn't going to be a quiet morning together, just getting to know each other, if she kept moving.

Wanting to hear the rest of her story, I put a hand on her hip and added pressure to keep her still. "So how did Big Red's ownership go from a gardener to you?" I tilted my head to place my lips on her bare shoulder, waiting.

She shrugged, my mouth moving with her. "My nan just got me, you know? Do you have anyone like that?"

I nodded even though she couldn't see me, though maybe she'd feel it. "Logan. My parents too, but being a twin has that baked in."

"That makes sense. At any rate, as a result, she was one of my favorite people on the earth. I'm not sure how she knew how much that truck meant to me. She used to drive it with Sam when they'd go to the store to get plants. She didn't *need* a gardener—she already had someone taking care of the yard—but she'd met Sam and he was bored to death in retirement, and the two of them teamed up. They were fierce friends in his later years, thick as thieves. Anyway, Sam's kids had him get a new truck when his old one died, and he got Big Red—"

"His name or yours?" I loved the feeling of Maeve in my

arms, her back to my front, cradled against me. We were in our own cocoon.

She laughed. "Mine. Sam continued working for Nan for several years, but then he got sick suddenly. He passed before any of us were ready for him to. In his will, he left Big Red to her and told her to use it to drive to the garden center in his memory or for something else she decided was worthy of his truck. Sam's kids thought it was great because they knew how much Nan had meant to him. Hell, he treated Allyson and me as the grandkids he hadn't been blessed with yet. And so Nan taught me to drive in Big Red—"

"Your parents didn't teach you to drive?"

She went stiff for a second. You ask a stupid question... Of course they hadn't.

"Sorry, go on."

She grabbed my forearm, which was resting against her chest, and squeezed. "Nan taught me, and Allyson would often go with us. We'd drive down roads that were far from the city; Nan would blare music and roll the windows down. Pretty soon I associated that truck with freedom and good memories of a kind man."

I felt wetness on my forearm, dripping from her face. Damn it, that had not been my intention. "Princess, we don't have to talk about this."

She cleared her throat but continued. "No, they aren't tears of sadness but gratitude that I did have good people in my life even if I forget it sometimes." Her chest rose and fell with a deep inhalation. "When I graduated high school, my parents weren't there. My dad had a work dinner to attend, and my mom went with him. They told me that it wasn't like I valued education and was planning an Ivy League education after. Needless to say, my plan to go to community college was beneath them. So they weren't there, but Allyson and Nan were. When we got home, we had cake that Nan had purchased to celebrate. After our small party was done, Allyson went out with a friend and Nan gave me a graduation card. In it were the keys to Big Red."

I could feel the tears falling harder on my arm, so I nestled in as close as I could. Sunlight streamed in my bedroom windows, bathing Maeve in a warm glow. I wanted to keep her here. To find her parents and ensure they never hurt her again. I wanted to give her the world and prevent her from sweeping everything we had away. I wanted to trust her. I didn't know how to do that because I had a feeling she was going to break my heart whether she intended to or not.

Maeve cleared her throat, oblivious to my mental gymnastics. "Nan told me it was my choice, but if I wanted, I could take it and go. She'd talked to Sam's kids and had their blessing as well."

I sat there, anger and sadness the emotions that were fighting for top billing. Her parents hadn't gone to her high school graduation. How did one even reconcile themselves with that kind of neglect? I swear, if I ever met those people, I couldn't be held accountable for what I might say.

I cleared my throat. "So Big Red was your ticket out of there."

"Yep. It allowed me to take that beautiful truck and some money that Nan passed to me and take off. I started at a community college, sleeping on the couch of a high school friend, and worked on my yoga certification. I took a few business classes as well. But once I was certified to teach yoga, I decided more schooling wasn't for me and started driving around the country, meeting people, checking out new places. I went where I was needed, where my heart took me. Friends I had from high school or my year in college always seemed to know someone who could use a hand. I drove from place to place, my skills for random jobs increasing with each new stop."

I nodded, seeing how liberating it would be to fly like a bird set free from a cage. What should have been her sanctuary, her home, had been a prison. With that thought, I traced the tattoo just inches from where my mouth was on her shoulder.

"I heard you talking to Lou when you first came to Highland Falls this time." I ran a finger over the birdcage. "We were at the brewery, and you mentioned your tattoos."

Maeve got quiet for a moment.

"And Sam was the gardener who was responsible for the peonies?" I asked as I slid my hand under her side to run a finger down that forearm where I knew the flower graced her forearm.

"No, not originally. It was the gardener she had when I was small. Tim, I think." She inhaled a shaky breath. "Then Sam came along and planted more peony bushes because we loved them so. Pink."

Wrapping her in my arms, I poured my feelings for this woman into a tight hug. She was killing me. I needed to find a way to make her feel supported. No, she hadn't had the love surrounding her as a kid that every child should feel, but she could as an adult. Even if we weren't together like I would prefer. I could do this for her.

"And the cage?"

"I think you know," she whispered.

"Humor me."

Her head was bowed as I strained to hear her voice. "It was my first. I got it after leaving Allyson behind."

Yep. I wasn't going to survive my feelings for this woman—she was breaking my heart. "Does Allyson know?"

"I mean, I think she likely suspects."

No, I didn't agree. Allyson would hate that Maeve was struggling with this. "Do you know that you actually aren't the villain here? That Allyson likely wanted you to get the fuck out of that hellhole? I know that just from knowing her for a year. And I never had the pleasure to meet your nan, but I sure as fuck know she made it clear that you should escape." I was worked up and told myself to calm down here. This wasn't about me; Maeve didn't need that.

Maeve rolled over to study me with wary eyes. "What are we doing here, Levi?"

My gut clenched, and I wished I could pull her against me once again. The internal battle for what I wanted raged on with no clear winners. We could keep it light and casual while she was here, connecting again whenever she was in town. I could reach deep and find the courage to ask for what I wanted, but that meant I had to trust that Maeve was who she appeared to be and hand over my heart.

Both options came up lacking for me. We felt far more than casual. But trust? When I knew she would be taking off for weeks or months at a time and I was just supposed to bank on the idea of her returning to me, still wanting the same things as when she left? Seemed like that was just asking to be disappointed.

"What?" she asked, her voice guarded as she apparently clocked my unease with our situation on my face.

"It's nothing," I said, wondering where to go from here. "And Maeve, laying it all down for you, I have no idea what we're doing." I took a deep breath, telling myself that she wasn't Tess and that I needed to trust her with the truth. It was a start. "If you were staying it would be one thing, but I don't know what this looks like when you go."

Her body became stiff as she rolled and looked up to the ceiling. "So you're asking me to stay." Her voice had a resignation to it, like she'd thought this was coming.

"Never," I said, emotion clouding my voice.

Her head swiveled my way in surprise. "What?"

"Maeve, it might kill me, but I will never make you stay. I'll be sad to see you go, but I know you need to and I won't stand in your way."

She rolled into me, burrowing to find comfort. "Thanks." When she spoke again, her voice was even quieter than before. "I'm sorry—I wish I was different."

I kissed the top of her head. "I don't."

Chapter 19

And the Walls Fall Down

Maeve

The Sanctuary Café was slammed this morning. Kate taught a gentle yoga class over at Nomad Yoga at nine. Clearly many of the attendees had made the trek here afterward for some morning caffeine.

I glanced behind the counter and saw Allyson and Andy moving as one, clearly no strangers to a crowd as they ensured no patron was waiting for too long.

"Need help?" I asked, raising my voice above the low din of conversations at the tables and the noise of the espresso machine.

Allyson shook her hand as she finished a transaction. "We're good." She nodded toward some low tables to her right. "Lou is over there. Said she was meeting you. Want me to bring over a vanilla latte?"

"How about a toasted-marshmallow mocha today?"

"Branching out." She nodded her approval. "Food?"

"Chocolate muffin?"

"You've got it."

I turned and scanned the tables that Allyson had indicated, quickly catching sight of Lou at a low one with her crew of two—Jeanie and Hattie. I'd told these three I'd meet them this morning since Allyson's party was tonight and I still planned on hitting the road tomorrow morning, the thought of which made my gut clench. Lou said she wanted the two of us to catch up before I "fled town like the Feds were after me" as she so kindly put it.

I was fascinated by Lou, had been since the first time I visited. While she and Nan certainly had different lives, I somehow knew they would have gotten along famously.

After starting off this visit talking to her at the brewery, we'd made time to meet up on several occasions over the past two weeks. She was a wicked gossip, cursed like a sailor, and seemed to be as loyal as they come. I could always use more people in my life who met that description. And Jeanie and Hattie, while far more mellow, still fit in well with all that was Lou. I'd been looking forward to our farewell—for now—coffee together.

"Girly, get over here," Lou yelled, waving from her table with her duo of friends.

"I'm coming." I weaved through tables and called out greetings to patrons I'd gotten to know in my many shifts here over the past year. As a result, it took me double the time it should have to make my way through the space. Small towns were certainly different than big cities, but I didn't hate the fact that I rarely felt alone.

Reaching their table, I plopped down in a leather armchair next to Lou and across from Jeanie and Hattie. "Hey, girls, what's up?"

Before they could answer, Allyson swooped in to give me my drink and muffin with a murmured *behave* directed at Lou. I cackled.

Lou looked disgruntled. "Like I have ever not behaved," she groused.

I raised my eyebrows at her.

"Fine, fine," she said while Jeanie and Hattie grinned at me. She cocked her head, scanning me head to toe. "Hmm." She looked at her girls. "Get a load of Ms. Maeve over here. She's clearly getting some."

I'd like to tell you I was shocked by her language, but that would be a lie. It seemed right on target for Lou. Still, we were in public and probably should shoot for some decorum.

"Lou," I said, shaking my head. "Lower your voice."

She rubbed her chin thoughtfully. "So no denial, just a request I don't broadcast it. I can work with that."

I shrugged, taking a sip of my drink. Damn, my sis got better at this barista gig all the time. "Not denying anything because it's not a secret."

Lou looked a tad irritated at me. "And we didn't warrant a text for this news?"

God save me from this woman. "Does everyone in town text you when they begin hooking up with someone new?"

She shrugged. "Several do."

Sweet Jesus. "Well, consider this me telling you in person. I've been a bit busy this week, but Levi and I decided to get to know each other better."

"Biblically," Jeanie murmured, and Hattie nodded, her little gray curls bouncing.

"Is he as delicious as he looks?" Lou asked, and all three of those seventy-plus-year-old women leaned in as if they were just waiting for the scoop. I looked from one beautiful and wrinkled face to the next, wondering what on earth I could possibly say to them, when the hairs on the back of my neck stood up and I looked to the café's entrance to see the one and only Levi Traub walking in.

I'd just left the man's bed an hour ago, but still I had to fight back the desire currently racing through my veins. It whispered to me that clearly the sensible course of action would be to go tackle the man so we could head right back to where we had been just sixty minutes ago. Logic had left the far reaches of my mind, and I was running purely on arousal.

Levi was heading to the counter—forest-green flannel hugging his biceps, his beard begging to be finger-combed, worn jeans cupping his ass—as my gaze stayed laser focused on him. Hell, I think my trio of companions were under the same spell. However, before he could reach Allyson, his senses must have spoken to him too and he turned, his eyes meeting mine, only to give me a sinful look that told me he'd shared my desire to return to his place and do some naughty things that were better left unsaid.

Damn.

"Well," Lou said, waiting for an answer as the four of us continued our stalker-like staring contest.

I didn't look away from the man as I worked to remember her original question so I could give the woman her answer. "Is he as delicious as he looks? More so."

"Knew it." Lou sat back with an all-knowing look, and we joined her in relaxing into our chairs. I couldn't speak for the crew I was sitting with and where their minds were, but I was going to need to actively ignore Levi being just feet away or the man might have stalker concerns.

Lou looked at me, clearing her throat as if to tell me I better be ready for the truth she was about to lay down as she shifted topics. "So, Ms. Maeve, you are abandoning us again starting tomorrow. Whatever will we do without you?"

I took another sip of the sweet coffee, debating how to answer. Side note, it really was a hell of a drink; I'd need to compliment Allyson. She got better and better each time I returned. Glancing around, I took in the café for a moment. A feeling washed over me of admiration for Allyson and all she had created here. I didn't tell her often enough, so I made a mental note to do that once I was done with the coffee. Maybe I could take her to the deli for lunch? Then we could talk about how she was going to dust off her acting chops so she could look really surprised tonight for her party.

Getting back to the matter at hand, I looked at Lou. "Now Lou, we've discussed this. You know the four of us are going to Zoom monthly for cocktail hour, but more than that, you know I'll be back. I have a nephew coming in a few months. I won't be missing that."

"I guess that is sufficient," she grumbled, clearly having more thoughts on the topic that she was holding back. Was that due to respect for me? That was new. Hell, as much as it hurt, and I hated to even admit it, people wanting more time around me was a feeling I wasn't used to. Damn childhood and the baggage we carry.

Before I could reassure her, the sound of a chair being dragged over to our group got my attention. I looked to my left and saw the one and only Levi pulling a chair up to join us.

"Miss me much?" I grinned, secretly pleased that he was apparently perfectly comfortable joining me while I was meeting with this motley crew.

"You have no idea how much, princess," he said, giving

me a look that spoke volumes. "Thought you all could do with a chaperone."

"Jeanie, Hattie, look at these two. Aren't they adorable?" Lou commented from my other side.

"That they are." Jeanie murmured her agreement as Hattie nodded her head.

I rolled my eyes to Levi, but then I noticed he'd leaned in over the low coffee table to make sure the crew heard him.

"Thanks, ladies. I happen to agree with you." He winked at them, I'm certain causing heart palpitations. "I think we're pretty adorable too. So what have I missed? You all sharing the hot gossip in town?"

"You mean beyond the two of you?" Lou leaned past me to give him a skeptical glance.

Levi shot her an assessing look over his coffee cup. "Now, Lou. I know your talents in this department. What's happening in Highland that doesn't involve the two of us?" He gestured at me, then at himself. "There has to be something interesting."

Lou pursed her lips, giving the matter some consideration. "Let's see, the baby train is still going strong. Ivy's Lorelai is only a few months old. Emma and Allyson are due at the start of summer." She tapped a finger on her lips, thinking.

Jeanie chimed in. "Oh, Elle—married to Nate at the library—is expecting."

Lou and Hattie look surprised, and Lou spoke up, clearly annoyed to be in the dark. "How did you know that?"

Jeanie shrugged. "I went to pick up some books on hold this morning, and Nate mentioned it. I believe he said they were due in May. Elle was there, glowing at a table and working on her next book."

"I thought she liked writing in their cute little house," Lou said gruffly.

"She said she goes to the library at least once a week to write. Reminds her of where they started and gives her new walls to look at when she's stuck."

"Anything else up in Highland?" I asked, fascinated that social media wasn't necessary here—you just needed to have the older town matriarchs on speed dial.

Lou, Jeanie, and Hattie looked at each other, and the look spoke volumes. The phrase *here comes trouble* came to mind. These three were up to something.

"We're working on setting Noah up," Hattie volunteered as Jeanie and Lou tried to hush her.

"Noah? Ivy's ex, Noah?" That could be fun. I mean, what small town didn't have a crew of well-meaning busy bodies playing Cupid? Good times.

Hattie nodded, ignoring the words of protest from her partners in crime telling her to stop sharing state secrets. "We decided we're interfering here because someone needs to. Noah's such a good dad—he needs to find someone, you know?"

I didn't know him well, but from all I had heard, the man was a good guy. "Who are you planning to set him up with?" Unfortunately, it didn't look like I'd be getting my answer since Lou and Jeanie had started a whispered conversation with Hattie. Oh well, Allyson would have to keep me in the loop. I was invested.

Levi tapped my hand and nodded his head to the side in a clear *come over here* gesture. We got up and walked over to a nearby couch that was empty while the ladies continued their hushed conversation.

"What's up?"

"This," he said, sliding his hand around my waist and pressing a kiss to my lips.

I let myself fall into his embrace for just a moment. It wasn't quick but also wasn't too excessive. Just enough to get me wanting more if I was being honest, but not give the café much of a show.

Stepping back once his hands on my waist loosened, I whispered, "What was that for?" My fingers slid over my lips, which were tingling from his kiss.

"Because we can." He linked his hand with mine. "I am still lost at what we're doing, but I don't ever want you to think I don't want this or that I think it's something that needs to be a secret." He squeezed my hand in his, looking down to where we were joined before meeting my gaze. "I am absolutely not pressuring you to stay, Maeve Murphy. I just need you to know that if you weren't leaving, what's going on between us would be a different conversation. Do you get me?"

Damn, I did. I hated that I got this man. Part of me wished he was asking me to stay while also being thrilled that he respected me enough to listen to what I was actually saying and not try to change my mind. It was a mind fuck for certain.

Several hours later, I was bumping along some country roads after an excellent Highland Falls afternoon. Allyson and I had hit up Goodman's Deli for lunch where I'd had a hell of a sandwich known as the Veggie and a delightful dessert, a scotcharoo. Emma and Maggie had joined us, which had been nice, and Allyson filled them in on the small detail that she was in the know about tonight's main event, her surprise party. Maggie found that beyond hilarious for some reason, and because these women were the best, we'd headed to Emma's place to debrief over some chocolate chip cookies—because who doesn't need a second dessert—while the crew speculated about who the gray-haired mafia might be trying to set Noah up with. Maggie even texted Ivy to get her opinion. Ivy's thoughts ran from "I love this" to "Do you think Lou would let me join them?"

Again, I loved these ladies.

Sitting around Emma's farm table in her kitchen, I'd marveled at the friendships I'd developed in Highland Falls without much effort. True, I had friends sprinkled around the country and enjoyed visiting every one of them when I could. But something about these women felt like if I were actually around for more than a week or two, I could let some deep friendships grow.

Which would make one ask why the hell I didn't stay put. Life would be a hell of a lot easier if I could. Honestly, when I sat with that thought for a hot minute, something deep inside whispered that maybe, just maybe, this time I could stay. Right on the heels of that came the absolutely certainty that I needed to go. My gut would tighten, my body would feel just off, and the itch would rise up. All I could think of was putting miles between me and Highland Falls.

And I hated that about myself.

The horizon stretched out on either side of me on top of barren fields, though I knew in just a few months the farmers would be out planting for hours on end and the landscape that surrounded me would look so different.

The Midwest had its own kind of beauty. I could see for miles, and Big Red and I were soaking in every one of them as we flew down the country lanes, singing our goodbyes to London with Taylor Swift, though my heart was grieving my imminent exit of this small little town nestled in the middle of Illinois. Who would have ever called it?

As I slowed to take a right and start heading back to Highland Falls, I was hit with the smell of pancake syrup.

That's weird, I thought to myself. *Am I now fantasizing about breakfast?*

And then, in the next second, smoke began rolling out from under the hood of the truck. Holy. Shit. I slowed down and pulled off to the shoulder, throwing the vehicle into park.

"Big Red, not cool," I said, my heart racing. "What on earth?" It was ridiculous how much this made me want to vomit. I mean, there was surely a reasonable explanation for why there was smoke coming out from under the hood.

"Get the hell out of the car, Maeve," I growled at myself, my survival instinct finally kicking in.

Phone tossed in purse, I grabbed the strap to slip it over my head and hopped out of the car, pulling the hood release as I went.

I stood in front of the truck and talked to myself, trying to gain the courage to open the hood all the way. The smoke coming out of the now marginally larger opening around the edge of the hood convinced me that I might, possibly, have lost my mind and reinforcements would be a good choice.

Reluctantly, I hit Levi's name. Yep, I said Levi. I mean, I could text Allyson, but she was pregnant and didn't need to be dealing with my headaches. I could call Logan, but see my last thought: Allyson would come with. So Levi it was.

"Maeve." His voice sounded growly, and it did something to me.

"Levi." I cleared my throat, somehow finding lots of emotions hitting me as I looked at my beautiful truck sitting sadly on the side of the road with smoke still coming from it, though not as intensely as before. "I need help."

"Where are you," he said, voice even deeper.

I heard what was clearly him grabbing keys and going out a door. Next I heard his car door shut and the car start up.

God, I loved that this man just acted. No long explanations. I asked and he would come.

"I don't know. I'm in the country, and Big Red has smoke coming from under the hood." At that, tears started an unbidden journey down my face. Dammit. Why was I crying over a truck?

Don't get me wrong, I knew why I was crying, but my distaste for vulnerability was a powerful force.

Levi's voice had become gentler. "Princess, can you find a crossroads? There will be numbers like 1100 North on a street sign at an intersection. I need those and I'll get to you. Then we'll figure out Big Red."

I looked to my left and there was a turn not far away. I headed in that direction as I spoke. "But Levi..." I gulped back the feelings that wanted to break free. Not now. "What if she isn't?" Reaching the sign, I rattled off the numbers.

"Maeve, I've got you. I'll be there in about five minutes. You say there's smoke?"

I nodded mutely before realizing he couldn't see me, so I whispered, "Yeah. Do you want me to look under the hood?"

"No, babe. How about you just keep watch? I'm going to call Jared to tell him I might need him. He has an auto shop in town, and he can meet us if we need a tow."

The thought of Big Red being towed did something to me. Was I grieving a truck? What was wrong with me? I was no fool—I knew I kept people out. My walls had been built through years of protecting myself. Was a truck really the thing that was going to bring them all down?

I cleared my throat. "What if they can't fix Big Red, Levi?"

"Maeve, we'll figure it out together. Two minutes—watch for me." I appreciated that he didn't bullshit me, but still. My heart whispered that my journeys with Big Red might be at an end, and I couldn't even wrap my mind around that.

"Okay," I said. "I'll see you soon." Hanging up, I walked up to Big Red. The smoke had dissipated, and the truck sat there, looking abandoned. I put a hand on her hood and found that it was cool in the January air.

Dropping my head to rest on the side of the truck, I stood on a country road miles from anyone and cried. Alone.

Chapter 20

Surprise!

Levi

I glanced over at Maeve and saw that she was in the same position as she had been minutes ago, forehead to the window of my 4Runner, eyes staring out at the fields blurring by. Her inner light was dim, and my heart broke for her.

Hell, pulling up on the road to her a half hour ago made me want to scoop the woman up, toss her in my vehicle, and head to a cabin somewhere where I could cocoon her in my warmth and pour in all the attention she needed. She hadn't even heard me on the road as she'd stood there, her head resting on Big Red the way it was now resting on my window. She'd looked so lost, so alone in this world.

I'd thought about her and Allyson's upbringing a lot over the past few days together. Hell, I'd been thinking about it since we'd met, but each time I found a new detail, it fleshed her early years out more, not that any of it was good necessarily. I realized now how privileged Logan and I were to simply have grown up with the parents we had. I had never given their love and support a second thought—

wasn't that what parents did? But now, seeing the invisible scars that Maeve's parents had left on her soul, I wished with everything in me I could erase them, and yet I knew I couldn't.

Life was hard. I knew I had work I needed to do on myself. I knew Maeve had her own. I wished for the ability to stop time, allow the two of us to sort out our shit and—hopefully—come back together, ready to try something out. Since that wasn't a power I possessed, I needed to trust her to do her thing while I did mine. I just had to hope that we would come back together in the end.

I slid my palm onto her thigh and gave her a squeeze. "You with me, princess?"

She looked over, wiping tears off her cheeks. "I'm so sorry. I promise I'll rally for the party—this is just silly of me."

"Maeve." My voice was gruff, and I couldn't help it. "You are allowed to have your feelings, and whatever they are, they're valid."

She fought to give me a small smile. "Thanks, Levi."

"Jared said he'd take good care of Big Red. Think of it like a spa visit for her."

Her adorable nose wrinkled at me. "Spa visit. Hardly, but I like the visual." She gulped. "I heard you and Jared talking. It could be a big problem."

"And it could be something simple like coolant."

"Still not cheap." She fiddled with the material in her jumpsuit, keeping her gaze on her lap. "I live pretty frugally—"

"Because you gave your inheritance to Allyson for the café," I pointed out.

A shoulder shrug from the seat next to me was the only acknowledgment I got.

"And from what your sister has told me, you send her money regularly as you work around the country so she can invest it back in the café." I'd just learned that one a few weeks back. Allyson said she tried to refuse, but Maeve wasn't having it, said she didn't have any need for the money and wanted the café to continue to grow.

The woman in question turned to the window once again. "I don't need money for the most part..."

"Except when a vehicle decides to take a trip to the spa, hmm?"

I could see her nod out of the corner of my eye.

I hesitated, having a feeling how this would go over. "How about you let me cover the repair?"

She spun in her seat in my direction. "Absolutely not."

Called that one. I turned the heat up a little since the January air was pretty cold and that jumpsuit and jacket didn't look especially thick, though we were almost to Logan's. "How about asking Allyson since you've sent your cash to her already?"

"No, that's not okay." She looked back to the window, leaning against it again like she couldn't possibly hold herself up anymore.

"Babe"—I squeezed her thigh—"I think you need to talk to Allyson. Investments in the café because you believe in her and want to be part of it are one thing, ones made from guilt for something you don't have any reason to feel guilty for are another."

I drove up the lane to Logan and Allyson's cabin, which was glowing from each window, even though I knew the two of them were at the brewery for the next hour. Big Red issues aside, we still had a surprise-not-really-a-surprise party to pull off. Our friends were already here, judging by the vehicles. Logan had been my next call after Jared, and

I'd explained the current dumpster fire. He said he'd get the group on party setup as long as Maeve still felt up to celebrating. Logan got the importance of that truck without my explaining, which was one more thing in a long list of qualities that I loved about him.

I'd checked with Maeve, and she was adamant that the show would go on, so here we were, doing just that.

"It's not guilt exactly. I just want her to reach her dreams..."

I almost missed Maeve's comment, her voice was so quiet, but I'd heard her. As soon as I parked, I turned toward her before she could escape the car. "Babe, what about your dreams?"

Her watery gaze met mine. "I'm not even sure what they are," she whispered.

Jesus. This woman was going to be the death of me. "Hold tight," I said, tapping her thigh.

I quickly got out, walked around to the passenger door, and opened it for her to slide out. She did, fitting right into my waiting arms.

I wrapped them around her so I could speak directly into her ear. "I think it's time for you to figure that out, and I'm here to help you in any way I can."

Maeve tipped her head back, the blond waves cascading over my arms and down her back. She stood there, meeting my eyes but not saying a word, as if she was still processing. Finally she gave a nod like she had come to some kind of decision.

"Okay. Thanks, Levi." Rising up on her toes, she pressed a kiss against my beard, then turned to go to the house.

I watched her retreating form and prayed that this woman wouldn't always be walking away from me.

Entering Logan and Allyson's was to walk into a beehive—there was action everywhere. Max was kneeling in front of the fireplace with Sully, getting a fire started.

"Levi, is your phone hooked to the Bluetooth here?" Maggie called from a spot in the kitchen where she was standing with Drew and Kate.

"Yep." I pulled it out of my back pocket, unlocked it, and handed it over. Knowing those three, they were going to be in charge of music all night.

From what I could tell, Jake was on the back deck with Nate and Aidan. Looked like they were grilling something.

And in the kitchen, smells wafted out, making my mouth water. Emma, Ivy, Elle, and Grace were commanding the area as Grace looked at a list in her hand and gestured to some open dishes on the counter. Apparently she was organizing the food for the night.

The place looked great, smelled amazing, and party prep seemed to be well in hand.

I looked down to Maeve and saw her taking it all in, wide-eyed. "You good?"

She looked up at me. "When you said this party would be a breeze, I didn't understand how you could be so at ease with the planning. But it's because you knew about this, right?" She threw a hand out to encompass the whole crew.

I thought about that and our conversations two weeks ago. Was it really only two weeks? "Yeah, I guess you're right, though I don't know if I could have explained why I wasn't stressed. But yeah, in the back of my mind, even without fully realizing it, I knew we'd never be alone. These guys have people over all the time. Parties are always a joint responsibility. Bring some food, bring drinks to share." I nodded to the lineup of bag coolers. "Hell, I bet they could throw a wedding in no time flat, though it would be super relaxed."

Maeve nodded, looking around again. "I mean, I have friends, but they're scattered all around. I'm so glad Allyson has this."

"You too," I said, reaching over and entwining our fingers together.

"Hmm?" she murmured, looking up at me.

"These are your friends now too. Just like they adopted me, they've taken you in. Better not fight that." I squeezed her hand.

She looked up at me, the brilliant smile on her face a welcome reprieve after the sad expression she'd had since we left Big Red. "That sounds pretty great."

The next half hour was filled with more guests, namely Logan's and my parents, and final party prep. Maggie had insisted on flowers and lit candles to give the atmosphere she wanted. Logan sent a text when they left the Homestead, so we knew we were on a countdown.

Since the food and drinks had been a joint effort; however, we were ready in plenty of time and were standing around visiting with a drink in our hand when Dad called out, "They're coming up the lane."

Logan and Allyson's first floor was an open concept, so it wasn't like there were many spots to hide, but everyone did a great job, tucking into the hall, behind couches, crouched down below the island in the kitchen. A cursory look before I took my place showed a welcoming space lit with candles, music playing, mouthwatering aromas from the kitchen, and a giant banner that Elle and Grace had hung that wished Allyson a happy birthday. So maybe hiding wasn't necessary, the jig would be up the minute she walked in, but Logan had wanted everyone to yell *surprise,* and that's what we'd do even though several of us knew how unsurprising the whole endeavor was.

"They're coming up the walk," I said in a low voice, sliding into the hall by Maeve, who had her phone out to take a picture or video, which one I wasn't sure. Standing by her side in the hall, I looked at all the photos that Logan had hung up here. My eyes locked on the one right in front of me. In it, Nola was staring back at me, her head tossed back, laughing. I remembered when it was taken—it was about a year before she passed. We were at a college football game for our alma mater. Nola was giving Logan hell about something and was highly entertained by his reaction.

The picture was taken at the tailgate—we were having a chili cook-off that day with our college friends. What I'm sure Allyson hadn't realized when she'd hung it up in her crusade to get Logan's memories that included Nola up on the wall was that Tess was in the picture with me. It hurt a bit to look at because I remembered being with her that day. Hanging out with my brother and Nola, so certain that in a few years we would have what they had.

Little did I know. Hell, little did any of us know.

The door opened, and the house seemed to breathe together as one. I saw Maeve hit the button on her camera as friends sprang from spots all around the first floor.

"Surprise!"

Allyson stuttered to a stop, her hand shooting up to cover her mouth as she took in the faces in front of her shouting their well-wishes. Even from here, I could see tears start their downward trek over her cheeks. Thankfully the smile stretched over her face told the tale that those were happy tears, not ones of sadness.

"You guys," she gasped as she was surrounded by arms pulling her into a hug from one friend to the next.

The vibe in the house switched from the one of anticipation that we'd all felt for the past fifteen minutes to one of a true party. Someone had cranked up the music, and clearly they'd found Allyson's phone to pair with the speaker because her favorite, Taylor Swift, was belting out lyrics. Come to think of it, Maeve loved the singer too. One more thing the Murphy girls had in common.

Speaking of Maeve, I turned to look at her and found her watching Allyson, a small smile on her face.

"You didn't mention your sister is an amazing actress," I murmured into her ear.

"Hmm?" She looked up at me, eyebrows quirked. She looked back to her sister, then back my way. "Oh, you mean her reaction?"

I nodded.

She shrugged, her own eyes getting a little damp. "I think that had less to do with surprise and more the feeling when people care enough to come together for you." She looked up at me. "You know?"

Once again, I was overcome with the strong desire to kick her parents in the ass. What those two did to their daughters might not be considered abuse, but they left a mark anyway. Fuckers.

Maeve was on the move, and I watched her walk up to Allyson, right into her arms where the two sisters embraced, rocking back and forth together. I'd followed and stood behind her, reaching over to give a fist bump to Logan, who looked beyond in love with his girl in front of him. He would slay everything he could for her, including remedying the bullshit of never having a birthday party thrown in her honor.

"Nicely done," he said with a nod to the happy crowd drinking, eating, and dancing around us.

"My boys!"

Oh boy, Linnie Traub was incoming in three... two... one. Yep, Mom's small solid form crashed into me, one arm squeezing my waist as she reached for Logan with the other.

Once he got the memo, he stepped up so she could hug the two of us. For a tiny woman, she was a force of nature, that was for sure. The woman was in her sixties, but she hadn't slowed down yet, and I hoped she never did.

"This was a good thing you boys did," she whispered up at us. Then, as quickly as she came, she was gone, off to grab Maeve and Allyson. Dad stepped up in her absence, giving each of us a quick hug.

"Nice party," he said gruffly.

Dad was the quiet one to Mom's exuberance. But the two of them were my foundation. I wanted what they had, desperately. What Logan had with Nola, what he'd found again with Allyson. I'd talked to him last year as he worked to gain the confidence to go for it with Allyson. Love after grief was hard. I knew I should just get over Tess's betrayal. However, it wasn't really Tess that was holding me back but my own judgment and how wrong I had been on who she was. How did I trust myself and my gut instincts again? I wasn't sure, but looking at Maeve talking to Allyson and my mom, I knew I wanted to.

Excellent realization when the woman in question was leaving town in less than twenty-four hours. Although with Big Red out of commission, would she?

Chapter 21

Follow Your Gut

Maeve

When Levi had originally asked me to help him plan this party for Allyson, I'd been leery of what he and Logan could possibly envision. However, this laid-back gathering at Logan and Allyson's wasn't all that different from other times I'd been with this crew. Well, that was with the addition of flowers, cake, and a few more people. Oh, and the gifts—all small but thoughtful and showed how well they all knew Allyson.

Was I jealous that my sister had found her place in this world in a community that was so accepting and loving? A little bit. Did I know I could have it too? Yes, but...

Something still held me back. I wished I understood what it was, but that itchy feeling was practically screaming at me and had been for the past few days. The difference was that now I had no way out. Big Red was in the shop, and I didn't even know how the problem with my truck would end. Would I somehow find the funds to fix her? Maybe I could stay a few extra weeks and work some shifts to save up the money for the repair. That's what made sense, but the idea of being here longer made me nauseated.

"Hey, you." Allyson came up beside me, hooking her arm through mine. "Want to come sit for a moment?" She tugged me toward a chair without waiting for my answer, but that didn't matter because the answer would have been yes.

We dropped into the kick-ass media lounger Logan had long before Allyson was on the scene. I had a feeling that Linnie Traub had helped him pick it out because it was exactly the kind of chair I would love to curl up in and I knew Allyson was the same, but I had my doubts that Logan would have ever had that thought when he was furnishing this place.

"So, you off on a new adventure tomorrow?" Allyson asked, drinking some sparkling water. I looked at her in surprise but then realized I hadn't filled her in on the adventures of the day since I hadn't wanted her standing on a country road as I dealt with a broken-down vehicle.

I took a small sip of the mango sangria that Maggie had insisted on bringing and I was glad for it. It was delicious and didn't taste strong, which might be deceiving. I guess we'd figure that out in the coming hours.

"Well, that journey might have gotten pushed back."

Allyson looked at me with surprise. "Why?"

I studied my drink and worked on my breathing. I had no desire for her to realize how upset I was about this. Tonight was for celebration, and I was not going to make this about me. "Well, Big Red decided today that she needed a break and decided to have a rest on the side of a country road after we had lunch."

Allyson sat up with some alarm. "What? When? Why didn't you call me?" She looked around the space while continuing her line of questioning. "Does Logan know? If so, I'm going to kill him for keeping this from me. What do you need? Is Big Red still out there? Do we need to go get her?"

I laid a hand on her thigh. "Breathe, babe. I called Levi."

Her head turned more slowly in my direction, her eyes now twinkling. "You called Levi?"

Oh Jesus. "Yes. You didn't need to stand on a country road in the middle of a winter afternoon in the Midwest. And I knew Logan would tell you immediately. So I decided on Levi, and he came and called a man named Jared who towed my girl to his shop."

She was nodding. "Jared is good. Super fair and reasonable. Did he call and let you know what was going on?"

"Not yet." I tried for relaxed when I replied. "I figure I'll just stick around a few more weeks and let her get fixed, then take off a little bit later than planned."

Her gaze turned far shrewder as I felt like our cocoon began to block everyone else out, letting her focus solely on me. "And how do you feel about that?"

My first instinct was to brush it off and tell her I felt fine, it was no big deal. But Logan and Levi across the room caught my gaze. The two of them were with a group near the fireplace, laughing about something. Their close relationship had been the impetus I needed a year ago to want to spend more time with Allyson. But we'd only deepen our relationship if I stopped keeping her at a distance, even if well intentioned. Some of that vulnerability I hated would need to happen here.

That thought in mind, I met her gaze. "I hate it." I took a deep breath, trying to calm my heart and the unease of sharing my feelings running through me. "I feel itchy and like I need to move."

"Scooch over, ladies." Maggie plopped down on the chair. "Maeve, hope you aren't offended, but I overheard you say you need to get out of here. And since I feel like we're so similar, thought I'd interject myself in this convo uninvited. What makes you want to move?"

"We're similar?" I asked, caught on that comment. Weirdly, I wasn't offended that she'd interrupted but was more interested in what she had to say. I really liked Maggie —she put me at ease as few did.

Maggie raised her class of sangria toward me in a silent toast. "Yep. We're both blunt, loyal to our friends, love our sisters—or in my case, sister-in-law / best friend—and have a desire to travel rather than stay in one place. And I think we look to travel for the same reasons."

I hadn't known that Maggie was a vagabond at heart, but the rest was all true. "And what reason is that?"

She sat up a little straighter as she leaned in, so Allyson and I leaned in too. "Well, in my case, I wanted to get out of Highland because I felt like people would get tired of me if I stayed. That they might notice I wasn't all that great, so I had a strong desire to just go."

My breath caught. "Is that so? What made you stay?"

There's no other way to describe it—Maggie began to beam. She lit up from within as she looked across the room to point at Sully, who was standing by the fireplace.

"That man's powerful sperm."

I choked on my sangria. "Excuse me?"

She nodded. "Yep. We hooked up. He had been my childhood crush, best friend's brother, blah, blah, blah. Broken condom, birth control pills go awry, and nine months later we had El." She shrugged. "You know, your average life-changing story and all."

I saw Sully look over and meet Maggie's eyes. They

exchanged a heated gaze that made me wonder if the two of them would be taking off sooner rather than later.

"Anyway, I was supposed to be moving when that all went down. I wanted to get out of this tiny town that I thought had one view of me. It made me itchy. And when I got stuck here living with that guy while I grew a baby, I realized that this community seeing me for who I was wasn't that bad but was actually pretty great." She clinked her glass to mine again. "So do with that information dump what you will."

Sliding off the chair, she walked over to Sully, who wrapped his arms around her and laid one on her. Yep, they'd be out the door soon. These women in this town, I didn't know that I'd ever met a group of women like them. They were incredible and showed how amazing female friends could be.

I looked from them back to Allyson, finding her watching me.

"How true was that for you?" she asked.

"What?"

"You heard me." She rocked a little to nestle back farther into the chair. "You know, I used to think that nothing Mom and Dad said affected you."

Well, that floored me. "Really?"

She nodded. "I looked up to you, you know. All younger siblings probably do. You were you no matter what they said or how disappointed they were by your actions. I wished for that because everything they said about me caused me to doubt myself."

Damn, that was a false impression. I didn't want to get into anything too heavy right then, but by that point of night, everyone left had settled into small conversations, so I figured we were okay. "I didn't seek their approval because I knew I'd never get it, but I wouldn't say I wasn't impacted by their view of me."

She gave me a slow nod like she was fixing up some thinking. "I guess I thought you didn't give a single fuck what they thought of you and that was an easier path."

My heart broke a little at the thought of a younger version of Allyson watching me and being jealous of what she saw. Hindsight being what it is, I could look back and realize that neither of us had anything to envy. "Babe, deep down in my soul, I *wanted* to give a fuck. Hell, I wanted them to step up and be decent parents. But I knew it wasn't going to get me anywhere. I left because they were breaking me. I wasn't recognizing myself. Still, I hated leaving you."

She leaned over, trailing her fingers over my shoulder where my birdcage tattoo was under my lacy, long-sleeved T-shirt. "I know. And you know that I wanted you to go. Nan did too."

I did know that—she'd told me several times over the past year—but I still struggled with it. "Maybe we both need to find ways to forgive ourselves for something that wasn't our fault?"

"That sounds good," she said, her voice sleepy, curling up to my side and resting her head on my shoulder.

"You fading?" I asked.

"Growing a baby is hard," she whispered.

I stretched out, holding her to my side. "Rest, Ally. I've got you."

"You always do," she said, growing heavier against me. Logan met my gaze and smiled, nodding at her. My sister by my side, a house filled with friends, and a fire ahead of me, warming the room. The itchiness subsided for the moment.

I knew it wasn't gone, but I could rest for the night as I soaked in the goodness all around me.

A few hours later, Levi and I looked around the living room and kitchen, making sure everything was put away. We'd sent Logan up to bed with Allyson, who had fallen asleep on me and not really woken up. Growing a baby was hard indeed. We'd promised we'd take care of everything so that when they came down in the morning, they wouldn't have to start their day with party. That wasn't a relaxing start to a Sunday for anyone.

"I think we've got it all," I said to Levi.

"I think you're right," he said, coming up behind me and sliding my hair over my left shoulder while he pressed his lips to the crook of my neck. "Heck of a party, Maeve."

"Mmmm," I murmured, distracted by the path his lips were taking. "Mr. Traub, what are you doing?"

"Have I mentioned tonight that this outfit was driving me mad?" He slid his hands up and down the lace sleeves.

I glanced down in amusement. "Umm, this jumpsuit is super baggy, and everything is covered. How on earth can it make you crazy?"

He spun me around so that I was facing him. "Princess, I'm beginning to think everything about you does it for me. And that jumpsuit doesn't detract from the see-through shirt you've got on." His hands slipped lower, squeezing my ass and making my core pulse.

I bit my lower lip, looked up at him, and ran a hand through his beard before tugging him closer. "Is that so? I wonder if we should continue this conversation in my bedroom?"

His gaze briefly dipped to my lips, then back up. "That's so, Ms. Maeve." And before I could even think of a reply, his shoulder dipped down as he tossed me over it, fire-man-carry style, and headed toward my room.

"Levi Traub," I hissed, pinching his ass. "I'm not light—put me down right now before you get hurt."

He slapped my ass as he headed up the stairs. "Light as a feather, babe. Now hush, you don't want to wake your sis."

Hours later in the early-morning light, I shifted in my bed. The warmth of Levi curled around me reminded me of last night and several orgasms that made my body sing. As always, he made me feel good—no, great. With him I flew, every single time. His mouth devoured me like I was his favorite thing. I'd never had that, and I'd had plenty of sex over the years. Yet each time with him, I felt closer than I'd ever felt to anyone else.

If I wasn't careful, I was going to fall in love with him, and that alone made me want to run like hell.

I slid out from under his arm, picking up my discarded clothes from the floor so I could go to the bathroom and not flash anyone else in the hall. As I found my shirt, I stubbed my toe on something large. Looking down, I saw my bag, still packed and ready to go like I'd planned originally. My heart sank. What in the hell was I going to do?

Ignoring that for now, I moved into the bathroom and looked in the mirror. My reflection stared back, a stranger in many ways. Sex hair was one way to describe my look. Shaken to my core was another. The woman looking at me looked scared as hell.

I felt all mixed up inside and somehow knew I wasn't going to figure out my mind while I was here. I needed space, solitude. But how on earth did I explain that to Levi? I couldn't expect anyone else to understand my need to go, but I absolutely had to follow my gut. I didn't want Levi to think it was a reflection on him, but it was me.

I dropped my head, so frustrated with myself, and noticed the paper on the bathroom counter with a set of keys.

It was a note from Levi. Who was lying in the bed in the room just behind me. He must have put this in here last night after I went to sleep.

M-

Princess, I know your plan was to leave this morning and Big Red being a diva has thrown a wrench in the works. I rented this truck from Jared so you could still head out in the morning if that's what you need. She's red too, but a little newer than your girl. Hopefully that will be a good replacement until he gets Big Red back on the road. Figured you can swap vehicles next time you're in Highland. Jared is a friend, so it's a nominal fee, more like a favor. His truck is just one he keeps around. No name, so feel free to get on that. And keep in touch while you're out there on the roads.

See you soon.

L-

Who the fuck was this man? Through tears, I scribbled a note back and grabbed my stuff before I could second-guess myself. This was for me. If I didn't want to lose myself and ignore who I was, I needed to get the hell out of this town and figure out my head once and for all. But it was also for him because my prayer, if I wanted to examine it deep down, was that once I figured myself out, I could come back here to him.

Tiptoeing up to the bed, I brushed a kiss across Levi's forehead. It was a chance, but I couldn't leave without doing it.

"Thank you for knowing me so well," I whispered. "You certainly aren't the lesser twin to me anymore." I gulped. "I don't know if you ever really were, but now I know you're the one that has my heart."

Tears slipped down my face as I found my courage to step back and walk out, shutting the door silently behind me as I stepped out into whatever came next.

Chapter 22

What I Want

Levi

I woke up to a cold bed and a faint memory. Just a few hours ago I'd been pulled from dreamland when I was roused by Maeve's voice as she'd said her whispered goodbyes. Tears had dripped down her face as she said what she'd needed to. I knew because they'd splashed onto me as I fought to stay still, pretending to still be snoozing. I'd wanted to pull her to me, to ask her to stay, to confess feelings that I hadn't sorted through yet. But that wasn't fair. Maeve felt, for whatever reasons, that she needed distance. I couldn't pretend to understand what was going on in her heart, so I had to trust her to go, and pray that she came back.

That was why I'd gotten her a truck. Logan and Jared had both shared their unsolicited opinions about what a mistake that was when Jared dropped it off during the party. The rest of the guys had agreed, though Drew had howled with laughter at one point, saying another "Highland Heart-throb" had fallen.

Whatever. I ignored them all. I just knew that Maeve

had a bird in a cage tattooed on her body. Her parents' home was that damn cage and like hell would I ever make her think being with me would be one. So I gave her wings. And now I faced the fact that she'd taken them and flown.

Felt like shit if I was being honest, but there it was.

I stumbled out of bed and across the hall to the bathroom, taking a good look at my reflection in the mirror. One, I looked far more hungover than I was. I passed a hand over my face, rubbing it to try to wake up. Two, I looked depressed. As I dropped my head, I saw the note I'd left Maeve. But this wasn't it. I picked it up, flipping it over. No, there was my note—the one on the front was to me from Maeve.

Levi Traub,

You are a king among men. I'm scribbling this to you at a little after five in the morning and don't have the words to tell you what this means to me. I need to go, and I can't pretend that makes any sense to you or anyone else, but I know I have to. I'm telling you now that I will be back. You know that, of course—my sister is here. But I'm also saying I'm coming back for you. Please be patient. I don't know how that will look or what it will mean exactly, but I know I want to, which is more than I've ever felt before.

Also, if I can ask for one last favor... Can we go radio silent for a bit while I sort out my brain? I'll let you know where I am in a few days, but I need some time. If that's too much, I get it.

Thank you for understanding me and being a friend when I needed one.

Maeve

Damn the woman. She made me feel so much more than I was ready for, or maybe I was just telling myself I wasn't ready. I'd been grieving the loss over what I'd wanted with Tess for so long, part of me wondered if I knew what was real and what was in my mind at this point.

And she considered me a friend. More? Who the hell knew? I'd stop trying to keep score. What we'd done last night was certainly more than friendly...

Whatever. Maeve was gone. I'd helped her leave. For now that was what mattered, and I needed to move on and focus on my own life. I took another look in the mirror and decided a shirt was in order before heading downstairs. I was sure my brother would have a lot to say about the fact that I'd been here for the night.

Charlie came and found me as I pulled on my clothes, his wet nose pushing into my legs as if he wanted to make sure I remembered him.

"Hey, pup. Maybe a run later." I rubbed his puffy head, noting the scent of bacon in the air. My mouth began to water as my stomach rumbled.

Jogging down the stairs, I followed the smell and headed toward the kitchen before coming to a screeching halt. Watching me from the other side of the island were my parents, Allyson, and Logan. They all looked as if someone died.

"Hey guys," I said, Charlie following me as I resumed my trek to the kitchen for coffee. When I reached the island, my mom moved in, wrapping her arms around my stomach as she began rocking back and forth.

"My baby," she crooned.

"Ten minutes older," I reminded her. Hell, Logan could always do with a reminder too.

The man in question rolled his eyes at me. Since Mom was still koalaed around my waist, I shot him a look. *What the literal fuck is going on here?*

He looked toward his wife. *Ask Allyson.*

I looked at my sister-in-law, who shook her head at the two of us. "I'm not trying your freaky twinspeak." She exhaled and turned fully in my direction, clearly working up some courage. "One, no shooting of the messenger. But two, Maeve's gone."

I nodded, waiting for more. When no more came, I looked at my dad and Logan since, as was already mentioned, my mom was occupied with hugging my waist.

Logan and Dad looked at each other, shrugged, and then Logan decided to speak. "That's it, man. We thought you might be more upset."

Okay, looked like we were starting our day with a Traub family let's-discuss-our-feelings moment. Hadn't had one of those in a while. I reached for my mom's hands, untangled her from me, and nodded at the coffeepot. "I'm good and we can delve into all this, but mind if I get some coffee first?"

"You really should have eight ounces of water before your first cup of coffee," Mom said as she got herself set up at the stove to continue making pancakes. Apparently she'd shifted back to advice mode.

"Noted, Mom. Already had some upstairs." I made my cup of coffee and then turned, counter to my back. Placing my mug down for a moment, I hopped up, picked the cup back up, and took a sip as I regarded the meddlesome crew in front of me that I loved, which was critical to remember right now.

"Okay, let's get into it. One"—I looked at Logan—"you already knew that I'd gotten a vehicle for Maeve to be able to stick to her plan today, so I'm not certain why this is a surprise."

Logan and Allyson looked at each other, then back to me. "Um, well, I guess I knew you'd arranged a truck for her, but I hadn't realized that meant she was out of here before dawn...."

Allyson picked it up from there. "And Maeve told me about Big Red breaking down, but she said nothing about another vehicle. I went to bed thinking she'd have to delay her trip, so I was surprised when Logan told me this morning about another truck. Still, I figured she must have decided to stay until I saw my texts." Allyson looked at her phone.

"How many pancakes does everyone want?" Mom called as Dad pulled some cooked bacon from the oven and began putting it on paper towels to drain.

We mumbled numbers to Mom while I waited to see if Allyson would go on. When she didn't, I decided maybe the texts weren't something she wanted to share, not my business, so I decided to lay it all out and get to the end of this conversation before I got the hives.

"I left Maeve a note in the bathroom last night along with the keys. I figured she'd see both in the morning—"

Dad interrupted. "Why didn't you just talk to her about it?"

I looked from him to Mom, who had a watchful expression on her face. Looking back to Allyson, I gentled my response, not sure if their childhood was triggering for her. "I can't imagine what it was like for you two growing up. While you didn't want for material things, it sure seems there was a lot you missed out on. From what I can tell with your sister, your parents didn't respect her enough to believe she knew her own mind. It feels like they made her doubt herself."

Allyson nodded at me, which allowed me to continue, and I looked at the breakfast crew while I tried to think of a concise way to wrap this up. "I don't understand why

Maeve needs space, but I know she believes she does and that's enough for me. I didn't want to influence her or make her feel bad, so I gave her a way out that she didn't have to say goodbye or justify her actions to anyone."

My mom and dad stood with their arms around each other's waists. I hoped they were proud of the way I handled this. They were my examples in everything. Damn, how lucky we were to have had them growing up.

"She will be back." I spoke from my heart and my deepest convictions. "I would like something more with her, but that remains to be seen. I just want her to feel settled and sure of herself if we're to try for that."

Allyson moved around the island to my spot on the counter. I slid down, and she leaned in for a hug. "Thanks for loving my sister."

My first instinct was to sputter that we weren't in love but strong like. But then, as Allyson tightened her grip around me, her small baby bump pressing in, I decided that I could let it go. This woman was pregnant and her only real family was Maeve. I knew Allyson also wanted her to be here more, but she wasn't begging her to stay either. We could support each other as Maeve left us in her rearview mirror.

"Okay, you two cavemen, pancakes are done, but Allyson, Dad, and I are all going ahead of you two." Mom slid the platter of pancakes onto the counter next to one of bacon and a bowl of fruit.

"One time we ate too many, Mom. One time," Logan muttered.

Her hands shot to her hips, a sure sign of what was to come. "Logan Traub, I had made a double batch, *a double batch*, which was at least forty large pancakes. And do you know how many were left for your father and me? Two pounds of bacon *and forty pancakes* and what were we left? Hmm?" Her voice had gotten progressively louder as she'd ranted.

"Mom," he said, digging his hole deeper, "we're talking about eighteen years ago during cross-country season when we were running a crazy number of miles a week."

"Young man, does that excuse bad manners?"

"No, ma'am."

"You're in trouble," Allyson said in a singsong voice.

I grinned. I loved these people. I stood back, watching Logan and Allyson bicker, my parents watching and smiling, Mom whispering something to Dad. And I sent off a wish into the universe that Maeve would find what she was looking for and come back here where people cared about her. She just needed to allow us all to show her.

Hours later I looked around my home office. I'd had a burst of desire to organize today, to get my work life in order while my personal life took a bit of a nosedive. It was Sunday, so I wasn't planning on calling Aidan to talk over upcoming jobs, but he'd texted to see if I wanted to head out on a run, so he was actually headed here now.

"Levi." A voice came from the front door. I'd told him I'd left the door open for him.

"Back here," I called, pulling the list I'd made out of the drawer so that we could go over it.

Aidan had started working for me last month. He was part time and would love to be full time come summer when Mia started daycare, but that was still in the planning stages. I'd offered for Aidan to join me because I was drowning in work, but the stress of being an independent contractor was that I was constantly worried the work would dry up even when it didn't show any signs of doing that.

"Yo, boss," Aidan said, walking in and looking positively naked without Mia strapped to his chest.

"No baby?" I asked as Aidan sat in the lounge chair in the corner of the office, near my desk.

"Nah, didn't feel like she'd want to do five miles in the stroller in this cold." He looked over the desk, then met my eyes. "You said you wanted to run something by me before we head out?"

I nodded, looking over my list. Running my finger over the first column, I tapped it and slid the paper in his direction. "That first column represents the regular clients I had before moving to Highland."

Aidan looked it over, nodding. He'd helped me with a few projects already for some of them.

"The second column is the clients I've added since moving here. I didn't count folks that I had only one job for, just regular customers who needed small film work done. That includes the university and some work for two manufacturing plants out of Decatur. The third column is folks who have reached out to me, but I haven't been able to get to..." I gave him a chance to look over the list.

"This is impressive. What's this ag one about?"

"Max and Logan recommended me for that. Their contact is at the University of Illinois in their ag department. When I moved on from only website work to adding some freelance film and video editing, the pool of potential clients exploded. These folks want to start a video series with farmers and their vet med program to help people understand what to do with crops and animals that are showing signs of disease. We'd be creating the videos and helping them to distribute to clients worldwide."

The topic wasn't on my list of things I wanted to learn more about, but I was excited about the potential. We could really do a lot of good with this video series. We'd have to go on location for some of the films, and they had a ton of different topics already in mind, but my brain was buzzing with possibility.

Aidan looked from the list to me. "So what are you saying?"

I gave him a wide smile. "I'm saying I was nervous about having enough work to make you full time come summer. But"—I gestured at the list in front of him—"when I finally took the time to write out everything we have scheduled and the potential jobs we have as soon as I give our official commitment, I don't think we'll have any worries about making you full time if that's still what you want."

"Hot damn." Aidan knocked on my desk. "This is awesome. How about in the interim? What can I do to help you more until we hit summer?"

I ran a hand through my hair, leaning back in the chair. "I know I need to do a better job delegating. You'd suggested meeting at the café on Monday mornings and making a list together. I think that would work great. Then we can have a plan of attack for each week. And having it in person won't let me turtle up and take it all on myself."

"Perfect." Aidan stood up, stretching as he moved to the door. "We ready to hit the road?"

I straightened the papers on my desk, then joined him to walk down the hall and toward the door. "Five miles?"

"Sounds great. Just enough time for you to share about how you and one Maeve Murphy moved from circling each other to kissing after watching a dog to whatever I've seen for the past few days."

I shook my head. "Not sure you want me to bring the run down, man."

"Traub, I already know that you got her the vehicle to

flee town in. I'm more interested in your mindset. How are you feeling about all this?" He opened my front door and stepped into the gray January-afternoon light.

How was I feeling? No idea. "Fucked up?"

"Sounds about right." He started to jog down my walk. "Let's go—we've got miles to sort out that mind of yours. Need to chat about how when you love someone, everything else falls to second place." He glanced back and gave me a leveling look. "Everything. Else."

Love? Shit. I mean, yay? Couldn't wait.

Chapter 23

Rocky Mountain High

aeve
It had been three days since I pulled out of Highland Falls, not that I was counting. I'd driven ten hours to a tiny town outside of Hays, Kansas. My friend Cindy owned a café that had what felt like every board game imaginable. She'd messaged last week that she had to take off for a day to help her mom out, so I penciled her in for my first stop and swung in to sub for her. Then I'd pointed the red beast west and reached Denver, Colorado, by nightfall.

Today I'd sat at the Wynkoop brewery, staring out the windows and wondering what on earth I was doing with my life. I'd left Highland, and every part of my body wanted to go home.

And when I said home, I meant Highland Falls. I wasn't planning on examining that too closely.

I took a photo of the tanks of the brewery, posting it to my Instagram. Scrolling back through my last few posts, I saw the backyard at Allyson's place, Charlie, an empty yoga studio, several of the Sanctuary Café, a pic of Big Red in the middle of a country road during better times, and a few pictures of Highland Woods. I also saw Levi's back at the bar of the brewery, and a pang of longing hit me.

So one might ask why in the hell I didn't just head back and live happily ever after? Because if I did that, and by "that" I mean leave my nomad ways behind, I needed to be certain. I also needed to face down some demons and sort my shit out.

For that reason, I'd had Allyson text me the name of her therapist at the start of my trip. That woman had given me a recommendation, and I was able to do a telehealth call with her colleague, Molly, this morning. We were considering Illinois my home base, and I was planning to see her in person whenever I was back in town, but I wanted to start doing the work I knew was needed while I was traveling on my own. Today's appointment had given me a lot to think about, and I had another call scheduled in a few days.

We had just a little bit to work through. Or thirty-two years of shit. Tomayto, tomahto.

John Denver's voice was coming through the speakers of the brewery, and I wished I could find the Rocky Mountain high he mentioned, though not necessarily at a dispensary. Not that I was judging, but I needed my overall mood to shift without being under the influence.

I felt lower than low. Not because of the therapy but because I'd clearly needed it. Why had it taken me so long to try this? Was I ashamed of getting help? Of who I was? And if Allyson hadn't mentioned trying it on her own, when would I have finally acknowledged I had a few things to work out?

Molly's voice popped in my head, her final words to me this morning playing on a loop—that I needed to be kinder to myself. We'd sorted out that my inner voice liked to mimic the criticism of my parents. Even I knew that was detrimental to my well-being. My job before our next call wasn't necessarily to change it—that would take time—but to recognize when I was being harsh.

My waiter brought over my fried pickles, and I munched on those as I looked around the space. This place was almost as good as the Homestead, but I found I missed the familiarity of the faces I'd grown to know instead of taking comfort in my solitude. There was a great balcony that would be lovely to sit on if it weren't the end of January.

I imagined I would head out in the morning, though I could be lazy about it. I was due in Boulder in two days to help at my friend's yoga studio. Abby and I had met in yoga instruction class all those years ago in Connecticut and kept in contact ever since. She and her wife had gotten married last year. It was their anniversary, and they were heading out on a trip while I took over her classes for two weeks.

I slid the appetizer aside as the waiter dropped off my fish tacos. He'd highly recommended them. With his vibrant purple hair, multiple piercings, tattoos, and kick-ass rock T-shirt, he seemed like a man who knew his own mind, so I took the suggestion. Three tacos were likely a bit much, but I'd eat what I could.

Picking one up, I debated how to attack this small but mighty dish. Deciding that the best approach was to just dive in, I took a sizable bite, and my mouth was alive with flavor. Damn, that was good if a bit juicy.

As I wiped my mouth on a napkin, I clocked a guy sitting with his back to me at the bar. Dark hair, tousled, beard visible from here. Not Levi, but he certainly put the Traub twin in my mind. Not that he'd left it much. Still, I thought I should text him and let him know I'd arrived. I both wanted to immediately and was worried. What if a reply from him was more than I could handle?

Get ahold of yourself, Maeve.

Was that nice? Maybe not. Oh well, Rome wasn't built in a day.

I opened my messages and fired off a missive to the man.

Me: *Made it to Colorado. Thanks again.*

My fingers itched to add another sentence, to add an emoji, but I held back. I'd asked for space, the man had been kind enough to grant it.

Except... now he was clearly typing. I didn't have to wait long.

Lesser Twin: *Thanks for the "made it safe" text. I hope you find what you're looking for, princess. Going radio silent again as was requested.*

I really should change the man's name in my phone, but I kind of liked it. And I hoped I found what I was looking for too. Time would tell.

* * *

Almost three weeks later, I was back in my borrowed version of Big Red and headed to Vegas. I was not a big Sin City girl, but my friend Mark needed some help at his café and independent bookstore in downtown Vegas. For Mark, I'd brave this town, but there was no way I could stay more than a week or two. Surely he could find new staff in that time.

Passing St. George, Utah, I noted that my phone got cell reception again. And with the return of reception, I saw that I'd missed a call from Allyson at some point in the past hour. I had to give it to her—like Levi, she'd given me some space. We'd chatted enough that she knew where I was, but she'd been remarkably restrained. However, Molly had encouraged me to start reaching out again, pointing out that this distance I insisted on was my literal and figurative way of surrounding myself in walls so I could try to control whether I was hurt by someone again. Who knew that my brain just snapped into gear to protect me without direction? Cool and a lot of work to unpack.

At any rate, Allyson deserved a call. I hit the button to dial her up, tapping Speaker so I could talk hands-free.

"Hey, my beautiful nomad. Is this a good time?" Allyson's voice caused an immediate sense of longing.

More to unpack.

"I'm good but driving through Utah to Vegas. Not sure if cell reception will hold. I'll call you back tonight if this drops." I took a quick glance at the canyon around me. Jesus, this was beautiful.

"Promises, promises," Allyson said with humor.

"I deserve that." I worked to pass an Airstream with Ohio plates. Yowza, they were far from home. A glance at the clock told me I might hit Vegas by dinner. Just a little under two hours left. I had this.

"So, my beautiful sis, how is the unlayering of the onion going?"

I drew my brows together, looking back to the phone like that would help me make sense of her comment. "I'm sorry, what?"

She laughed before attempting an explanation. "That's what I told Logan therapy felt like. I figure one layer out and damn it all if there isn't another layer of BS hanging out right below."

I snorted. Truer words had never been spoken. "Yeah, that's pretty much it. But honestly, it's good. Feeling lighter in a way." I paused and considered I didn't want this to be all about me. "How goes it for you?"

She was silent for a moment, to the point that I thought I'd lost her. But then she spoke up. "I mean, it's good, but there's a lot. I knew Mom and Dad did a number on us, or I guess I shouldn't speak for you, but they definitely did on me."

I shook my head at her comment. "Oh, babe, you can speak for me there. I'm right with you."

Silence again.

"Allyson?"

She sounded choked up when she came back. "Yeah, Maeve, you are always right with me. That's one thing I've faced."

What? "Hold on, Ally." Up ahead there was a sign for an exit at a scenic overlook. I flipped on my blinker and pulled off. I had a feeling this conversation needed to happen when I wasn't driving. "Okay, I pulled off. What's going on?"

"I'm sorry." She was clearly crying. "Pregnancy hormones are no joke."

"Babe." I was alarmed. My sister held it together during the times she *should* let go. I wondered if I should text Logan.

"No, no, this is good, Maeve." I heard her take a deep breath in, then a long one out. "I've just been struggling with how to say this to you."

"Now I'm nervous." I looked out over the red rocks in mesas and buttes as far as the eye could see.

She sniffed. "Maeve, I don't think I've ever appreciated all you did when we were growing up to try to protect me."

I immediately wanted to brush off her comment. "Oh, Ally, it wasn't that much."

"Babe, you have a scar on your lip that says otherwise."

I ran my finger over it. I knew it was barely visible at this point. "Ally, I was doing what any sister would do."

She made a sound of disagreement. "What I hate, Maeve, isn't that you needed to do it, but that you have beaten yourself up for over a decade for leaving me when I wanted you to go. That you feel like you need to flit around this country without settling down because you aren't sure who you could trust to actually be there for you. That you need to pour your money into my dreams because you've chosen that dreaming for yourself isn't something you can do."

She took a deep breath as my heart threatened to beat out of my chest at her words, which felt like they were ricocheting around the cab of this truck.

"And mostly I hate the fact that you are one of the best people I know and you don't even see it."

I touched my cheek and realized it was wet. The tears had come unbidden and unnoticed as I struggled with how to reply to my baby sister.

I went with humor. "So therapy is going well."

She snorted. "Yep, but don't think you can avoid this topic."

I took a deep breath and then went with the truth. "You know I'd do it all over again. Every time. I regret none of it."

Allyson sighed. "I love you; you know that, right?"

I smiled. "Back at you, babe."

She chuckled as I watched an eagle soaring over the space in front of me. "Nan would be so proud of us."

I thought about that for a minute. Would she? Nan wasn't of a generation that did too much with therapy—there was far more of a stigma for them. But maybe? She'd be happy that we were talking. She'd be even happier if we were together.

More to think about. "I think she would be proud of us," I murmured.

We sat in companionable silence for a few minutes as I felt that tug of longing to be back in Highland Falls once again. It was getting stronger, which was something I was working out.

"Can I ask you something and you promise not to get mad?" Allyson's voice was tentative.

"Oh boy." I braced. "Go ahead."

She waited a few beats before saying anything. "Have you ever thought about *why* you feel this need to travel so much?"

My gut clenched. Hell, that was all I had thought about over the past three weeks. Molly and I'd had numerous conversations about it. It was messy; the insecure part of me felt it was silly. I was still trying to figure out the easiest way to verbalize it and wasn't sure if I even wanted to talk about it. But for Allyson, I would.

"I think... Well, I think that I worry if I stick around anywhere too long, people will get to know the real me and not like what they see." My tears were back in earnest.

"Oh, Maeve, babe. I hate that we're on the phone, because I want to wrap you up in my arms and reassure you that that's simply not true." She paused, and I worked to get ahold of myself. "I can tell you that everyone in Highland Falls only wishes they got to see more of you, not less. *Everyone*, especially a certain twin you know."

I wiped my nose because I was getting that gross. "Yeah, I know Logan thinks I'm pretty awesome." I grinned.

I could picture Allyson shaking her head. "I'll let you

joke right now because I'm not there, but you know I'm talking about Levi, though Logan loves you too."

"I know," I whispered. I glanced at the clock. "Ally, I'm sorry to do this, but I need to get on the road so I can hit Vegas before rush hour."

"Okay, but call me tonight." Her voice was reluctant, and I didn't blame her. If I'd called her and she'd had an emotional moment, I'd hate the fact that I wasn't there. Seems I'd had that goal a year ago for the two of us to become closer and I'd achieved it. Funny that it made my heart feel even more tender as a result.

"Promise," I said, pulling my shirt up and just doing a whole wipe-down. What a mess.

"And babe, while you're out there helping every friend you've ever made, maybe find a way to take care of yourself? You're worth it, and I want you to see it." Her voice was gentle.

"I'll work on it, I swear," I said. "Love you lots."

"Love you more." She paused. "I sure hope I see you again soon." Before I could reply, she'd hung up.

I soaked in the landscape as I sat with the truth. I wanted that too.

Chapter 24

Texts... So Many Texts

Levi

It had been days, no, weeks, since Maeve Claire Murphy put Highland Falls—and me—in her rearview mirror. I'd told myself not to reach out. The woman was a bird that needed to fly the trappings of a small town that were akin to a cage preventing her from being free. But January had become February, and we were days from the end of the month of love with still no word from the boho princess, though I'd been following some of her journey on social media.

Logan told me Allyson had talked to her, so I knew she was in one piece, flitting around somewhere in this country. Still, it stung that she hadn't reached out beyond a text when she got to Colorado that told me she was fine and thanks for loaning her the truck. I'd thought we were more, but now I was second-guessing myself.

And so I'd been holding strong, giving her the space she'd asked for, until this morning's website job. It just wasn't keeping my attention, and in a moment of weakness, my fingers flew over my phone and I sent a text out before I could take the words back.

Me: *It's been almost four weeks since you raced out of town like your ass was on fire. You okay? I miss my friend.*

Maeve being, well, Maeve, meant it was two days before I heard back. Not that I had that kind of willpower. When I saw a message from her, it took mere moments to reply.

Maeve: *Checking out my ass? I promise it wasn't on fire even though I ate some of Logan's spicy dip at Allyson's party. And did you lose Aidan?*

Me: *Why would I have lost Aidan?*

This woman was a puzzle, as always. What did Aidan have to do with anything?

Maeve: *You said you were looking for your friend. Logan then? Max? Another Highland Heartthrob?*

One, punch to the gut. The more I got to know Maeve, the more I saw the deep-seated insecurity she tried so hard to always keep hidden. Her parents had done a bigger number on her than she wanted to admit. Two, why the hell was she using Drew's "heartthrob" nonsense? Ignoring that for now. And three, why in the hell was she replying after two in the morning?

Me: *You, princess. I was looking for you. Whatever else we were, we are friends, right? Sue me, but I miss you.*

Me: *And what are you doing up so late?*

Maeve: *True, I am missable. And it wasn't that late, I'm on Pacific time right now.*

Maeve: *And yeah, we are friends.*

Pacific time? That made my heart clench. She was so far away.

Me: *That gives me a narrowed-down window of where you've gone to, I suppose.*

Maeve: *You could just ask.*

I laughed out loud at Maeve's text as I walked into my house after a grueling run with Logan. The roads were icy, and I'd felt certain I'd wipe out any moment. But Maeve telling me she was, essentially, an open book and all one had to do was ask for information? Laughable. The woman typically held all of her truths like a dragon guards its hoard. Reading her through text was even harder. But if she really wanted to open up, I was all in.

Me: *Okay, where have you gone, Ms. Maeve? And how are the borrowed wheels?*

Maeve: *Whoa, you want to know where I am or where I've been?*

Maeve: *And the wheels are fine. I sent Jared my thanks to make sure I was still okay. But I do miss Big Red.*

Yeah, she was an open book all right. And a smart-ass to boot. I debated mentioning that I'd seen Big Red recently but decided to hold on to that secret.

Her sarcastic nature was fine—I could give it right back. I exchanged texts with her between showering, getting dressed, and some easy meal prep of egg tacos for dinner.

Me: *Andy Reid misses you too.*

Maeve: *Who?*

Me: *Never mind. I'd love to know what you've been up to since I saw you last.*

Maeve: *Let's see. I stopped in Kansas to work in my friend's café for a day.*

Maeve: *Denver, then two weeks in Boulder where I subbed for my friend Abby at her yoga studio. Texted you right before I got there.*

Maeve: *And then two days after that I got to Vegas where I've been filling in for a barista at my friend Mark's downtown bookstore and café. Been here for, what, two weeks? I'll move on once he gets someone trained.*

My mind spun with all the miles she'd racked up as she tried to stay as far away as possible, but I fixated on one little word in that diatribe.

Me: *Who is Mark?*

Maeve: *Did you growl when you wrote that? In my mind, you growled.*

Me: *Who. Is. Mark?*

Maeve: *Oh, I love this.*

Me: *Maeve Claire Murphy...*

Maeve: *I'll be sure to let Mark's husband, Chad, know your feelings about his partner.*

Me: *Was that so hard?*

Maeve: *You could have just said you were jealous.*

Me: *I thought that was obvious. So you're in Vegas and working at Mark's café and bookstore. Any thoughts on when you'll be back in the Midwest?*

I waited for three little dots to appear to tell me she was typing. Five minutes, ten, forty went by. After several hours I went to bed, hoping to hear back from her in the morning. Had I pushed too hard? She had to know I missed her.

Maeve: *Not sure. Jared says he's waiting on a part for Big Red, so I figured I'd make more stops to do some jobs and build up the cash to pay for the repair, not to mention this truck loan.*

Would it be bad form to beg for a swift return?

Me: *You know that you owe zero dollars, not even a penny, for the rental, and I offered to pay for the repair.*

Maeve: *Hush. You know my thoughts on that.*

An hour and one text from Drew Spencer later, I had a lighthearted excuse to reach out again to her.

Me: *In case you're interested, Lou has somehow convinced Mike Newman, editor of the county newspaper, to give her a weekly column.*

It took her an entire workday, but eventually she messaged back.

Maeve: *Jesus. What is the column about?*

Me: *She's calling it Highland Happenings.*

Again, hours went by without reply. Was she out with friends? Working? Had she met someone else? Was she just not as attached to her phone as the rest of our generation? Questions swirled in my brain as I went to bed. When I woke up, a text had come in overnight once again.

Maeve: *Nice alliteration. So town gossip?*

Me: *Exactly.*

Me: *Your absence in Highland Falls will be an upcoming column, she tells me.*

Maeve: *That's not necessary. I'll text her. I'm wondering if Jeanie and Hattie are co-contributors. Maybe they could do a write-up on each Highland Heartthrob? I'll mention that to her.*

Me: *Hush, you.*

I wondered if I could get Lou to sway Maeve into a return trip sometime before the spring thaw. For that she could write about any heartthrob she wanted.

Maeve: *Do you ever worry that Logan sees you as less than you are?*

I woke up on a gray Thursday morning to that text, which caused my gut to clench. Somehow I knew she was not just asking a curious question. This was as close as Maeve came to baring her soul. And I was worried. What was going on with this woman?

Me: *This seems deep for a Thursday morning. You okay?*

Me: *And yes, I do worry about that sometimes, but only when I'm struggling myself.*

Me: *Maeve?*

Me: *Maeve? You're worrying me.*

Me: *Maeve? Seriously, check in.*

Three days and no reply. I messaged Allyson and Logan to see if they'd heard from her.

Maeve: *Dude. You don't call Allyson to worry her.*

Me: *Sorry, not sorry. You don't leave that message where I'm worried about you and then go incommunicado for several days.*

Maeve: *I didn't mean to worry you. Just thinking about things. Allyson and I had a good conversation before I got to Vegas. It was cathartic but also made me face some shit.*

Maeve: *And I drove out to Arizona after my original text to you a few days ago to help a friend with her coffee shop in Williams. Cell reception isn't great out here, so I didn't check back right away. Sorry.*

Maeve: *I'll do better.*

Maybe that was it. I hadn't traveled the west much, who knew? Cell reception could indeed suck. But somehow, in my heart of hearts, I thought it was more.

Me: *Want to talk about it?*

I didn't want to talk about this via text. I wanted to be next to her in bed, her head on my chest while I traced my fingers over her back, letting her unload all her fears. I wanted her to know that there were more people on her side than her sister. That it was okay to stop running. That it was okay to open up. That it was okay to be vulnerable.

But for now I had to sit here, phone in hand, and pray that she would continue reaching out. I needed to be here when she wanted me to be. And I needed to do it all on her terms. And I went to bed, hoping I'd hear from her again soon.

Maeve: *Real talk, sometimes I just think Ally looks at me as less than an independently functioning adult. I don't* *have the typical "adult" life—stable job, relationship, home. I don't know why I'm worrying about that, but I've been thinking about it a lot since I left. And I think it is bullshit— I don't really believe she thinks that, but my insecurity gets the best of me.*

I woke up to the text and read it a few times. Was that how she thought Allyson saw her or was that how she saw herself? One thing I'd learned over the past few months was that Maeve was her own worst critic. From what I could glean, her parents had gaslighted her childhood self before she'd had enough and hit the road. The fact that she didn't know her own worth was both not surprising and heartbreaking. And she put up this wall of confidence and easygoing nature to keep everyone at a distance.

I wanted to take a sledgehammer to that wall and absolutely annihilate it. For now, however, I'd go down this rabbit hole with her.

Me: *Real talk back to you—do you think it's because Allyson now has the stuff you mentioned, is going to be a mom, and that you are reevaluating your life in what you think is her point of view of what a successful adult looks like?*

Maeve: *Maybe?*

Me: *Maeve, can you answer this? Are you happy? Truly?*

Maeve: *I don't know.*

Yep. My heart cracked in two. I felt like I was coming out of my skin. She was hurting. She was reevaluating everything she knew to be true. And what was I doing? I hadn't held her in four weeks. I needed to see her. She should hear from my own lips that she was everything that was good in this world. That if she wanted those rungs on the "adult life" ladder that Allyson had, she could have them. But if she wanted to travel the world and never settle down, she could do that too.

I just wanted to be with her for that.

Holy shit. My stomach turned over, and I reexamined that last thought. Yep. Wasn't changing. I'd moved to Highland Falls and loved it here, but it didn't feel complete now that the whirlwind known as Maeve had been here and gone. Would she accept traveling the world with a companion by her side? I had no idea, but I needed to find out.

If you'd asked me six months ago if I'd give up the stability I'd found to follow a woman, I'd have laughed in your face. Now? I knew there were no guarantees, but the idea of not leaping into this thing with Maeve was scarier than trying for something lasting between the two of us. I mean, my job was remote. Aidan and I had just gotten my business more organized that it'd ever been. Our Monday coffee chats for planning were awesome, but I could be anywhere in the world and do that too. And I loved being near my family, but if I was choosing between them and Maeve, I was picking her. I could always visit.

I just had to get her to agree.

Holy shit.

Me: *Just putting this out there—it's okay to reevaluate your life and change your mind about what life looks like for you.*

For example, making your life about the two of us, not just her. But I'd save that for when I'd processed a bit more.

Maeve: *Levi, that's pretty much what this trip is about.*

My heart rate sped up. Did that mean she was reevaluating the two of us along with her life? Our time together had come right before this extended road trip. Was it too much to hope for that I wasn't alone in wanting more? I needed to talk to her.

Me: *Can I call you?*

Maeve: *Thanks for asking, but I promised Jennifer I'd do morning shifts for her this week. Need to get to the café in five. Maybe in a few days?*

I felt a certainty down to my soul that I needed to see Maeve Claire Murphy now. Like I was already running late. I wanted to tell her what she meant to me. That she was perfect as she was. And that wasn't something I could do through text.

Me: *Take care of yourself. Maybe do something just for you. Make sure you're treating my friend well. She deserves it.*

Maeve: *Thanks, Levi. I'm heading out to the Grand Canyon in a few days. I've always wanted to see it, so I'm taking a long train ride to the South Rim and back. So consider that me following your advice. I'll call in a few days.*

And with that, an idea took shape. I opened a browser on my laptop.

Me: *Talk soon.*

Maeve: *Thanks for being here for me, Levi.*

Me: *Anytime, my princess.*

Chapter 25

Hell of a View

Maeve

I stepped off the historic railway car that had taken me on a ninety-minute journey through a variety of terrains. Following the directions of the staff and the passengers who had been ahead of me, I trudged up the path, across the street, until only open space lay head. My breath caught in my chest; it was the Grand Canyon. Finally.

My brain worked to process the view. The South Rim was as awe-inspiring as I'd dreamed. It had been on my bucket list of places to travel to since we studied the geography of America in my fourth-grade class, but Patrick and Mona Murphy were simply not there for any kind of trip that involved sweat. Hell, they also weren't there for any of their children having a say on how they spent their time or money, and I'd known better than to push it.

Somehow, in all the years since I'd left their home, I'd never made it out here. This week at Jennifer's café, I'd overheard some tourists talking about the train to the South Rim, and Jennifer had filled me in. When she learned that

I'd wanted to visit for most of my life, she insisted on telling me I could ride the train out and back and let the railway worry about parking and traffic in and out of the park. Though I'd assumed March was not a high-volume time, it still sounded like a win. When Jenn threatened to close the café and go with me even though it would mean losing a day's profit, I laughed and ordered a ticket immediately, allowing her to stay and keep the café open and stop her meddlesome ways.

The train had pulled out of the depot that morning at nine thirty, and the temperatures had been so much better than I'd anticipated. It had been a little above thirty degrees leaving Williams but should be around fifty at the South Rim. I mean, not bathing suit weather, but I also wasn't going to be sweating as I hiked along the edge.

The ride out had some entertainment—musicians, actors pretending to be a sheriff and outlaws, along with some snacks and drinks. The miles flew by and before I knew it, I was there, and I was trying to comprehend the sight in front of me.

I'd looked at the trail maps before coming and knew I was going to take the out-and-back path that ran parallel to the rim. I'd be able to take in the view the entire way, but in no way would I risk not making my three o'clock train home.

There weren't as many people here as I'd expected, but I guessed summer would be their busier season. Still, I headed to the wide rock wall that looked out as far as I could see and sat down for a moment. I pretzeled my legs right up on the top of the wall while I leaned back on my hands, taking in the gorgeous view that was there for us all. How do you even begin to wrap your mind around beauty like that? Maybe I should FaceTime Allyson so she could see it? Or Levi?

I felt goose bumps rise at just the thought of him. Funny, that was usually how I reacted when in the man's presence. I guess the thought was enough now. But he had encouraged me to take care of myself, and I was finally doing it. FaceTime might be a bit much, but a text couldn't hurt.

I held my phone up, taking a picture that in no way captured what I was staring at, but it was a start. Without letting myself think about it too much, I sent the pic and then fired off a text.

Me: *This really doesn't share how awesome the view is but wanted you to know I was following your advice.*

I laid my phone down next to me on the wall and decided to soak it all in a little longer before starting my hike. As I was doing just that, someone came up to the wall on my left.

They cleared their throat, which I ignored, assuming they were getting someone else's attention.

Instead, they spoke to me. "You're right, princess. It's a hell of a view, but a picture can't do it justice."

My head swiveled quickly to the side as I took in the one, the only, Levi Traub standing there in the flesh. I gasped far more theatrically than was normal for me.

"Levi," I said, hand to chest as I shot up a prayer of thanks that the shock hadn't sent me tumbling over. "What are you doing here?"

He shrugged, coming to sit next to me. "Heard the view was incredible; thought I might take it in." He turned in my direction and gave me a smirk that I'd come to know well in the past year.

I leaned over, bumping my shoulder into his. "I'm not saying I hate this surprise visit, not at all." I swallowed, thinking of the feeling I'd been filled with for the past four weeks. Seeing this man, I was easily able to define it now—loneliness. I'd *missed* him. I mean, sure, I missed a lot of people from Highland. But I knew this feeling was one I needed to examine a little closer.

Levi leaned to one side, pulling something from a back pocket before settling back down. I looked over and saw the back of a sealed envelope. Had he brought a piece of mail here? Color me confused.

Levi worried the paper between his fingers while he cleared his throat again, obviously a little nervous, which made me pay more attention.

"Last week I stopped by Jared's to check on Big Red—"

"Aw, that was kind of you, but I've kept in contact with Jared. He's great about keeping me in the loop."

He continued rubbing a thumb over the envelope. "I know. I just wanted to check for myself. At any rate, while Jared and I were talking, one of his mechanics brought this envelope. They found it below the manual and some other crap in the glove compartment."

My heart slowed down as I took in what he was saying. "Levi..." I started, uncertain.

He continued looking at his hands as he turned over the envelope. My name was on the front in Nan's handwriting. "I saw your name on this and, well..." He cleared his throat again. "I thought it might be important and wanted you to have it."

He passed the envelope to me as my vision became watery, my brain overwhelmed.

His voice was gravelly. "Sorry to intrude on your trip, Maeve. I arrived last night and drove out here this morning. I just wasn't sure when you were coming back through Highland, and it didn't feel right for me to have this and not you."

I lifted my face to look into his warm brown eyes. "Levi..." I worked to find an inner calm, but it had been lost in the wind. "This is Nan's handwriting."

He nodded, reaching out to clasp my hand near him. "I thought it might be."

I glanced at the envelope, then back at our clasped hands, then up to his face. "You didn't want to just give it to Allyson?"

He shrugged, looking bashful for a moment. "Wasn't her name on it." He let go of my hand and leaned forward. "And if I gave it to Allyson, I couldn't do this." He put one hand on the wall near my hip and leaned forward, tipping my chin up with his other. When our lips met, mine parted on a breath. Yes, this was what I had been missing.

I lost myself in our kiss for minutes before he pulled back, much to my dismay. I must have made a sound of protest because he shot me a smile. "Can't put on a show for the folks here—don't want to detract from the actual sight they came for."

I mean, that was the right thing to do... but I also had a moment of wondering if the hotel here was booked. As I shifted, I felt the envelope in my hand once again.

Nan.

Levi looked at me with understanding. "No pressure. If you don't want to open that when I'm around, I can take off. Or give you some space." He glanced back to the parking lot. "Hell, I can go ahead and get back on the road to give you the solitude that you're looking for."

I put a hand on his forearm to stop both his ramblings and the idea of him leaving. "I don't want you to leave. Not now, not tonight, if that's not too much to ask." I could feel my neck flush at that pronouncement but stuck to it.

He bit his lower lip and gave me a good eyebrow

waggle. I laughed, tugging him forward by his bearded chin to place a smacking kiss on his lips.

"So, I'm not a downer on your plans?" he asked, looking unsure.

I couldn't blame him after all my "I need to be by myself" talk he'd put up with. But what I'd been putting together was that maybe, just maybe, I'd done enough work on my own.

Instead of diving into all of that right then, I simply shook my head. He was, of course, not to be put off.

"So you're checking out the South Rim today…"

"And Antelope Canyon in Navajoland tomorrow"—I paused, then gave him what he was looking for—"before starting my drive back to Highland."

Levi laid a hand on my thigh. "For how long?"

"TBD?"

"I can work with that." He glanced at the envelope in my lap. "What would you like to do with that missive?"

I thought about my nan. About how much I missed her. I felt her here—I mean, truly I felt her everywhere, but somehow more here right now as I was close to something that could only be described as majestic.

"I think I'll open it here." I placed my fingers on his lips before he could speak. "And I'd love you to sit right there."

"Okay. No need to share unless you want. I'll just be over there taking in the view and sending pics to Logan."

Oh boy. "Umm, do he and Allyson know you're here?"

He chuckled. "Who do you think called Jennifer to find out your ticket time and date? Allyson could become a travel agent. She got me booked out here, a car to rent, and a hotel in no time."

"Never underestimate my sis when she has a goal," I murmured, marveling that she'd figured out who to call.

Though Jennifer's café was the only one in town, so likely not that difficult since Allyson had known where I was.

I took a deep breath, then another. With a glance at Levi, I saw that his gaze was now firmly locked on the beauty of the canyon in front of us, giving me space in the only way I was allowing him at the moment. That gave me the courage I needed, and I tore the envelope open, sliding out a handwritten letter. Opening it, I got a whiff of Nan's floral perfume. Whether it was truly there after all these years or a figment of my imagination, I didn't care. Nan was here.

Unfolding the paper, I read.

My darling princess,

I stopped, sitting up straight. She'd called me princess—how had I forgotten that? She hadn't always said it, and sometimes it was more teasing, but often when she needed me to soak in her love, that's what she called me. No wonder I'd felt comfort when Levi began to use the endearment too.

I felt awash with a comforting warmth and started over.

My darling princess,

Tonight you will graduate from high school, and I am so proud of you I could burst. My daughter and her husband still have their heads firmly stuck up their asses and won't be there. I've tried to impress upon you and Allyson that the failings here are solely at their feet, with not one bit at yours. I also must reckon with the notion that I have some hand in this. I have no idea what happened to my daughter that she married a money-hungry businessman and is obsessed with her status, but I often search for answers that never appear.

*I know you do the same. Maeve, I watch you searching for explanations to their behavior. You are constantly trying to both stay out of their line of sight so they don't pass judgment on you **and** trying desperately to get them to finally see* *you. What you don't seem to get is that **they are so very unworthy of the air you and your sister breathe.***

You, my dear girl, are so much better than they could hope to be. Your heart is pure. Your curiosity is a marvel. And so, even though it is beyond heartbreaking for me to contemplate, I am giving you the keys to flee tonight. Don't mistake my words—I want you to go. I know, deep down, Allyson does too. Maeve, I fear they will break your spirit if you stay, so I need you to leave.

Use Big Red, as you love to call her, to gain your freedom. Soak in your life, feast on the marrow, and know that I see you. So does Allyson. We love you for everything you are and everything you hope to become. I wish your mother and father could wake up and realize they've missed out on the joy of their lives, but they are far too narcissistic for that.

Spend no time looking back—go forward and live, my beautiful princess. Live your life out loud and be the beautiful person that you are. Spending the last years with you and Allyson has been the joy of my life. You two are my legacy, and I'm beyond honored to belong to you both.

All my love,

Nan

It was hopeless to stop the tears streaming down my face, so I didn't try. Instead, I scooted toward Levi on the wall as he turned and straddled it. I moved forward, my legs going over his, leggings snagging on his jeans, before I could be flush against him. I wrapped my legs around his back so I could lean on his broad chest and finally cry.

Without looking up, I held up the letter in my hand so he could take it to read. Once he had, I wrapped my arms around his torso and poured out all the tears I'd held back upon losing Nan. If I paused to think about it, I was sure I looked like a mess, but it felt so good I rolled with it.

Levi ran a hand up and down my back, whispering the letter into my ear as he read it, wrapping me in Nan's words.

"I'm sorry," I whispered. "This is silly. I knew Nan saw me, it's just..." My voice trailed off as I struggled to verbalize what it was about that letter that had rocked me to my core.

"Shhh." Levi smoothed a hand over my hair and down my back. "One, it's okay to feel however you feel. And two, it's never a small thing to hear from someone you didn't think you'd hear from again, let alone someone you miss as much as Nan." He paused, then squeezed my waist. "She seems like a badass."

I huffed out a laugh. "That she was."

He tucked my head under his bearded chin. I laid my head on his chest, staring out into the canyon to my left.

Levi's voice interrupted my thoughts. "Makes sense that you take after her then."

Eagles soared over the canyon, the sun bright in a brilliant blue sky, layers of rock gorgeous in the early-spring light. The air was brisk, but Levi's body and Nan's words kept me warm as I soaked in the feeling of rightness of this moment. I felt at peace.

Chapter 26

The Road Home

Levi

I watched Maeve sleeping in the light coming through the curtains in our hotel room. To think that last night I'd been asleep in a hotel in Flagstaff and unsure if I was making a horrible choice, interfering where I was possibly not wanted. To be lying in a hotel in Page, Arizona, next to this woman felt like a surreal dream.

We'd spent the morning and lunch at the Grand Canyon. Maeve had let the folks at the train know she wouldn't be making the return trip with them since I'd driven up to the park in my rental. Once she'd gotten her fill of the beautiful landscape, we headed out in my car so we could pick up her truck in Williams by the café. She'd already been packed up, so it was a quick stop before heading to Flagstaff to drop off my rental, then a fast dinner at a pizzeria with a wood-fired oven that Jenn had recommended, and then a long drive up to Page. Somewhere along the way, she'd secured a ticket for me for tomorrow's tour.

I'd kept the conversation light, knowing she'd had a hell

of a day and not all dragons needed to be slew, or even faced, at once. We'd talked about Lou's new column at the paper, Aidan's and my Monday meetings, and Allyson.

Maeve had wanted to know how much bigger Ally's baby bump was, how Logan was doing with everything. At that, I'd given her a look. She hadn't hesitated to give me one back.

"Come on, Levi. I know your brother. He is the ultimate protector, and after what happened with Nola, I can't imagine this pregnancy doesn't bring up some complicated feelings."

I'd lifted her hand to entwine my fingers with hers. I loved that while she held herself back from others, she was constantly seeing exactly who her friends were. The secret she hadn't been let in on was that while she thought she was a mystery, I think far more people saw the real Maeve than she'd believe. And I was ready for her to embrace that fact. We all deserve to be known, especially Maeve.

"To answer your question, yes, Logan struggled with the pregnancy at first. Having more people in his life that he doesn't want to chance losing is rough for him. But he's met with his therapist and talked through it with her and with Allyson, so I'd say he's doing good." I was damn proud of Logan for all the work he'd done in that regard.

Maeve had been satisfied with that, and we'd spent the final part of our drive in comfortable silence for much of the time with her making comments about a song or artist on the playlist and something it reminded her of.

What I was struck by was the notion that for the first few months I had known this woman, she'd driven me crazy. However, I hadn't been paying attention to the fact that while we indeed did argue at times, I was more myself around Maeve than I was around anyone else beyond my brother.

That was another thing to think about.

We finally made it to the hotel, and as Maeve stared at the large bed, I knew what was on her mind, so I addressed it. "Princess, I'd love to pick up where we left off at the Grand Canyon this morning, but I am absolutely beat, and we have to be up in seven hours. How do you feel about cuddling and sleep?"

She visibly relaxed. "God, that sounds good." She dropped her bag and fell face-first onto the bed.

I laughed. "You want the shower?"

Hours later in the low light of dawn, I marveled at how lucky I was. Could I make a life of this? Of hotel rooms, a vagabond lifestyle? It honestly wasn't my first choice. But if it meant I would go to sleep and wake up to this woman every day? It would be worth it.

I roused Maeve with promises of coffee as we packed up and rushed to the Navajo Nation. As we drove, she explained how Jenn had told her about these slot canyons that had only been open to the public since the late nineties when the area was made a Navajo tribal park by the Navajo Nation.

"I mean, Levi, they didn't have to allow a bunch of tourists to traipse all over their sacred land, but they did, and all the tours are led by members of the Navajo family that runs the tour company. Jenn said it was the best thing she did when she moved out here." She was practically bouncing in her seat.

I took in her long blue skirt and tee proclaiming her love of Ms. Taylor Swift. "You sure you're going to be warm enough?"

"Yep. I've got a hoodie to throw on and some sneakers

when we get there." She wiggled her bare toes, which had been in Birkenstocks. "This isn't a huge hike, but I think it will be pretty dusty, so I brought options."

We had all our stuff behind our seats anyway because once we finished the tour, we were starting the road home. I glanced at her shirt again, a thought nagging me, though I couldn't bring it to mind at first.

"Yes, love this song," she said, singing along with Swift.

"Hey, wait a minute," I said, looking from her T-shirt to the radio to her face. "When we were texting and you said you missed Big Red, I said Andy Reid missed you too."

She looked my way, batting her eyelashes. "Yeah?"

"Maeve Claire Murphy, you acted like you didn't know who that was, but anyone who is a fan of Taylor Swift knows that Andy Reid is known as Big Red and coaches for Travis Kelce's team."

"Well, I'm not a huge football person, but also..."

I glanced over again. "Yeah?"

Her smile was blinding. "I was messing with you."

I laughed, loving how relaxed she was, wondering if that was going to be her new normal.

"Oh, turn here," she said, starting to pull on socks and get her shoes ready.

I pulled into a dusty lot with a low building on one end, some porta potties just beyond. Maeve jumped down just before I rolled to a complete stop. I quickly put the truck in park and hustled to catch up.

"Princess, we're not late," I said, striding up to the ticket window with her.

"I know, I'm just excited." She proceeded to check us in for the Upper Antelope Canyon tour. As Maeve stood there, I marveled at her ease of conversation with the woman at the ticket window as she encouraged the woman about some medical test she apparently had coming up. I'm not sure how I'd never seen her natural curiosity about people before, but it was readily apparent right then. Maybe that explained all the friends across the country? But how many of them really knew her? She was there for them when they needed someone—were they there for her? Would she let anyone be?

About ten minutes later, the guides were out, helping us load up into the beds of pickup trucks that had been tricked out to have covered bench seats in the back. Maeve was in her element, chatting with the other people on our tour. One family was from North Carolina, the other one from France. That group didn't speak a whole lot of English, but Maeve had already taken their picture for the mom.

As the drive got underway, we all stopped talking to focus on holding on to our seats. To say driving over the dunes was bumpy would be an understatement. Maeve and the kids from North Carolina seemed to love it. Maeve couldn't stop laughing as we'd hit a bump and all fly off our seats, then check to ensure we didn't lose our phones or any other possessions.

Within twenty minutes of starting out, our guide pulled up outside a giant rock that had a slit from the bottom to top. As I watched other trucks unload, I realized we were headed inside that opening. I'd never heard about this place before yesterday, so I was unsure what would be so amazing about this rock, but I was willing to give it a try for this woman.

As our group gathered in front of the upper canyon, our guide mentioned how sacred this area was to the Navajo Tribe. She cautioned us to make sure we didn't leave any litter behind and said she'd help us get great pictures once we were inside. As we headed forward, she had us pause for a moment of silence, then led us in.

"Aren't you excited," Maeve asked, coming up beside me.

I laughed at her clear exuberance. "I mean, the rocks look pretty, so sure."

Maeve laughed, sliding her arm around my waist. "Levi, what do you know about these canyons?"

"Um, exactly what you've told me and not one fact more."

"I thought so. Well, beyond what I've told you about how interesting their formation is and how honored we should feel that we're allowed to visit, they are also magical in pictures." She gestured ahead of us. "The rocks on the other side of that opening are simply breathtaking." She leaned her head against me as we walked.

"As are you, babe. And I'll follow you anywhere, so let's go." I slid her arm from my waist to hold her hand so we could go through the opening.

"Follow me anywhere?" She glanced back at me, eyes twinkling with her smile. "Watch out or I'll hold you to that."

I wanted to tell her to go ahead, but we'd stepped inside and my jaw dropped. We were just feet from the entrance, but already I was at a loss for words.

Our guide came up beside me, sensing my confusion. "The canyons were formed by erosion just like the Grand Canyon. Your wife said you visited it yesterday?"

I didn't bother to correct her because I was struck by how much I liked Maeve being referred to as my wife.

"We can have flash flooding here, so the guided tours are necessary. But the water has created these passages." She pointed to the ceiling. "Light streams through that opening throughout the canyon. The beautiful shafts of light come through and hit the rocks just right. As a result, the purples and reds of the sandstone become even more vibrant." She put a hand on my arm to stop me and called Maeve over as well as our group.

The guide asked for Maeve's cell phone and told the rest of the group what settings to use in their camera apps to get the best pictures. Then she took one of Maeve and me, showing all of us how the rocks photographed.

They were beautiful to the naked eye, but in the picture? Unreal.

We made our way through the slot canyon, our tour guide continuing to point out great picture spots, telling us stories about the history of the canyons and why they were so revered by the Navajo. All too soon, we were at the end and walking up and over the canyon to make our way back to the trucks.

The ride back to the ticket office didn't seem as long as it had been on the way out. Our whole group was quiet again, but this time it felt different. Like we had just witnessed something sacred and were soaking in the last moments of it before returning to civilization.

Once we reached the parking lot, Maeve said her good-byes to both families and we headed toward the truck. She was looking at her phone as she walked, talking a mile a minute. "Levi, do you think you'd be good to drive for several hours, then stop for food, or do you want something to start, then drive? I'm fine either way."

I caught her elbow before she went to open the door and spun her so that her back was to the truck. Before she could say anything, I tipped her chin up and let my lips meet hers, caressing her mouth until it opened and we could fall into each other, even if only for a moment.

Once I felt like I'd at least expressed my gratitude, I pulled back. "Maeve Murphy, I'm glad I came out to Arizona for many reasons." I bent to kiss her neck below her ear. "I'd never seen the Grand Canyon." Kiss to her collarbone. "I'd never even heard of a slot canyon." I tugged the neckline of her shirt to the side to kiss the top of her breast. "And I get to spend time with you at a time that you have happiness practically beaming out of your pores." Straightening her shirt, I tucked a stray lock of hair behind her ear. "I just wanted to express my thanks to you for allowing me to tag along on part of your trip."

She stepped back into my arms, wrapping hers around my waist as she rested her chin on my chest. "Levi Traub, I'm so glad you butted into this journey, but now I'm really ready for you to show me the road home."

I leaned down to kiss the top of her head. "Happy to, princess. Let's go."

Chapter 27

Looking for a Barista

M^{aeve}
I'd returned to Highland Falls a week ago, and in many ways, it was like I'd never left. Levi and I had taken a little over a full day for the trip, driving through the night and taking turns sleeping. But I'd shown Levi the way I liked to travel—two-lane highways and small towns. We'd found some great spots for coffee and meals, and I couldn't help but notice how easy it was to be with him.

Coming back to Highland had been providence of sorts. Allyson'd had some spotting last week, and the doc wanted her off her feet for a few days. I'd felt anxiety flood my body at the news, but Allyson had reassured me that everything was fine; the little bean was just asking her to slow down for a hot minute. So I'd subbed in for her, taking a yoga class or two when I could to work on my own mental state.

As a result of my work schedule and influx of yoga classes, I hadn't seen much of Levi. We'd texted, but deep down I knew I was avoiding him for the first few days. We'd been thrown together in such an intimate way, and he'd seen me with my walls down, and I wasn't sure what to do with all that. Did we just move on like we were dating? Did we need to have a conversation? All of that was new territory for me, so I was in the dark and needed some guidance. Before I could find any, the man headed up to Chicago for a few meetings with clients, and I wasn't sure when he would be back.

I looked at the messy kitchen counter in front of me. Allyson's second-in-command, Andy, was out at the second café, Sanctuary in the Park, and I was on the closing shift for the town location. I'd been prepping everything for the next day, which had been good for my head. But now that it was all done, I was realizing I should have cleaned as I went because it looked like a bomb had gone off in here.

Glancing at the six-foot-tall cardboard cutout of Jason Momoa that Allyson had here for reasons I didn't fully understand, I found myself confiding in it. Allyson called him Flat Max, a nod to our friend Emma's husband Max. I decided to lay it all out there to him. Surely a cardboard figure could guide me better than I was doing on my own.

"Flat Max," I said, lowering my head to a flour-covered counter as I fought the urge to bang it and knock some sense in my brain, "please remind me in the future to clean as I bake because there are no elves coming to help the shoemaker here." I worked in some calming breaths. "And truth time, I'm an idiot because prepping this many baked goods didn't help me figure out what to do about Levi Traub. Shocking, I know." I closed my eyes, fighting back tears. "It just made me miss him more."

My phone rang from its spot on the counter with a FaceTime call, and I clicked Accept before processing that the name of the caller wasn't Allyson like I'd assumed but my mother.

This day was not looking up.

A tone of judgment wafted over me, bringing me back to childhood with a bang. "Maeve, I'd love to tell you that you look good, my dear, but what a lie that would be." My mother's strong disapproval was evident even from almost a thousand miles away.

"Thanks, Mother. Always good to see you." I propped my head up and noted the flour dusting my hair and face in the small picture of me. I couldn't find it in me to give a damn. "Is there a reason you're calling other than wanting to cheer me up?" Sarcasm tended to go sailing right over her head.

Her face twisted in an expression that looked like she'd just sucked a lemon. "Why on earth would I want to cheer you up? One, you have flour all over your face, and two, you clearly haven't been taking care of yourself. You've easily put on several pounds, and you know your frame just doesn't carry that well." She shook her head in clear disgust. "Anyway, I just got off the phone with your sister."

Oh, poor Allyson. Why would she take a call from this woman? Then again, I was currently facing a similar predicament. Maybe Allyson and I could commiserate tonight over a plate of warm cookies.

"Yes? You talked to Allyson?" Maybe if I agreed with her, we could get to the end of this conversation sooner.

"Yes, I did, and Maeve Claire Murphy, I know you are only concerned with yourself, but how could you be so selfish that you would be gallivanting across the country when you could have been helping your sister? And now she's on bed rest! I cannot even remotely understand where your father and I went wrong with you." She was gesturing like she was begging God to tell her where she had strayed. I had some thoughts on that if she'd care to listen.

Before I could fire back a response or break down at the simple fact that my own mother did not have the first bit of compassion for me, a movement in the doorway from the kitchen to the café caught my eye. Levi.

He was leaning against the frame, and the anger on his face made it evident that he'd heard every word my own mom had just spewed in my direction. The cords in his neck stood out as he braced himself on the doorframe, holding on to the top of it like he was concerned about what would happen if he let go.

It's okay, I mouthed. Belatedly, I realized I was on video, not a call. However, a glance at my phone showed that my mom was still having a conversation with herself. All good.

No, it's not.

He moved into the room and stepped to the other side of the island from me, then whispered low enough that I seriously doubted my mother would hear. "Want me to talk to her?"

The pounding of my heart reverberated through my body. Did I want him to grab the phone, look at my mother, and tell her to take a long walk off a short pier? Yep. But did I feel deep down that I needed to tell her myself? Unfortunately, yes, I did.

I gave him a quick shake of the head that didn't faze my mother as she was still ranting about my failings. Right then it seemed to be focused on my lack of a stable job and how I was relying on the kindness of strangers and likely the welfare system.

Levi nodded his agreement and moved around the island so he was standing perpendicular to where I was with the phone in front of me, propped up against the flour container. I slid my hand out of camera range, and Levi immediately claimed it, rubbing a thumb over the top of it over and over. Soaking in the strength from him that I needed, I interrupted her.

"You know what, Mother? I don't have time for this."

She spluttered, "How dare you—"

I held up the hand that was not currently attached to Levi. "Nope, we're not doing this." I leaned closer to my phone. "Hear me when I say this—you and I are done. I have wished for all my years on this planet that my parents weren't narcissistic assholes that were only concerned with themselves, but we're all who we are, so I guess I need to accept it."

Shocked silence came from the phone.

I was on a roll, and years of what I wanted to say spilled out of me. "I am floored that you have it in you to even concern yourself with Allyson, but please know that my own sister doesn't blame me for her medical condition because that would be ludicrous. Unfortunately for Allyson, one thing she inherited from Dad is a strong work ethic. That can be admirable at times but needs to be kept in check. She's learning that and will get better with her being surrounded by people who love and care for her because of who she is, not what she can do for them."

I took a giant breath and kept on trucking. "And if you were as concerned as you say you are, you'd have your ass on a plane and come out here to visit your daughter: to see her businesses, to celebrate her wedding, hell, to meet her new family. But you haven't done that anytime in the past three years, so I'm certain I won't be seeing you anytime soon." I knew tears were working their way down my face as I looked straight at the phone. I let them fall. I wasn't ashamed of my tears. If anyone here should be feeling some remorse, I knew it wasn't me.

For the first time that I could think of in my life, I

wasn't concerned if one of my parents really saw me or not. Because I was shocked to realize it didn't matter. Don't get me wrong—I'd lost out in the parent department for sure. But look what I'd gained. My sister and I were growing closer than ever. Nan had been there for me when no one else had. And I was developing real friendships that I knew could be my new foundation. As I took in my mom's expression—one that was aloof and impatient—I suddenly realized that she wasn't worth the heartbreak that I'd given her. I didn't know what her life was really like, but she'd created it. If she ever wanted to atone for all that she and my dad had done, I'd hear her out. But I was done prostrating myself for them. It was time to take care of me.

She still hadn't spoken because I'm sure she was shocked that I'd said what I'd said. Time to wrap this conversation up.

"Mom, I wish you nothing but the best, but you and I are done. If you ever want to apologize for the neglect you've heaped on me from my childhood or the verbal abuse you've sent my way since, I'm happy to hear it. But otherwise, feel free to lose my number."

Even in the small screen of a phone, I could tell she was drawing her posture up. "I cannot believe you'd speak to your mother this way, Maeve, but maybe I shouldn't be surprised—"

Levi's finger had slid over so he could click to end the call. He looked at me with some remorse. "Sorry, princess, I wanted to let you handle all that. I'm a little concerned my mom might pop up and swat my head for this, but babe, your mother is a bitch."

I couldn't help it—for some reason that did it, and I threw my head back and laughed. Yep, Mona Murphy was absolutely a one hundred percent bona fide bitch. No question about it.

When I finally came down from my ridiculous laughter, I looked at Levi, who stood by my side, watching me. I noted that he was still holding my hand and hadn't let go since he got here.

"Maeve, you know that woman was spouting complete bullshit, right? That you are no more responsible for Allyson's short stint of bed rest than any other resident of Highland Falls?" His eyebrows were drawn together with concern.

I looked at Levi and saw him. Scenes flashed to mind: seeing him pulling up to Allyson's with a smirk the first time I met him, teaching him how to make a vanilla latte after my mom had called Allyson last spring, his smile at Logan when he and Allyson had gotten married at the courthouse, his sleep-rumpled face when we slept with Charlie after the chocolate incident, the first time we kissed, our first time together at his place, his face when he came all the way to Arizona to give me a letter from Nan, his eyes on me as I took in Antelope Canyon. Those scenes all blended, and I realized he had certainly become my metaphorical home, and I wanted that to continue until the end of time.

I loved this man. Holy shit. I *loved* him.

I worked to breathe normally. In a kitchen surrounded by quite possibly every dish that Allyson owned at this café and a metric shit ton of flour was not the place that I wanted to confess my feelings. I'd also like to be able to tell the man the plan I had for the two of us being able to stay together. That was beginning to come together, but I still had a little work to do, namely a conversation with my sister, before I could unload on him. So yeah, I needed a hot minute or two.

"Maeve?" Levi was looking concerned, likely because I'd suddenly become mute. I shook my head, getting my thoughts in order.

I squeezed his hand, which still held mine. "Thanks, Levi. I do know that she is full of shit. Unfortunately, that wasn't even the worst I've ever seen from her."

His frown deepened. "Maeve, that's terrible."

I held up a hand. "No, I know. But what I realized this time was that it wasn't hurting as much as it usually did. Because I think therapy is helping and so are you."

I'd mentioned my new foray into therapy on our drive back. Levi had, of course, been a huge proponent of talking with someone. I learned that he had after Nola's passing and still saw someone from time to time to work out new issues.

"At the risk of sounding egocentric, how am I helping?" The man still looked confused, like he didn't realize all that he did for me.

I held up our joined hands. "Having you here was huge. And"—I swallowed because, as I've established, vulnerability wasn't easy for me—"the fact that you share how crazy you are about me helps me find my worth." I looked away for a moment, locking eyes with Flat Max over there in the corner. "Sorry if that makes me seem needy."

Levi tugged me forward and wrapped his arms around me. "It makes you seem human." He pressed a kiss to my neck and started to trace it with his tongue.

I liked where this was going, but now that the pieces were lining up in my mind, I needed to talk to my sister. "Umm, sorry to put a halt to this, but I need a big favor."

Levi stopped immediately and looked at me with serious eyes. "Anything."

I bit my lip and looked to the side. "Well, is there any

way you could clean this up so I can go talk to Allyson? I'm so sorry to leave you with it—"

Levi stepped back and slapped my ass. "Take off, princess. Logan should be here in a moment; he and I are heading out on a run in an hour, and we decided to hit you up for some baked goods as a pre-run snack. We'll get this and then leave."

One more item for the Levi-is-too-good-to-be-true column. I pressed a quick kiss to his lips. "Welcome back from Chicago. Extra muffins and scones are in the case."

"You are the best." He pulled me back for another smacking kiss. "You can repay me later for the kitchen—go see your sis. And Maeve, how's dinner tonight sound? My place?"

My heart thumped in excitement. "Sounds good. Six?"

He nodded and I wanted to stay locked on his eyes, but instead, I took off at a jog through the café and out the door, shouting my hellos to Logan, who was coming up the steps, and hurrying to my borrowed truck and out of town to Allyson's.

Reaching their cabin, I walked in without bothering to knock. "Ally, it's Maeve," I called as I kicked off my shoes at the door.

"Couch!"

Ally was indeed propped on the couch, her red hair piled high in a messy bun, covered with a fuzzy white blanket, and one snoring Charlie at her feet. His fur blended with the blanket. She was holding a plate of cookies and looked up at me with a touch of guilt.

"I've had six," she said, her mouth partly filled. "Mom called."

"Before we go there, what is the report from the doc?"

"Everything looks good. I can do a part-time bed rest

starting next week but need to take it easy." She grabbed another cookie.

"That's great," I said, feeling a whole lot of relief. "And unfortunately, I knew Mom called because she called me too."

Allyson rolled her eyes as her head dropped back. "That woman drives me to madness." She looked at me as she nodded to the end of the couch that wasn't taken up by her or the pup. "Was she terrible?"

"She was our mother, so of course." I ran my hands over my leggings before looking back her way. "Levi was there, so that made it a bit easier."

Allyson looked surprised. "I'm floored she'd be negative in front of Levi. You know, wanting to impress men and all. She doesn't get nasty if Logan's around, but I hang up on her a lot more now than I used to."

"Maybe we should just block her calls. I did tell her that she and I were done, and Levi hung up on her, but I'm sure she'll be back."

"Yep, just like a bad smell. But Levi was there, hmm? Want to tell me what has become of the two of you now? I'll give you a cookie..." She held the plate up again and grinned.

I snagged a cookie and looked down at the sleeping Charlie before locking eyes with Allyson. "Umm, any chance you're looking for a barista permanently?"

Allyson screamed, dropped the plate on the coffee table, and crawled over a confused Charlie to throw herself into my arms.

My smile couldn't be contained. "So, I take it that's a yes?"

Chapter 28

Here's to the Future

Levi

Logan walked into the café's kitchen and scanned the scene in front of him. "What the hell blew up in here?"

I was moving dishes over to the sink so I could wipe down the counters. "Maeve."

What I loved about my brother was exemplified right then. He nodded, shrugged out of his windbreaker, and started to help. "Saw Maeve hotfooting it out of here on my way in. You all good?"

I'd filled Logan in a little once Maeve and I got back from Arizona. He knew we'd had some breakthroughs but that she was still a little skittish about commitments and I didn't want to push her but was hopeful. Then I'd had to head to Chicago to handhold a new client. That had morphed into a meeting with another potential account, and it had been three days before I could get back home.

What I'd realized, or I guess I'd already known but had it confirmed for me when I was away, was that Maeve was it for me. I'd given her a little space when we arrived back in

Highland Falls because she was slammed with the news that Allyson needed a week of bed rest and the woman snapped into fix-it mode. I knew she was going to need to do everything in her control to set the situation to rights and then she'd be fine. So I gave her that time, then got pulled away.

As I'd driven back from Chicago that morning, a conversation with Logan told me exactly where I'd be able to find Maeve when I got to town. My plan had been to check in with her, make plans for dinner, and then lay it all out how she made me feel and that I wanted a future with her. I even planned a run with Logan for this afternoon so I could process it all with him first.

It was funny—all this time I'd been worried that I wouldn't be able to love again for fear I'd be looking back at what I'd had with Tess. How could I find it in me to trust again when my judgment had been so mistaken before?

With Maeve, however, I've always known she had a foot out the door. She was more skittish about relationships than I could ever be. And yet my heart was undeniably hers. When she came into town back in January, everything I had been trying to hold back since we met got upended. Once we tried for more, I knew I'd never be able to go back, that I was lost to her. That was just reinforced after Allyson's party when she left town.

A month without Maeve made me feel like I was missing a limb. I tried so hard to keep my distance, not because I wanted to but because she'd asked for it. But I reached the point where I couldn't ignore the pull this woman had on me. I went to her and wanted nothing more than to lay it all out and agree upon a future together. Part of me felt like she wanted that too. Another part told me I was a dumbass and was preparing to get my heart broken.

Looking up at Logan, I realized he'd been standing there waiting while I got my thoughts together. "I love her."

"No shit, Sherlock. Tell me something Allyson and I didn't clock six weeks ago." He pushed up his sleeves and began scrubbing a bowl, then nodded toward the counter. "Bring me the dishes and start helping while we get this place back to rights. While we're doing this, you can tell me what you're finally going to do about the Maeve situation."

I laughed and grabbed some dishes while the two of us plotted what we'd ever do if Patrick and Mona Murphy came to town. Long story short, it wasn't going to be pretty. However, we both agreed that we'd be a breeze compared to Mom and Dad, especially Mom. You didn't fuck with my mom's kids. And like it or not, Allyson and Maeve Murphy had been adopted. Though Mom was small, she was mighty. Come to think of it, I might actually like to see my mom and Mona square off. I bet we could sell tickets.

We got the kitchen put in order in record time, snagged some baked goods, and headed out for a quick run in town. Usually Logan and I hit the trails, but Aidan decided to join us and running in town was just faster. As the three of us let the miles go by, I felt the stress of work and my anger at Maeve's mother pass. We weren't setting any time records here, but bullshitting with these two about the NHL, concerts we wanted to go to, and the new bar opening off the square gave me a settled feeling of being home. They also helped me work out any worries I had about what came next.

When I moved down here last spring, I was flirting with depression. I knew it and made a change to stop it. Almost a year later, I sometimes failed to appreciate how much better my life was. My work-life balance was far healthier. Adding Aidan to my fledgling company allowed me to be less alone even if it stressed me out at times. Being near Logan brought me back to center. Through Logan, I'd built up a hell of a network of friends. And then there was Maeve. With her, I saw a future.

Saying goodbye to the guys, I jogged home and got ready for Maeve. It was March, and the weather was doing that Illinois thing of alternating between winter and spring every other day until finally making a decision. That night there was still a nip in the air, so I decided to go with my aunt's hamburger stew.

Mom's sister, Susie, had shared the recipe with me when Logan and I went to college, and it had become a staple once we were out of the dorms. It was ridiculously easy, felt relatively healthy during a time of my life I didn't eat a ton of vegetables all the time, and could be ready quickly if you were hungry.

I diced up the carrots, celery, onions, and potatoes and got the whole thing simmering while I hopped in the shower. Once I got out, I pulled on a pair of joggers and a thermal. Hitting the living room, I looked around. Living by myself meant that everything was where I'd left it, which was great, I guessed. But when I went to Logan and Allyson's, I felt like their place was alive with the two of them, a dog, soon a baby. If everything went well tonight, maybe Maeve would be here more often than not? I wondered what her thoughts were on dogs. We could find one that didn't eat chocolate.

I powered on the candle warmer Allyson had gotten me for Christmas. She had joked at the time that all girls love a good-smelling house. Now I just had to hope that Maeve liked the smell of—I glanced at the label—vanilla bean. It was the best I could do.

I had everything under control and was looking in my

fridge while I decided on a drink when I heard the door open. I stood up and glanced toward the front of my house.

Maeve had let herself in, which absolutely fucking delighted me. I was likely reading too much into it, but to me that said she felt at home. She kicked off her Birks as she walked in, some crazy-patterned socks on her feet. When she looked my way, she let out a sigh of relief.

"I was hoping you went for comfortable clothes since we're having dinner at your place, but on the way over I got worried I'd misread and you'd be dressed up. But now I know I fit in." She gestured to her outfit, caramel-colored leggings and an open cardigan with a T-shirt. All of it looked so soft, I felt the need to touch it to find out.

She shot me a bright smile as she walked straight up to me and pressed a kiss to my lips. Yep, I was a fan of this woman. Damn. She moved to step back, and I slid my hands down to her ass—the pants *were* incredibly soft—keeping her against me.

"Now, Maeve. Where are you going?"

She looked up at me, then around my side to the stove. "Well, Levi, it looks like you're cooking, so we need to stay in here."

I leaned over, turning the burner off. "It will keep, princess." I grabbed her hand and headed toward my bedroom without another comment, and Maeve had laughter bubbling up as she jogged after me.

Now, I'd wanted to sit down and have the conversation I'd been looking forward to over dinner, maybe have a beer, offer her one as well. In other words, have a civilized night. But the woman had walked in looking like every fantasy I'd ever had come to life. No jury on earth would find that I was in the wrong here. This woman was my end and my beginning, and I needed to get her into my bed now. There would be time for stew later. Say, in an hour.

We hit my room, and I noted that I'd left a bedside lamp on. Nicely done, past Levi, that way I could see this gorgeous woman as I divested her of her clothes in the next ninety seconds.

"Want to tell me what the hurry is?" Maeve said, coming up behind me and wrapping an arm around my stomach.

I ran my hand over hers, then spun to face her, spilling my honesty. "You walked in looking like this." I stood back, waving my hand up and down. "And I couldn't wait to get you in here." I had the good sense to feel a bit ashamed of that comment. "Sorry, does that make me sound like a caveman?" My face heated up. "Apologies, Maeve, I didn't mean to drag you off. We haven't even really had a chance to talk, chalk one up to temporary insanity..." My voice trailed off with uncertainty. I wanted this woman so much and yes, part of that was sex, but I also felt the nerves of what was unsaid, my worries about how she was feeling. It was all a jumbled mess in my head.

Maeve studied my face for a moment, then guided me to sit on the edge of the bed. She climbed up onto my lap, straddling me so that we were chest to chest and our height difference didn't put our faces far apart. "That's better," she said. "What's going on?"

I groaned, dropping my head to her shoulder. "I got ahead of myself because you are unbelievably sexy, but there are things to say, and I think they made me nervous."

She leaned over and kissed my cheek. "You are good for my ego, Levi Traub. And I have things to say too. Do you want me to go first?"

I lifted my head and met her eyes. The blue color pulled

me in every time. Here we were—she'd had a rough conversation with her mom this morning. Actually, that might be the understatement of the century. And the woman was trying to make this easier on me. I needed to dive in. If I wasn't lucky enough for her to return my feelings, maybe she could get there one day. I could love her enough for both of us because I knew one thing for certain—I wanted to give Maeve Murphy all the love she'd been missing, because she was worth it.

"I love you." It popped out, before I was ready. Her eyes widened, but I just plowed on like someone had given me truth serum. "I don't know when I started loving you—it's hard to remember when I didn't. I mean, you did drive me crazy at first—"

Her smile was wide when she interrupted me. "Ditto, evil twin, you drove me mad."

I was choosing to take her amusement as a good sign, so I plowed on. "And I was nervous at first because I know you don't like to be tied to one place, but I've thought about it, Maeve. I've also talked to Logan and Aidan. And if you're willing to have a home base, and that home base being Highland Falls, I'm good with traveling around and not being here often. Whatever you need, I just want to be with you."

Tears sprang up in her eyes, which was concerning. "Oh, Levi, you are too good, but that's not necessary."

My heart began to pound with worry. Did that mean she didn't want to be with me? "Umm…"

She apparently realized I was having a momentary freak-out. "No, Levi. I'm screwing this all up." She looked down for a moment as if to get her bearings, then looked back at me. "I love you too."

Whoosh. All the air left my chest in a rush as I leaned

down and pressed my lips to hers. Fuck it. I didn't care if my home was an Airstream, I'd deal with whatever if this woman felt the same.

She put a hand on my chest and pushed me back a bit. "Hold on, sir. Let me get this out."

I held up my hands. "Sorry, sorry. Continue, princess."

She laughed. "Okay, what I meant a moment ago is that it's not necessary to treat Highland Falls as our home base so we can travel because I think I'm ready to slow down and be here."

I looked at her with concern. "Babe, are you sure? I don't want you to have to be something you're not to be with me."

She leaned forward, pressing another kiss to my lips. "This. This is why I can make that decision." She put her hands on either side of my face and looked me straight in the eyes. "I have processed a lot of shit over the past month and still have more work to do. One thing has become crystal clear—I've avoided growing roots in one spot because I was convinced that if I stayed somewhere for too long, people would see the real me and decide I wasn't worth their time. So I moved on before that could happen." She slid her hands down to rest on my chest as she waited for my reaction.

My heart broke again for the little girl who had been taught she was unworthy by her parents. It would be the honor of my life making sure she learned just how amazing she was.

And if she said she was ready to stay in one place, I was going to believe her. "That sounds amazing. Do you know what you want to do here?"

Her eyes began to twinkle in what I was now familiar

with—her expression of complete happiness. "Yes. That's why I went to Allyson's today. She's always called me her silent partner since I invested in the business with her. And apparently she's had a separate savings account over the past few years where she'd put what she considered my portion of the profits for me. So I'm joining her and Andy in managing the cafés. I'll do her schedule for most of the rest of her pregnancy so she can take it easy and work when she feels like it. I'll also work her shifts for at least twelve weeks after the baby comes. Once she's back, we'll adjust to a new schedule where the three of us share managerial duties." She drew a breath before continuing. "I also told Kate and Kristine I was up for teaching at least one yoga class a week, maybe more."

"Yoga and coffee shops, those are your jam." I pressed a kiss to her neck, wanting to wrap her in my arms and never let go.

"Yep." She looked proud as she continued with her plans about joining Emma's book club, lunch dates with Lou, and more.

When she finished, I brushed the hair back from her face. "So, you love me?"

Her smile was blinding. "I love you."

"And you're moving to Highland?"

She kissed the tip of my nose. "I'm moving to Highland. And I can tell you a secret that might be a terrible idea, but I'm willing to risk it."

I raised an eyebrow. "All ears for terrible ideas, babe."

She leaned forward to whisper in my ear. "I don't have anywhere to live yet."

My heart picked up speed. Was it possible to get everything you were looking for in one night? Looked like it. Instead of shouting for joy, I glanced over at the bed and went for levity. "Are you saying this bedroom isn't up to your usual standards?"

Her eyes twinkled as she watched me. "I mean, I guess it's okay. You are missing out on one thing..."

My mind raced. Was she serious? If so, what was I missing? "What?"

She shrugged, "Charlie and I have gotten pretty close."

I laughed and slid my hands to her waist to tickle her. "When you aren't trying to kill the pup."

"Hey, we were both there," she said, gasping for breath as she laughed.

I continued to tickle her until she finally begged for mercy. At that, I dropped down on the bed next to her. We rolled to our sides until we were facing each other.

"Hey, Maeve," I whispered.

"Hey, Levi."

"I'm really happy."

Her beauty astounded me as she said, "So am I. Finally."

I pulled her against me and thanked whatever is out there for bringing this woman to me. Here's to the future—it was looking better than I'd ever thought possible.

Chapter 29

Never

M*aeve*

Levi's arms were still wrapped around me as my mind swirled with thoughts that I didn't know how to sort through. He loved me. That one was worth shouting from the rooftops. He loved me and I loved him.

Whoa.

And I was moving to Highland Falls. More importantly, I was moving in with Levi.

Double whoa.

Come tomorrow I'd be acknowledged as an equal partner with Allyson in the cafés and a regular instructor at Nomad Yoga. Part of me felt like I'd been preparing for the move for years.

Scratch all that. Levi Traub loved me. He saw me for who I was and loved me. My entire body seemed to break out in goose bumps as I soaked in the beautiful feeling of being truly known and loved by someone. It made my toes curl. I felt a wave of warmness toward this man and looked at him to find him staring right back at me.

"What?" I asked, wondering what he was thinking.

He shook his head. "Just trying to figure out how I got so lucky."

Part of me wanted to curl up in his arms and bask in the warmth of his body. The other part of me wanted to show him how much I cared about him by driving him mad. Sex, in the past, had been chasing release. Sure, there was attraction, but it sure hadn't felt like sex with Levi, even the first time. It was like I'd been in the minor leagues and here I was now, hanging out with an all-star in the majors.

Would sex just keep getting better and better? One way to find out.

I rolled Levi so I could climb back on him. He gazed up with an amused expression.

"You taking charge, Maeve?" His voice was husky, and that alone made my core clench.

I faltered for a moment. I was not one to lead during any sexual experience of my life, save a solo one. Was that okay?

As if he could read my mind, Levi brought a hand up to my chin and tipped it to look down at him. "You know that's good, right? If you want to be in charge, go for it. If you don't, say the word."

I took a breath and nodded at him. I was typically confident, though not every partner had brought that out of me in the bedroom. Still working through that. This was Levi, I told myself. I could ask for what I wanted or, hell, I could take it. He'd be okay with any of it and would tell me if he wasn't.

"How do you feel about being in charge to start, then when it's your turn, I'm up?" I asked, thinking of a fantasy I'd had for a while.

He raised an eyebrow at me. "You mean you want me to get you off, then you'll do the same for me?"

I gave him a nod.

"And you don't want to kill two birds with one stone, so to speak?"

I thought about that for a second. "You mean sixty-nining? Nope. Not today."

He considered that. "Two things. One, you need to know that I think it's hot as hell when you ask for what you want."

That made me heat up. "And two?"

His expression could only be described as fiery. "Game on, woman." He sat up, flipping me over so that my head was on the pillow, and within a matter of seconds, we were both naked as the day we were born.

Holy shit. That was hot as fuck.

Levi crashed his mouth to mine, and I got lost in his kisses. He was at once devouring and cherishing me. Waves of want washed over me again and again. I tried to bring my legs together to do, I don't know, *something* with the rising feelings, but Levi was there. Hell, he was everywhere. His hands roamed my body at will, caressing, pinching my nipples and then replacing his fingers with his mouth before sliding his hands down to rub circles at my clit. Then he slid down my body before I could put it all together, and his mouth found my center.

Well, this wasn't going to take long. That roller coaster feeling I was so familiar with from years of sex was another level with this man. He knew what he was doing and took me straight there. His movements were consistent, which my body-mind connection needed to be able to tip over the precipice, and tip we did. The sensations of my orgasm washed over me in a wave of sensations, and I felt alive.

Levi, knowing I'd be oversensitive, had moved his mouth to nip at my inner thighs, then my stomach, then my breasts as he worked his way up to my mouth.

"You good, babe?" he asked as his mouth moved from mine to my neck, to my earlobe, back to my lips. "We can be done here if you want."

Umm, was hell no an acceptable answer? "We had a deal, Lesser Twin. You're getting off and then we're having sex." I slapped his ass, or as close as I could. I reached down for the confidence I knew I had but needed to use. "I need you to keep moving up."

He stopped his small kisses and looked at me. "Move up?"

I waited for him to put two and two together. He wasn't getting there, so I tapped at either side of my shoulders. "Knees here, hands on the headboard, got it?"

A look of surprise washed over his face. "But then aren't I still in control?"

"If you think you're the one in control in that situation, you aren't paying attention."

"And you want that?"

"Sure do." I thought it was hella hot, but we could get into that later. And Levi's rock-hard cock against my thigh was telling me he was in favor of it too.

He lowered his mouth to mine, almost kissing me but talking instead. "Maeve Claire Murphy, when will you stop surprising me?"

"Levi— Holy shit, I don't know what your middle name is." How in the hell was that possible?

His mouth met mine as he whispered, "Jameson, princess. And just think, we have so many things to learn about each other."

Jameson. Sounded right. "Okay, Levi Jameson Traub, get up here and let's go."

"At your service, princess." His gravelly voice was evidence of his arousal as he slid up my body until his cock was in front of me and I could envelop it with my mouth.

I slid my hand up his leg and squeezed, letting him know he could move with me if he wanted.

It was, as I'd thought it would be, awesome.

A little bit later, we were sweaty and sprawled out on the bed, breathing hard and coming down from a second orgasm each. I was right—each time with this man was better than the last. At some point we'd have to plateau, but I looked forward to trying to find out when that was.

Rolling toward me, Levi pulled me into his arms and pressed a kiss to my temple. "How you feeling, princess?"

I lay there with his arms encircling me, low light warming the room around us, delicious smells coming from the kitchen for the dinner we'd need to get back to. I took a deep breath in and brought it all the way to my belly, paying attention to the sensations in my body, searching for what was normally there—the itch to go, the unease of staying in the same spot. Nope. Nada.

I turned to look at Levi, who was watching me and waiting, like he knew his question had a bigger meaning than was evident at face value. As a result, I gave him a wide smile as I slid a hand up to his beaded jaw and pulled it down to me.

Pressing a kiss to his lips, I drew back and met his gaze. "I feel good. Like I'm home."

His face lost any tension that had been there, and a look of contentment washed over him. "That's good to hear, Maeve."

An hour later we were curled up on the sectional, mugs of his aunt's stew in our hands. We'd warmed up some French bread and had it between us as we watched *Diners, Drive-Ins, and Dives*. Guy was in Omaha at some taco place.

"Come on, how can Omaha have an awesome taco place and we have to drive to Champaign for great Mexican," Levi grumbled.

"I mean, we have Homestead, Giuseppe's, and Goodman's. Plus the new place opening up this fall."

He gave me an imperious look. "Mexican, babe." He gestured at the television. "They're in *Omaha*."

I gave him a look of confusion.

"Omaha, the middle of nowhere."

I grabbed my phone, tapped out a few things on my browser app, and slid my phone his way. "A population of almost a half a million is just a touch higher than ours at just north of ten thousand, but sure, middle of nowhere, *babe*."

"Don't confuse me with the facts, princess." He gave me a look of amusement, then put his food down on the coffee table and grabbed mine to do the same. Once the food was out of the way, he slid me down on the couch and came to lie down snuggled up to me on our sides.

"Haven't had enough of me tonight, Lesser Twin?" I grinned, twirling my fingers in his hair.

"Never, Maeve." He pressed a kiss to my neck, then met my gaze again. "I have two thoughts."

"Oh, Levi, it's okay. I'm sure there are more than two thoughts in that pretty head," I said, realizing that I was more myself with him than I'd ever been with anyone.

He shook his head with amusement. "Now you're going to feel bad when I share what I was thinking."

"Hit me with it."

"One, I was thinking how much I love this. Just being with you here—dinner, TV, bullshit conversation, and knowing we get to do it again and again."

My eyes welled up as I whispered the truth of it. "Me too."

He pressed a kiss to the tip of my nose. "And as we watched that show in particular, I thought of all your travels over the past year."

I started to go stiff. Did he not believe me? Did he not trust that I wanted to stay put?

He looked down, likely sensing I was freezing up. "Easy, babe. I can see your mind swirling and yes, I absolutely believe you. I know you're staying. What I was thinking is that you love to travel. Do you think that's something you'd still want to do once or twice a year? We could pick places to go based on a show like we were watching, or where you had a friend to visit, or a place you'd always wanted to see like the Grand Canyon. Is that something you'd be interested in?" He brushed back my hair.

Tears slipped down. I envisioned years of trips with this man. Driving along the coast, over the mountains, through the plains. Windows down, music pumping, but being at home because my home resided not only in him but in me.

I felt at peace.

I laid my head on his chest. "Yeah, Levi, I'd like that. I'd like that a whole lot."

He rested his chin on my head. "That's good, princess. One more question?"

"Sure," I said, exhaustion beginning to creep into my voice.

"At what point are you going to change my name from Lesser Twin on your phone to my actual name?"

I laughed. "I didn't know you knew about that."

He pinched my ass. "Logan told me, and that wasn't an answer."

I tipped my head up to meet his eyes, which were dancing with amusement. Sliding up, I got my mouth right at his ear and whispered my answer. "Never."

He roared with laughter.

Chapter 30

Finding Home

Levi

I was meeting Maeve at the brewery tonight and had a surprise for her, not that she knew that. She'd taught her first official scheduled class at Nomad Yoga tonight at five. She mentioned something about a "flow" class, not that I knew what that meant. I told her I'd be up for taking one of her classes sometime, something that had made Drew Spencer, who had been near us at Logan's, dissolve into laughter. His girlfriend, Kate, explained that Drew had once come to her class thinking it would be easy and had melted into a puddle of sweat.

I'd given him a skeptical look at that, and he'd whispered that he'd almost died. I planned on finding out more about that later.

Our friends Jake and Sully were both behind the bar tonight. Typically they took turns with who was managing or even left their manager, Finn, to handle the place. But Finn was off with his family on a trip, and those two had been giddy over some new hazy beer they'd been working on.

"Hey guys," I said. "New beer ready?"

"Yep, *Into the Mystic* should be good to go next week," Jake said, wiping down the counter. "Come by on Thursday and we'll do a ceremonial tasting."

"Shoot me the time."

"So," Sully said, leaning across the bar from me. "Any special reason you're so jumpy tonight?"

I shrugged, trying to play it cool. "Nah, just lots of caffeine."

"Or you were waiting for her?" Sully jerked his chin toward the door.

I spun on my barstool and soaked in the dream headed my way.

It was ridiculous. It had been over a week since Maeve told me she was staying, and I was still as thrilled to the marrow of my bones as I had been when she'd first spoken those beautiful words.

I watched Maeve make her way across the room. She was gorgeous. Her blond curls were piled in a messy bun on the top of her head. Her black leggings hugged the curves I adored. She wore an open light jacket with a cropped top underneath. Over the past week, she'd confessed that while she loved her ample curves, she did still hear her mom's criticism from time to time. As a result, I was making it a personal mission to worship said curves as often as possible.

Maeve stopped to talk at no less than eight tables on her way to the bar, but I was in no mood to hurry the woman. The folks were stopping her, and even from here, I could see it was residents she knew from town checking in with her. I wanted her to soak in small-town life, to see that the people here would know her and care about her. In Highland Falls, she could be who she really was and would only be appreciated for it. We had thirty-two years to make up for after all.

That reminded me... I pulled out my phone to fire off a text to Allyson and Logan. Maeve's birthday was coming up next month, and you'd better believe I was going all out. She was fascinated by the pirate birthday my mom had thrown Logan and me as kids, so we were doing a sexy-pirate party mashed up with a Taylor Swift theme. It was absolutely one hundred percent ridiculous, and I knew she would love it. Logan had even worked up a way to have a plank walk like we did as kids over a wading pool, but this version involved a shot, spinning around, then walking the plank. It promised to be good fun and would make Maeve laugh, which was really my entire goal.

She finally made her way to the bar only to get waylaid at the opposite end from me. Taking another glance, I realized she was with Lou, Jeanie, and Hattie. Oh boy. I got up to head down there. Otherwise, they might convince her to join them for dinner, and I had plans for the woman.

As I neared the group, I noticed a dark-haired woman closer in age to Maeve and me than the other three women, but I didn't recognize her. Coming to stand behind Maeve, I slid a hand to her waist and felt her lean back and give me her weight.

"Hey," she said with a tired smile on her face. I knew she loved it, but she really was working a lot right now. That would even out after Allyson had the baby came back from maternity leave.

"Hey, princess." I kissed her temple before looking up at the woman she was with. Lou gave me an approving nod. "Hey, ladies."

"Levi, I have someone for you to meet," Lou said,

gesturing to the woman next to her. "This is my niece, Jules. She just moved to town."

I reached out a hand. "Nice to meet you, Jules. What brings you to town besides Lou?"

Jules blushed, clearly not wanting to be the center of attention. I leaned in as she spoke—her voice certainly didn't carry in this crowded bar tonight. "I got a job at the local accounting firm."

I decided to let her off the hook. "Well, welcome to Highland."

Maeve looked up. "I gave her my number so we can have her to a gathering soon. Make sure we're introducing Jules to the crew, you know?"

Lou leaned forward, tugging on Maeve's arm. "Make sure Noah is on that party list."

Jeanie and Hattie nodded in unison as Jules sat back, shaking her head. Well, clearly Lou had found her target. Good luck to Jules and Noah.

"Hope you ladies have a great evening, but I need to snag Maeve from you if that's all right."

Lou waved us off like she was done with us. I shook my head at her. The woman was a menace in all the best ways.

I grabbed Maeve's hands and began to reverse in the direction she had just taken, bringing her toward the front door.

She tugged my hand. "Hey, aren't we eating?"

I looked over my shoulder. "Can't wait—need to do something first."

Her laughter warmed my insides. "Levi," she called. "Show some restraint."

"Never," I replied, waving to Laurie at the hostess stand and then pulling Maeve out the door and around the block, the opposite way from the yoga studio. I hadn't wanted to chance her coming this way.

We took three steps around the corner, and I knew the moment she saw it because she came to an immediate halt.

"Big Red," she breathed out, dropping my hand and walking to her truck as if in a dream. "But…" She looked back at me. "Jared said it would be weeks before the part came in."

"Well, I have to confess something," I said, coming to stand next to her, still at least fifteen paces from her best friend. "The part was in immediately."

Confusion clouded her eyes. "What? Why did he tell me it was back-ordered?"

I grabbed her hand, needed to anchor to her. "Because I asked him to. Jared let me work on her in my spare time, fixing your hose and coolant issue, but also a few other things. That way you only needed to pay for materials."

The look she shot me was indescribable. "You worked on Big Red?"

I nodded. "I did."

She dropped my hand and walked up, running her hand over the hood. She paused, resting her head on the truck for a moment in a silent conversation. After a few moments, she moved around the car and had small exclamations as she noted minor dents and scratches fixed. Opening the door, she first shouted that the squeak was fixed, then that the interior had been detailed. I'd also installed a better sound system, knowing her love of music. All the small issues and a few big ones had been taken care of with a little sweat and a lot of borrowed knowledge from Jared. He'd been glad to give it, especially when I offered to look at his business's website.

But I would have paid all the money I had to see Maeve as she was now, glowing.

"Can we go for a ride?" she asked breathlessly.

"I'd be disappointed if we didn't." I tossed the keys to her.

Sliding into the passenger seat, I buckled up as I listened to Maeve murmuring some conversation with Big Red that I had no part of. That was just fine, I knew my place in this relationship.

She started her up, shooting me a look as the truck quietly turned over, much smoother than she had before. We pulled into the road, and Maeve made an immediate right to head straight out of town.

We drove in silence for just a few minutes before Maeve hit a few buttons to get the first notes "28" from Zach Bryan.

She tugged her hair out of the knot on her head and let the waves fall down before giving me a glance. "Sorry, Levi, I know it isn't exactly warm out, but there is only one way I can rechristen Big Red."

I looked at the woman I loved, the fields outside of Highland Falls passing by outside this bubble we'd created.

"I got you, Maeve," I said, hitting the button to roll my window all the way down.

She did the same, then reached over to squeeze my hand. "I know you do, Lesser Twin. You always have."

She took a right onto a country road and pointed us toward the horizon, her hair flying around the truck cab and music pouring out of the speakers and windows as we chased the sun. Fields flew by, and the scent of promise was in the air. We'd head home when we got hungry, but for now we had miles to go and songs to sing.

Epilogue

How Lucky Are We?

Two Years Later

Maeve

It had been a hell of a week. Allyson and I were busier than ever at the two cafés. We'd had an opportunity to expand to a third location last year, but we'd turned it down. We decided we'd rather run two great shops and have some sort of work-life balance than spread ourselves too thin. Look at us, growing and shit.

It had been two years since I'd decided I was ready for a home base and, much to the surprise of some, I hadn't regretted it for a minute. Staying in Highland had allowed me to find a feeling of steadiness that I hadn't known I was missing. Levi said I was more "me," whatever that meant.

Looking down, I took in my wedding band. It was still shocking to me that I, Maeve Murphy, was married. Married! We hadn't wanted to wait because I knew in my bones that Levi was my forever, and he felt the same. Much like Logan and Allyson, we had zero need for a big wedding. We'd followed their example and gotten married at the courthouse shortly after I'd moved in with him. We'd celebrated with friends in the backyard of Frank and Linnie's place. They hadn't thought we were too nuts for the rushed wedding. Turns out they got married months after meeting all those years ago. When you know, you know.

Those two had become a vital part of my life. Who knew that by getting together with Levi, I would get something I'd always wanted and never believed I would have—parents. Frank and Linnie were more than I could have dreamed. Allyson and I still heard from ours once in a blue moon, but in the five years Allyson had been here, they'd still never set foot in Highland. I think all visits would be on their terms and at their place.

I didn't feel inclined to go out of my way, which my therapist supported. So when Levi and I took a trip to Boston a year ago, we stopped by for lunch. I'd kept our visit brief because I knew it would be all my man could do to not lose his shit with them. He'd done a great job, but you could only push him so far. Grandkids were a reason for them to come out here, but they were content to mail a card. Allyson and I already knew from personal experience that they weren't really nurturing to kids, so cards were excellent.

I lay down on our couch, nudging our two-year-old goldendoodle, Bogey, to scoot over and give me some room. I'd babysat Will for Logan and Allyson today so the two of them could have a lunch date, and the toddler had worn me ragged.

Bogey snuggled right up to me as I tugged a warm blanket up over me. Maybe I'd just take a quick five minutes before getting dinner ready. Yeah, just five minutes.

I awoke to a kiss to my temple and opened my eyes to meet Levi's warm brown ones.

"Hey," he whispered.

"Sorry, I didn't get to dinner," I whispered back. "It's Bogey's fault. He's too cozy."

Levi nodded seriously. "So not because you likely ran all over Highland Woods with a two-year-old who could give a nuclear reactor a run for the money on energy levels?"

I gave that serious consideration. "That might have been a factor."

He placed a hand on my belly. "Or, quite possibly, the little peanut you're growing?"

I shrugged. "Another likely answer, but now that I'm out of the first trimester, I think there's less of a chance."

Levi rubbed his gloriously bearded chin. His tousled hair still made me crazy. Hell, let's be real, everything about this man did it for me.

"And nothing to do with getting so little sleep because of a certain grumpy man last night."

"Oh, you need to be kinder to yourself," I said, my smile starting, and I was hopeless to hold it back.

"Mean Maeve," he said, eyes twinkling as he leaned over to start tickling me.

"No fair, Levi, you know I can't handle this." I started to howl with laughter.

"Mama!" Speaking of toddlers, though this one was seven months younger than his cousin. Little feet pounded in my direction, a bit unsteady, but I could hear Beau's laughter as he made his way to us from his play area over by the kitchen. When he reached the couch, he fell into my waiting arms.

"Hey, baby," I said, kissing his sweaty head. My baby. I'd had no idea how much I would love being a mom. To be honest, it scared the shit out of me at first. I mean, as

Allyson and I had talked about when she got pregnant, it wasn't like we had great role models. But Levi had been my cheerleader the whole time. Well, he, Allyson, and Linnie. With their support, I dove into motherhood and flourished.

My arms filled with Beau, I marveled at how much my life had changed in two years. Levi handed me a basket of books so Beau and I could do his favorite pastime—reading the same books over and over ad nauseam. But that was okay, I'd do it all day every day for our little man.

"I've got dinner," Levi said, kissing first Beau, then me. I watched him walk away, Bogey following him, and I sent up gratitude to Nan at any part she had to play in my life so far. It was more than I could ever have hoped for.

"Book, Mama," Beau said, nestling back against me, sliding his little legs under the blanket.

I pulled a board book out and got ready to start, but Beau's arms went around me as he pressed an open-mouthed kiss to my cheek.

"Mama," he said happily.

"Love you too, baby," I whispered, meeting Levi's gaze as he watched us from the kitchen. He shot me a sexy wink with a mouthed *Love you*. I replied in kind.

Some days I simply couldn't get over it. How lucky were we? Home felt pretty damn good to me now.

Acknowledgments

Book eight is complete and I wish I could say it got easier as I have gone on this journey, but the truth is there is some point in each book that makes me wonder if I'll write another. Levi and Maeve kept drawing me back in, every single time I wanted to quit. I loved his quiet appreciation for Maeve and her sassy attitude. As a result, I returned to this story again and again.

Thanks, as always, to the people I surround myself with that cheer me on: friends, family, students, and my community.

Thanks to readers who have reached out to tell me what they love about my characters.

Thanks to my husband who was willing to dress up for Halloween as Max and Emma from Coming Home, book one in this series. Also a shout out to him for reading every book before it ever goes to anyone else.

Thanks to my ARC team for reading my books and giving me great feedback.

And thanks to my dad for letting me borrow Big Red on the regular. When I do, I roll down the windows, crank up Taylor Swift on my phone (because the radio doesn't work) and sing at the top of my lungs driving down those country roads. That trait was a gift I gave from me straight to Maeve. We both know that you sing when you need to sing and Ms. Swift is the perfect artist to sing along to.

About the Author

Kat Ryan is a middle school teacher by day and a budding romance author in the free time she steals for herself. She loves to write about small towns, found families, strong women, and cinnamon roll heroes that love them. She's a sucker for a HEA and more than a bit of steam in the stories she writes.

Kat lives in the Midwest with her husband and her two sons where she consumes a steady diet of coffee, chocolate, and romance books. And while her students and sons plan to never read the books she writes, her husband has and continues to cheer her on.

Want more from Levi and Maeve? Subscribe to Kat's newsletter on her website, https://katryanwrites.com. All "extras" for each of Kat's book are linked in the newsletter that comes out every month.

Also by Kat Ryan

Coming Home - Max and Emma

Finding Beauty - Sully and Maggie

Loving Ivy - Jake and Ivy

Follow Your Dreams - Nate and Elle

Starting Over - Drew and Kate

Running on Empty - Logan and Allyson

Wrapped Up in Us - Aidan and Grace

The Road Home - Levi and Maeve